Every Earl Has a Silver Lining

Earls are Wild
Book One

Anna Markland

Dragonblade Publishing, Inc. is an imprint of Kathryn Le Veque Novels, Inc.
P.O. Box 7968
La Verne CA 91750
ceo@dragonbladepublishing.com

Produced in the United States of America

First Edition March 2021
Print Edition

ARE YOU SIGNED UP FOR DRAGONBLADE'S BLOG?

You'll get the latest news and information on exclusive giveaways, exclusive excerpts, coming releases, sales, free books, cover reveals and more.

Check out our complete list of authors, too!

No spam, no junk. That's a promise!

Sign Up Here

www.dragonbladepublishing.com

Dearest Reader;

Thank you for your support of a small press. At Dragonblade Publishing, we strive to bring you the highest quality Historical Romance from the some of the best authors in the business. Without your support, there is no 'us', so we sincerely hope you adore these stories and find some new favorite authors along the way.

Happy Reading!

CEO, Dragonblade Publishing

Additional Dragonblade books by Author Anna Markland

Earls are Wild Series
Every Earl Has a Silver Lining

Clash of the Tartans Series
Kilty Secrets
Kilted at the Altar
Kilty Pleasures
Kilty Party
Kilts in the Wind
Kilts Ahoy!

The Viking's Gift (A Novella)

Dedicated to the memory of Gracie Fields,
a lassie from Lancashire.

Sometimes,
not getting what you want
is a wonderful stroke of luck
~Dalai Lama

More Anna Markland

Anna has authored more than sixty bestselling, award-winning and much-loved Medieval, Viking and Highlander historical romance novels and novellas. No matter the setting, many of her series recount the adventures of successive generations of one family, with emphasis on the importance of ancestry and honor. A detailed list can be found on her Amazon page with more complete descriptions at annamarkland.com.

Foreword

A word about the weather. Although it doesn't play a major role in this story, it should be noted that 1816 is often referred to as the *Year without a Summer*. Temperatures were the coldest on record between the years 1766 & 2000. This resulted in major food shortages across the Northern Hemisphere. Even in Canada and the United States, crops failed, and people went hungry.

The anomaly was a volcanic winter caused by the massive April 1815 eruption of Mount Tambora in the Dutch East Indies (known today as Indonesia).

On a personal note, this story is the first one (of the more than 60 I have written) set in Lancashire. Since I'm a Lancashire lass born and bred, I took the opportunity to use several names of places and streets familiar to me. Farnworth, Crompton, Blair, Harwood, Withins and Thicketford all evoke fond childhood memories.

TWIST OF FATE

Island of Saint Helena, 1816

"**M**Y COUSIN'S DEATH has sealed my fate," Lieutenant Colonel Gabriel Smith reluctantly confessed to his batman.

Standing beside him on the windswept clifftop, Corporal Bradley remained silent, though the faithful servant must be hoping he would be sent back to England with his master. What career soldier wouldn't want to escape the thankless duty of playing nursemaid to Napoleon Bonaparte on a godforsaken rock in the middle of the South Atlantic?

"The regimental commander has always resented the respect I've earned from the men. He's been looking for an excuse to send me home, though I trust he doesn't know about the convulsions."

Bradley grimaced. "Sir, I hope you don't think…"

Gabe held up a hand. "No. I know your loyalty. In any case, my unexpectedly inheriting an earldom means he can be rid of me without jumping through military hoops."

His batman squared his always-rigid shoulders. "I'll have to get used to addressing you as *my lord*, sir."

"S'truth, man," he replied. "A title is something I never aspired to. The Earldom of Farnworth has been in the Crompton family since the twelfth century. It's incredible I've inherited the title, and I'm not sure I want it. I'm a second cousin twice removed, for heaven's sake.

"I've never even been to the estate in Lancashire. The original castle is apparently a ruin and the manor house was built hundreds of years ago. It's probably crumbling and will likely need a tremendous amount of capital investment."

"Still, sir, er…my lord…you're better off getting away from here," Bradley replied. "This climate will kill the best of men."

Looking out at endless miles of gray ocean in every direction, Gabe doubted moving to a drafty old house in northern England was the solution to the deteriorating state of his health. He had a deep-seated suspicion his worsening malady had nothing to do with the weather. "I'm not dead yet, old chap."

Bradley studied his feet. "What I meant, sir, is you'll feel better once you're back in Blighty, especially now the war's over and we've got the Little Corporal wrapped up nice and tight here."

Gabriel inhaled the salty air, hoping to ward off a premonition that another embarrassing fainting spell was imminent. Unlike the men in his battalion, he'd initially welcomed the stark beauty and isolation of the island of Saint Helena. It was a place to forget his fiancée's betrayal with his best friend. But his heart was still as barren and bleak as the rock on which he stood.

What little news filtered through from England spoke of thousands being thrown out of work now that Napoleon was no longer a threat. The victory at Waterloo had brought an end to the war effort. "One thing about a war," he mused aloud, "it's good for the economy."

Bradley didn't react, probably used to his commanding officer's nonsensical outbursts by now.

Gabe gripped the hilt of his sword. It was time to face reality. "Jackson has already appointed a new battalion commander as my replacement."

"I'll get started packing then, shall I, sir?"

"Yes, although, who knows when the next navy ship will put in."

"Expected in a fortnight, sir."

Gabe chuckled. Bradley had clearly been anticipating their departure but he would never ask for any favors. He was too proud, too much of a stickler for form. "By the by, I've requested you be allowed to accompany me, since I don't intend to resign my commission just yet."

His batman drew himself up to his full five-foot-nothing height and saluted. "Thank you, sir. I'll get cracking."

Left alone on the chilly hilltop, Gabe took a last look at the sparse trees clinging to the cliffs, all bent to the will of the relentless wind. "Earl Gabriel Smith," he muttered. "Ridiculous."

At the age of twenty-six, he'd spent ten years in the army. It was the only world he knew. The prospect of taking on the responsibilities a title brought with it churned his gut. However, an inner voice whispered it was of little consequence—the mysterious ailment that had taken hold of his body would likely kill him before the year was out.

TRAPPED

EMMA CROMPTON SET aside the tea strainer and offered the cup of Twinings' pekoe to her sister, hoping Priscilla wouldn't notice the rattle of the Sèvres porcelain cup in the matching saucer. "Matthew's death has sealed my fate," she lamented. "I am no longer the Countess of Farnworth. I must be gone from Thicketford Manor before the new earl arrives; he won't wish to be burdened with me and my child. I should have moved out months ago."

Seated on the rosewood and brass inlaid sofa, Priscilla smoothed a hand over the stripes of the pale blue upholstery and leaned forward to accept the tea. "You'll miss all this," she said with a hint of envy, her eyes roving over the walnut sideboard, the works by Rubens and Rembrandt, and the champagne silk draperies flanking the tall windows. Her gaze finally came to rest on her sister's chinoiserie tea caddy.

"I will," Emma conceded, swallowing the bitterness in her throat. She'd grown used to the plush warmth of Axminster carpets underfoot. "But we'll manage."

"You're welcome to come live with us at Bradshaw House," Priscilla replied after some hesitation. "Although, the dog…"

It was a generous offer, but an impractical one. "I thank you, Sister, but your home is barely big enough for you and your family, and I'd prefer to stay in Lancashire." She refrained from adding that Priscilla's socialist husband wouldn't welcome her. Warren had no time for the "idle rich", though Emma thought his attitude was born of jealousy.

As well, the prospect of living with six unruly nephews was enough to fray anyone's nerves and Emma craved peace. She loved her sister, though they'd never been close. However, Priscilla had no control over her sons. Her husband encouraged their misbehavior. "Boys will be boys," he was fond of saying.

The holy terrors would likely pick on Emma's shy seven-year-old daughter. Patsy hadn't yet fully grasped the reality her father wasn't coming back and hadn't spoken a word since the funeral. She carried her toy poodle around everywhere she went. Strangely enough, the normally temperamental Wellington didn't object. Patsy didn't need to be bullied by six cousins, and Priscilla clearly didn't want a poodle in a house ruled by Warren's three mastiffs.

"So, where will you go?" her sister asked, her voice betraying relief the offer of shelter had been declined.

Since her husband's untimely death, Emma had thought long and hard on the matter. Her mother and father had sold their comfortable home and were presently touring India, spending freely on what they called "their golden years". The one thing the two sisters could agree on was that their parents had lost their minds.

Emma loved her suite of rooms at Thicketford Manor. Matthew's father had spared no expense in his efforts to modernize parts of the centuries-old structure. She'd never cared for the depressing green décor the old earl had chosen for the master's chambers, but her bedroom and boudoir were beautifully decorated. The pale-yellow walls offered sorely needed solace.

Since Matthew's demise, she hadn't ventured through the door connecting her bedchamber to his. Too many memories lingered there. Soon, another man would lie in the enormous four-poster bed draped with dark green velvet curtains where she'd surrendered her virginity to her handsome husband. She recalled the experience as akin to being cocooned in an underwater grotto.

Patsy was fond of the nursery and her governess but still sought the consolation of her mother's chamber at night. The legalities of Matthew's estate hadn't yet been settled in the seven months since the accident that had taken his life. Neither of them had expected him to die so young. As a consequence, he hadn't paid the attention he perhaps should have to the disbursement of his holdings. Emma didn't blame him.

The estate's battery of lawyers kept assuring her she wouldn't be *penniless* when all the documentation was sorted. The oft-repeated phrase caused her to doubt she'd end up with sufficient funds to keep Miss Ince employed. It was a miracle the elderly spinster had stayed on, though Emma suspected she had nowhere else to go. Hired on as a nanny when Patsy was born, the retired schoolteacher had been persuaded to take on the role of governess as well.

"I suppose I could purchase a cottage," she sighed in answer to Priscilla's question.

The daughter of a prosperous spinning mill owner, Emma had unexpectedly married into the nobility and achieved wealth beyond her wildest imaginings. At first, she'd been somewhat offended by Thicketford's overwhelming opulence and grandeur but had to admit she'd become accustomed to living in a magnificent house with a fabled history.

The Farnworth estate should have been Patsy's birthright. A son would have inherited his father's lands and titles. Instead, the prize had fallen into the lap of some distant relative no one had ever heard of—a soldier of all things. Generations of Crompton ancestors must be twisting in the family vault. The Earldom of Farnworth might never recover.

Emma clenched her jaw, painfully aware it would be pointless to confide her resentments to her envious sister. Summoning the cool exterior Matthew had taught her to adopt, she lifted the teapot. "More tea, dearest?"

Passing her cup for a refill, Priscilla took Emma completely off guard. "Have you thought of marrying again?"

Emma admitted inwardly she dreaded the prospect of a lonely widow's life, but Matthew hadn't been dead a year. "I'll pretend I didn't hear that, sister dear," she replied, handing back the cup and saucer. "I'm not out of mourning for my husband."

"Still," Priscilla continued undaunted. "When the year is up, I'm sure you could find some eligible bachelor to take you on. That fellow from the neighboring estate who came to the funeral, for example."

Emma's stomach turned over. "Arthur Coleman?"

"Yes, isn't he the son of Baron Whiteside? He seemed very solicitous of your welfare at the reception after the funeral."

Emma had to put her teacup down on the side table lest she toss the contents at her sister. "The wretch tried to proposition me with my husband not five minutes in his grave."

"Oh, I think you must be mistaken. He seemed an honorable sort. And very handsome."

Emma snorted. Priscilla never did have any inkling when it came to men—witness the skinflint she'd married. "Arthur Coleman is a ne'er-do-well. Even Matthew recognized him for what he is—a wastrel who is frittering away his father's wealth at an alarming rate."

"Still, he's the heir to the Whiteside barony, isn't he? I know you're a countess but beggars can't be choosers, my dear. You could do worse than marry a baron."

Emma laughed out loud, sounding mildly hysterical even to her own ears. "Oh yes," she replied bitterly. "Why not plan to marry the Smith person who's inherited what should have been Patsy's?"

Sticking out her little finger at an exaggerated angle, Priscilla sipped her tea. "Don't be silly. You can't marry someone with a name like Smith."

Emma closed her eyes, vowing to avoid moving in with her sister at all costs.

LOW EXPECTATIONS

URING THE TEDIOUS ceremony to hand over command of his battalion to a snooty young officer name Smethurst, Gabe thankfully managed to salute at all the appropriate times and remain upright—despite the best efforts of the bitter wind.

Dismissed by his commanding officer, he boarded the tender that would take him out to *HMS Dreadnought* moored in Rupert's Bay. His feelings were mixed. He was relieved he hadn't made a complete cake of himself by convulsing at the feet of Colonel Jackson. Nor was it his problem that Bonaparte's acerbic tongue would quickly whittle Smethurst down to size. However, *Dreadnought* hardly seemed auspicious for the journey he was about to undertake.

The ship was a relatively new, second rate 98-gun ship of the line, launched in 1801, according to the midshipman who greeted Gabe after he'd been piped aboard. He barely listened to his young guide's narrative as he was escorted to his quarters. His belly churned at the prospect of weeks of seasickness. He'd never been a good sailor, even in times of robust good health.

A scant year ago, during the ten-week voyage to Saint Helena aboard *HMS Northumberland*, he'd kept up his men's spirits. Many were disgruntled at the duty imposed on them. The rank and file, and even some non-commissioned officers, complained they hadn't signed up to watch over an arrogant Frenchman on an uninhabited island in the middle of nowhere.

Gabe didn't blame them, but Saint Helena was as far as he could get from the feckless Georgina Plant and he'd looked forward to the isolation. He'd enjoyed the voyage, despite occasional seasickness.

Thankfully, he hadn't been directly responsible for the infamous prisoner. The portly Corsican spent much of his time on deck leaning with his arse propped against the barrel of a 32 pounder, staring out to sea. Even in gale force winds, the *bicorne* stayed firmly wedged on his head, almost covering his eyes. It became a standard jest among the men that the hat must be nailed on. Boney stood motionless for so long that Major Ibbetson was able to render several watercolor drawings of him.

Perhaps the emperor was reliving dreams of past glory and the nightmare of defeat at Waterloo. Gabe had fought on the side of the victors and would never forget the horror of Waterloo either.

"Give the Little Corporal his due, though," Bradley had remarked. "His uniform is always spotless and the gold braid shines like new."

"Small wonder given the army of servants and retainers he's been allowed to bring," had been Gabe's usual reply.

As the *Dreadnought* weighed anchor, Gabe acknowledged he wouldn't miss the isolation. It hadn't healed his heart nor soothed his resentment. Thicketford Manor might turn out to be a medieval ruin but it was still a more preferable place to die than Saint Helena. A man with the very ordinary English name of Smith ought to be buried in his native land.

He spent most of the interminable voyage in his bunk, plagued by *mal de mer* which aggravated the constant throbbing headaches. However, when he ventured on deck for fresh air, he thought the weakness in his limbs might be improving slightly.

He was exhausted by the time he and Bradley disembarked *HMS Dreadnought*. As a senior officer, he'd been obliged to dine at the captain's table. Driscoll held forth endlessly about the ship's illustrious history, including her role in the Battle of Trafalgar. Gabe heard the tale so often, he could recite it verbatim.

Dreadnought was the eighth ship in the lee division to enter the action. She started firing on San Juan Nepomuceno at two o'clock and fifteen minutes later forced her to surrender after her commander was killed in action.

Gabe didn't begrudge Driscoll his pride in the vessel he commanded. However, as he stood on the Bristol dock and inhaled the air of his native land, he acknowledged with a chuckle that he could probably recite the whole blooming history of the ship from the day she was launched.

His amusement was short-lived. There was something about the air in Bristol that smelled…

The ever-efficient Bradley thrust a kerchief into his hand just in time as he sneezed, then sneezed again.

"What is that smell?" he asked his batman, after blowing his nose. "It's making my eyes water."

Bradley stuck out his chin and inhaled deeply. "Good old Blighty. Nothing like it, eh, sir?"

Gabe hadn't remembered the air in England being so pungent but supposed his nose was used to salty Atlantic sea breezes. And Bristol was an industrial city as well as a port.

He'd planned to make his way north without delay, but Driscoll invited him to stay at his home in the town for a day or two. While it meant listening *ad nauseam* to the stories about *Dreadnought*, a comfortable bed would renew his energy for the trek to Lancashire. In any case, it wasn't likely anyone at Thicketford Manor was eagerly awaiting his arrival.

>>>«««

GRIPPING THE BRIEF missive handed to her on a silver tray by the butler, Emma gritted her teeth. "I suppose this explains the delay," she huffed.

"My lady," Frame acknowledged with his usual deferential bow.

The man had served the Crompton household for longer than she'd been alive. He trained all new staff, keeping on only those who met his high standards. His word among the servants was law, but he never bullied. A softly-spoken reprimand or a raised eyebrow was all it took to keep them in line. There was nothing she could do to ensure the butler was retained and hoped the new earl recognized the treasure he had inherited.

Upon first noting the letter had come from her husband's solicitors after months fretting about the uncertain future she and her daughter faced, she'd assumed it contained news of the monies left to her. A lack of funds had rendered it impossible to make arrangements for alternative accommodations. It seemed increasingly likely they'd be forced to lodge with Priscilla for a short while at least. The prospect only tightened the knot in her stomach.

Her heart lurched when she re-read the letter she'd only scanned briefly. "According to this, the new earl's ship—HMS Dreadnought for goodness' sake—docked in Bristol a week ago and he intended to proceed here forthwith. But, it has taken the lawyers three days to get word to us. The man might arrive any day. And where on earth is Saint Helena?"

"I believe it's a barren, uninhabited rock in the Atlantic Ocean, my lady," Frame replied. "Napoleon Bonaparte was exiled there after his defeat at Waterloo."

A chill stole up Emma's spine. She recalled hearing something of the sort and couldn't imagine the British Army posting its best officers to the middle of nowhere. Gabriel Smith might be a lieutenant colonel, but her expectations of him weren't high. "It seems anyone can buy a commission these days," she muttered.

"Quite, my lady," Frame agreed. "All is in readiness for his arrival. However, might I suggest the maids move your belongings to another chamber, perhaps on the attic floor for the time being? It's my understanding the new earl has no wife, but..."

Emma felt like an idiot. Of course she couldn't stay in the suite of rooms adjoining the master's bedchamber. She wondered if grief and fear would ever loosen their paralyzing grip on her wits. "Thank you, Frame," she said as she rose from the blue sofa. "I'll sorely miss your wisdom. This is a good time for me to oversee the move while Patsy is with Miss Ince in the nursery."

"As you wish, my lady."

CHANGES

EMMA SAT STIFFLY in the wooden rocking chair in the claustrophobic attic chamber, thankful Patsy had finally fallen asleep in her lap. Her daughter had wailed fretfully, not understanding why she couldn't sleep in the usual place. Only after Emma allowed Wellington to curl up with them had the child calmed.

Her back ached but she didn't dare move. Another weeping session would severely test the floodgates of her own sorrow. A yapping poodle might tempt her to violence.

It would take some time to get used to sharing the small bedroom with her daughter. Before her father had made his fortune, she and her sister had shared a bed. The memory wasn't a pleasant one. However, Patsy certainly wasn't the bully Priscilla had been. Emma consoled herself with the promise the situation would only be temporary. As soon as the solicitors sorted out the will…

However, a child couldn't be expected to comprehend such matters, especially one who hadn't spoken since her father's funeral.

The attic chambers, intended originally to accommodate the master's valet and the mistress' abigail, were tucked under the eaves. The ceiling that sloped alarmingly on either side of the bed was already closing in. Emma had a phobia of enclosed spaces and dreaded waking during the first night feeling trapped in new surroundings.

The tiny armoire and mismatched set of two drawers were completely inadequate for all the items in her wardrobe. Poor Lucy had heaped the overflow on top of the only other chair.

The light gray walls badly needed repainting and the once plush Axminster area rug was threadbare in places.

Used to her own private boudoir, she wasn't looking forward to traipsing across the hallway to the shared facilities, though Frame had assured her the other bedroom had been vacant since the valet's departure for another position. Her abigail had been packed off to the servants' wing, a move Lucy would likely consider a demotion.

It wasn't to Emma's credit that she had never realized her personal maid slept in what amounted to a cupboard in the attic.

She ought to be grateful the butler had also made sure the room was spotlessly clean and aired. She was confident the bed linens would be crisp, the pillows soft and the blankets warm. On the morrow, she'd mention the need for a mirror.

"We'll just have to make the best of it," she whispered to her sleeping child, hoping she had the fortitude to bear the presence of the usurper who was due to arrive any day. The only course of action would be for her and Patsy to avoid this Smith person completely.

⇒⇒⇒⋘⋘

GABE ENJOYED THE first few hours of the journey north. The air smelled fresher once they left Bristol behind. The scenery was very different from Saint Helena—mile after mile of verdant fields, English oaks, wide, lazy rivers, and tidy farmhouses. He began to feel he really was back home. It was years since he'd read any of Blake's poetry, but "England's green and pleasant land" played over and over in his head.

The coach was well sprung and reasonably comfortable, if chilly. The other passengers who boarded and disembarked at various coaching houses en route seemed disinclined to engage in conversation, for which Gabe was grateful. It seemed *the year without a summer* had soured everyone's mood.

Bradley made sure their bits of luggage were secure in the boot before cheerfully climbing up top behind the guard and driver; no doubt he intended to talk the men's ears off with tales of Napoleon.

It was as well Gabriel had followed his batman's advice and traveled in uniform. They were treated with respectful deference in the coaching inns and provided with clean accommodations, vermin-free linens and, occasionally, complimentary food. He suspected Bradley of putting it about that the officer he served had fought at Waterloo. It was unlikely his servant would have mentioned his own bravery on that bloody battlefield.

He wasn't sure at what point he became aware of the troubling numbers of ragged men begging in the streets of the larger towns they passed through, some of them amputees. The rumors of widespread destitution after the collapse of the wartime economy were evidently true. It churned his gut to see soldiers who'd sacrificed limbs having to beg for their bread. He was more grateful than ever that he and Bradley had survived the carnage unscathed. If only that held true for all the men under his command.

His optimism eroded further as they ventured into the industrial heartland of the nation. By the time the coach dropped them at the Punch Bowl Inn in Manchester, the fetid air had made breathing difficult. The autumn sun that might have burned off the fog was obliterated by the effects of the volcanic winter it seemed the whole world was enduring. The incessant wind had spared Saint Helena, though the island was never what one might call warm. He hoped Thicketford Manor was located in a greener, more bucolic part of Lancashire.

His chamber was cramped, but clean and well supplied with towels, a ewer and basin and a small set of drawers. He'd slept in worse and it was only for the one night.

The dining room proved to be busy and too noisy. Born in the south of England, Gabe found the northern brogue difficult to understand. It seemed northerners were also less inhibited about other folks overhearing their conversation than their southern countrymen. After a passable meal of lamb chops, potatoes and gravy, he extricated himself from the cacophony and retired to his chamber. He slept fairly well considering the drunken revelry that went on below for hours.

The next morning, having forced down a couple of fried eggs, he was studying a substance on his breakfast plate the pimple-faced waiter had informed him was black pudding when Bradley approached and saluted. "Morning, sah!"

It might be Gabe's imagination, but his batman seemed to have an even stiffer ramrod up his backside than usual. Perhaps the man was also apprehensive about their imminent arrival at Thicketford Manor. "There's no need to salute me," he muttered, shoving the black pudding away from his queasy stomach. "We're not on duty."

"Sah," Bradley replied, clicking his heels and remaining at attention. "Thought you'd like to know I've procured nags to take us to the solicitor's office."

Gabe wasn't feeling remotely well enough to organize transport. Indeed, the prospect of keeping his appointment with the solicitors charged with overseeing the earldom's finances filled him with dread. They'd know as soon as they met him he wasn't up to the task.

However, the ever-dependable Bradley had simply gone ahead and taken care of the matter. "Good man," he said, relieved yet unreasonably irritated he would need to rely more and more on his servant as his illness progressed.

THE WILL

I T FELT GOOD to be back on a horse, though the gelding Bradley had rented from the stables was old and docile. Gabe hadn't ridden on Saint Helena. His world there had consisted of long hours spent in Napoleon's cottage and the compound surrounding it. He nursed a hope the stables at Thicketford housed a few good steeds, until his conscience reminded him any fine horseflesh he might have inherited had come to him only by dint of his cousin's death.

He was glad of Bradley's assistance in forging his way through the crowded, foul-smelling streets of Manchester. Again, he was struck by the numbers of people begging, toothless women and ragged urchins among them.

The streets eventually widened into elegant thoroughfares and, soon, there wasn't a beggar in sight. Impressive, three-story stone houses came into view. A shiny brass plaque affixed to the front door of one such house indicated they'd arrived at the offices of Messrs. Rowbotham, Bootle and Radcliffe.

He'd written to the solicitors from Bristol to explain he couldn't guarantee an exact time of arrival and been assured by return post he didn't need an appointment.

It was clear from the sorrowful expression on the lean face of the ancient clerk who eyed their uniforms with disdain that anyone who arrived without an appointment had no hope of seeing any of the partners. Annoyance, coupled with the reek of leather-bound books, decaying paper and ink, stirred Gabe's headache.

Again, Bradley took charge. "I don't think you realize who you're talking to," he said, his nose an inch away from the clerk's. "The earl has come all the way from…"

The fellow nigh on fell off his stool. "The earl? Of Farnworth? Why didn't you say so? Mr. Rowbotham himself will see you directly, my lord. If you'll follow me."

Gabe didn't know that he liked the toadying deference the mention of his title had brought about. As a lieutenant colonel, he'd earned the respect of his subordinates. He was an earl now, but he was still Gabriel Smith, a soldier who might not be hailed as a hero of Waterloo, but who'd fought bravely. A man should be respected for his accomplishments, not his title.

Mr. Rowbotham's scowl disappeared quickly once the clerk explained the identity of his unexpected visitor. "Come in, dear chap," he said in a grating voice that scraped Gabe's nerves. "Have a seat."

He indicated a well-worn leather chair in front of his massive desk, but didn't rise from his own seat behind the towering piles of papers. Rowbotham's sallow, wrinkled skin, bushy mutton chop sideburns, untamed white eyebrows and stooped shoulders bespoke a man of advanced age, so it was hardly surprising he didn't get to his feet.

Rowbotham perused him for what seemed like long minutes. Gabe began to wonder if the ancient solicitor had dozed off. Fearing the floor-to-ceiling bookshelves crammed with too many giant tomes might collapse and bury them both, he wished Bradley had entered this inner sanctum with him. Annoyed with himself, he shook off the pathetic notion. He was becoming overly dependent on his servant. "Thank you for seeing me," he declared, hoping he sounded like an earl. "I understand you have papers for me to sign."

"Indeed."

Gabe expected several of the teetering towers of documents to tumble to the floor as Rowbotham sought the pertinent papers on his desk. Dust motes filled the air.

At length, a file box with the documents was located. Rowbotham sifted through the contents. Finally, he peered at Gabe over iron-rimmed spectacles—probably made in the last century—and announced, "The whole estate and all the properties, rents, etcetera, etcetera, are left to the late earl's heir."

Gabe blinked. His dead cousin had married. He and his wife must have children. They were surely his heirs.

Rowbotham cleared his throat and continued his gravelly pronouncements. "Under the terms of the will, with the exception of twenty-five pounds per annum, everything goes to you."

Gabe gripped the edge of his chair as a bout of dizziness swept over him. "Twenty-five pounds per annum?" he asked, grasping at the only words that had registered.

"For the widow. And I believe there's a child. Female, unfortunately," he tutted, as if Matthew had sired an abomination with two heads. "Else she'd have inherited."

Gabe later had no recollection of signing papers. He must have shaken Rowbotham's hand, left the offices and ridden back to the inn. All he could recall as he sat on his bed with his head in his hands was that Matthew's widow had been ousted from her home with a meager twenty-five pounds per annum to support her and her child. He had to assume she came from a wealthy family who would take her and her child in and look after them.

He fervently hoped he would never meet the woman. He wouldn't be able to face her, though it was hardly his fault Matthew had made such poor provision for his family.

EMMA KEPT UP a steady stream of conversation about nothing in particular while Miss Ince finished dressing her daughter. Patsy didn't react to anything she said, her attention on Wellington who sniffed every corner of a chamber with which he was unfamiliar.

Emma prayed her little girl would one day get over her grief and recover her voice. She shuddered at the thought of what might happen when the new earl arrived. She'd tried to explain their need to keep out of his way, but doubted Patsy fully understood.

She resolved to hide her own disdain for the man, lest her frustration only add to her child's confusion.

Since Smith hadn't yet arrived, she saw nothing amiss with breaking her fast in the morning room. It would likely be her last chance to eat in elegant surroundings. Arrangements had already been made for trays to be delivered to the attic chamber for her and Patsy.

She gave up trying to coax her daughter into eating her sausages and turned a blind eye when Patsy fed the meat to Wellington waiting expectantly under the table. Matthew had always forbidden the presence of the dog during meals, but Emma had given up trying to enforce all his rules.

A polite cough heralded Frame who offered his silver tray with a letter. "The post, my lady."

Her heart fluttered when she saw the return address. At long last, it appeared the solicitors had settled the estate. With trembling hands, she slit open the envelope using the pearl-handled letter opener Frame had thoughtfully provided.

ARRIVAL

BACK AT THE Punch Bowl, Gabe couldn't get his mind off the pittance allotted to Matthew's widow. He'd never met the woman, and assumed he never would, but she had a right to be bitter about the way things had turned out. It seemed unlikely he would ever marry but, if he did, he'd make damn sure adequate provision was made for his wife after he was gone.

The innkeeper served a lunch of liver and onions shortly after their return. The food was well prepared, the portion generous, but Gabe couldn't rid himself of the bitter taste in his mouth.

Bradley left to confirm earlier arrangements about transportation to Thicketford Manor. Upon his return, he hovered, staring at the far wall.

Gabe sensed there was something he was reluctant to say. "Well?"

"The conveyance, sir, it's not exactly fitting for an earl, sir. It was the best I could do."

Gabe got to his feet, gripping the edge of the table to ward off a spell of dizziness. Perhaps he should have eaten more of the liver that was reputed to have fortifying properties. "I'm sure whatever you found will get us there safely."

"The driver says he'll be waiting outside the inn in a half-hour, sir."

"And how long a journey is it?"

"He says two hours, sir."

Gabe's spirits perked up. Two hours would take him far from the overcrowded, grimy town of Manchester.

⇶⫷

NOT RECALLING HOW she'd managed to make it up the stairs, Emma sat in the rocking chair and stared in disbelief at the letter from Mr. Rowbotham. Her initial reaction had been to tear it to shreds and toss the pieces into the glowing coals of the fire burning in the hearth, but that wouldn't change the dire circumstances in which she found herself. Things were much worse than she'd ever expected. She and Patsy were destitute. Having to beg Priscilla for a roof over their heads loomed large. The prospect lay like a lead weight in her belly, especially since she knew for certain the earldom was wealthy and prosperous.

Her tears had long since dried up, to be replaced by a knot of anger every time she looked at her sleeping daughter curled up on the bed with Wellington. "How could you let this happen, Matthew?" she whispered hoarsely. "Your little girl will have none of the finer things she's entitled to."

The daughter of an industrialist, Emma had never experienced a London season of balls, musicales and other refined gatherings. They were the reserve of the nobility into which she had unexpectedly married. Matthew's title meant more to her parents than to her, but she'd looked forward proudly to the day Patsy would make her shining debut into society.

She was the dowager countess—a title that made her feel ancient. Patsy was still the daughter of an earl, but a London season was expensive and completely out of reach on twenty-five pounds per annum. Unless she could find a patron. Perhaps the new earl. She cringed when her derisive snort prompted a growl from Wellington.

The crunch of hooves and carriage wheels on the gravel driveway drew her out of her reverie. Visitors had arrived. Her body tensed when she realized the visitor might be the overdue earl come to exert his claim. Despite a resolve to stay where she was, her feet carried her to the window.

Peering through the streaked glass, she was sure she'd been mistaken. An earl would never arrive in a rustic wagon pulled by drayhorses. When a tall, black-haired man in uniform was helped down from the contraption by another soldier, she was tempted to laugh out loud.

However, the new earl was much younger than she'd anticipated. She held her breath when he looked up at his new domain. There was no possibility he could see her given the grime on the pane, but she was transfixed by harried features that spoke of pain and weariness. She suspected he'd once been a handsome man, but would wager he was definitely ailing.

The sinking feeling the new earl wasn't long for this world should have filled her with satisfaction. Instead, she felt only pity and a deepening sense of uncertainty.

ARRIVING FROZEN TO the bone in a hay-wagon wasn't the way Gabe had hoped to make his appearance at Thicketford Manor, but he supposed beggars couldn't be choosers. He'd told Bradley that several times during the journey, yet the man kept apologizing.

They had eventually left the industrial town of Manchester behind, but the countryside they encountered wasn't what Gabe expected. Every few minutes, their driver hollered at sheep seemingly wandering at will across rough roads that traversed barren hills and wild moorland of a shade of green he couldn't name—if, indeed, it was green. He'd heard of the Pennine chain, the so-called backbone of England that formed a barrier between Lancashire and Yorkshire. He hadn't realized it consisted mostly of rolling moorland and rocky outcroppings, relieved occasionally by vibrant swathes of purple heather. The sky loomed as gray and foreboding as the landscape.

The scenery changed abruptly after they started downhill into a verdant valley. A ray of sunshine, rare in this abysmal summer, broke through the clouds, illuminating a huge edifice in the distance, an imposing presence set amid green fields and towering oaks. He allowed himself to hope it might be a good omen.

They passed through a tiny village consisting of a few cottages and arrived at a set of ornate wrought-iron gates. After belatedly tipping his cap, the gaping gatekeeper lumbered out of a sentry box to open the gates of Thicketford Manor. The house itself loomed like a mirage at the end of an incredibly long driveway lined with majestic weeping willows. "Bigger than I thought," Gabe mused aloud.

"Aye," the driver agreed. "A grand hall ye've inherited."

He deemed it wiser not to voice his first impression that Thicketford Manor looked like it had been drawn straight from the pages of Miss Radcliffe's gothic novel—except the stone from which it was made was almost beige in color. It didn't help that the sun had again retreated.

"Shame about the earl dying," the driver lamented. "Him being so young an' all. With a little kiddie. Didn't doubt ye'd be arriving soon."

Gabe got the feeling he was in a part of the country where everyone knew all there was to know about their neighbors.

When they came to a halt at the front entry, he allowed Bradley to assist him down from the wagon with as much dignity as he could muster, given the weakness in his knees. He hoped he appeared worthy of the inheritance that had fallen into his lap. There was no porte-cochère so the lack of rain was a blessing.

Exhausted and thrown off balance by the journey and the meeting with the solicitor, he looked up with some trepidation at the expansive exterior of his new home.

He thought he glimpsed a face at an upper window, a servant

perhaps. A gaunt man, probably the butler, was chivvying the household staff into a receiving line on the front steps. He reminded Gabe of Sergeant Major Hooper—a look and a quiet word was all it took.

"Frame, my lord, at your service," the man intoned when he was apparently satisfied his troops were ready to greet their new master. "Welcome."

Frame's tone of voice suggested Gabe wasn't, in fact, welcome, but he'd expected a cool reception. Or perhaps butlers naturally behaved like stuffed shirts.

Bradley shouldered Gabe's kitbag.

"The footmen will see to the luggage," Frame told him.

"No, Mr. Frame," Bradley replied. "The earl's belongings are my responsibility."

Frame didn't argue, but Gabe sensed from his rigid features it wouldn't be long before a confrontation occurred.

WELLINGTON

A FRAID TO WAKE Patsy and her dog, Emma tiptoed to the door and pressed an ear against the rough wood. She was under the impression Frame wasn't pleased about something the second soldier had said to him. And who was this person anyway?

The butler had introduced the new earl to the staff assembled on the front steps. She felt a twinge of pride when the maids curtseyed properly and the footmen bowed politely. As far as she could tell, the new earl hadn't uttered a greeting to any of them, though he'd shaken hands with the footmen. *Gauche.*

She'd have to have a word with Smith about Tillie; the cheeky maid was already ogling her new master's broad shoulders.

She gritted her teeth. There'd be no friendly, helpful conversation between the earl and herself. She mustn't be swayed by his impressive stature and broad shoulders; he'd have to find his own way with the servants, though Frame, being the stickler for rules that he was, would probably overcome his distaste for the new master and explain the lay of the land.

Her room was on the fourth floor and she could hear only muffled voices coming from the foyer. If she opened the door just a crack…

She gasped when Wellington squirmed through the narrow gap and scurried down the stairs, yapping loudly.

WISHING THE BUTLER would stop droning on about the architecture of the huge foyer and which of the preceding earls had purchased various naked statues and innumerable urns—after verifying their provenance, of course—Gabe was almost relieved to hear the rapid clicking of claws on wood and the barking of a dog. Except, the insistent yapping of the brown poodle nipping at his heels could hardly be called barking. He'd expected the estate to be home to dogs, but this wasn't what he'd envisaged.

"A poodle?" he asked. "Whose dog is this?"

For the first time, Frame's icy demeanor cracked. The hesitation was almost imperceptible, but there nonetheless. "Wellington is part of the estate, my lord."

Bradley snorted. He too recognized a lie when he heard one, or perhaps Gabe's servant was merely amused by the thought of the famous duke's reaction to having a poodle named after him.

"So, I suppose Wellington belongs to me," he replied, though he decided against petting the snarling animal. He wasn't overly fond of dogs in any case.

"Yes, my lord, I suppose he does," Frame replied as he calmly scooped up the dog and handed him over to a maid.

The poodle immediately ceased yapping.

Gabe felt something of a coward. Clearly, Wellington wasn't the ferocious hound he had feared. "Perhaps he doesn't like strangers," he said, instantly wishing he could take the words back. The dog's animosity would perhaps prove to be typical of what he should expect.

DITHERING OVER WHAT to do about the commotion Wellington had caused in the foyer, Emma slammed the door when Patsy began to wail. She hurried to take the child into her embrace. "Hush, sweetling. Mama's here."

Her daughter had woken and become upset to find her poodle gone. She must also have heard the dog barking downstairs because she tried to pull away from Emma to get to the door.

Emma hated having to keep her daughter confined to their room and Patsy screamed all the louder to be allowed to leave.

"This is ridiculous," Emma muttered as she rocked the weeping child squirming to get out of her mother's arms. Much more of this and Patsy would begin to resent her. "We cannot stay cooped up here indefinitely."

A tap at the door heralded Tillie, the last person Emma wished to see. The servant made a half-hearted attempt to curtsey before releasing Wellington from her arms. "The new earl's arrived," she announced with her nose in the air. "Quite the 'andsome gentleman, if I do say so."

The maid couldn't have made it clearer she knew Emma no longer held sway in the household.

"Yes. Thank you, Tillie," she replied. "That will be all."

The cheeky maid swanned off, copious breasts thrust out, hips swaying in a most unladylike manner. Probably the kind of tart the new earl would enjoy.

Trying to calm her lonely heart, Emma leaned her forehead against the closed door, relieved that at least Patsy had stopped crying.

NOISES IN THE NIGHT

G ABE STARTLED AWAKE the next morning when Bradley drew back the heavy draperies of his four-poster bed with an annoying flourish and announced it was time to rise.

"It's barely dawn, man," he groaned, his heart thudding in his chest. "We're not in the army now."

He didn't mention being awakened periodically from an otherwise exhausted sleep by the occasional yapping of the infernal poodle. But something else was bothersome. "Did you hear a child crying in the night, Bradley?"

"Sir! Coming from one of the rooms up top. Dog's there too, I reckon."

"Up top?"

"Fourth floor, sir. Where my room is."

Gabe felt badly. He was so used to Bradley fending for himself he hadn't given a thought to where the man had been billeted. "Is your room comfortable?"

"Better than Saint Helena, sir," his batman replied with a grin.

Gabe nodded, gesturing to the canopy of the huge bed. "I know what you mean. I doubt I'll ever get used to sleeping in this monstrosity. The green draperies alone are enough to make a man ill."

"Bed's big enough for two, sir," Bradley said, the cocky grin still in evidence.

Gabe should reprimand the servant for his cheeky and uncharacteristically forward suggestion, but it was true that his bachelor state didn't serve the needs of the estate. He might not have long to live but, if he passed without an heir, the earldom would be thrown into even greater disarray. Who knew how far and for how long the solicitors would be obliged to search for the next eligible relative? Gabe might not be what most considered earl material but it was incumbent upon him to do his utmost to keep the earldom prosperous. Tenant farmers, the large staff and, indeed, the community at large depended on the Farnworth estate. He wouldn't want it passed on to a wastrel.

"Shall I have a tray sent up with your breakfast, sir?" Bradley asked, drawing him out of his reverie.

It was tempting to simply hide away in his chamber but, sooner or later, he'd have to start behaving like the master of the house. He swung his legs out of bed, pausing until the dizziness left him. "No. It's time to face the foe."

Bradley looked relieved. "Just as well, sir. Mrs. Maple wasn't too keen on the idea of a tray. Said the late earl always broke his fast in the morning room."

Gabe struggled to recall the scores of servants he'd been introduced to. "Mrs. Maple? As in tree?"

"The housekeeper, sir."

And so it begins, Gabe thought as Bradley helped him don his robe. "Perhaps I'll feel more equipped to face the day after my shave."

EMMA OPENED THE door to admit Frame, closing it quickly to prevent Wellington's latest escape attempt. "You shouldn't be the one bringing our trays," she said as the butler set the breakfast fare down on a small table. "Surely one of the maids can do it."

"I don't mind, my lady," he wheezed. "Good exercise."

Much as she appreciated his loyalty, Frame wasn't a young man. Climbing five flights of stairs from the kitchens carrying a tray laden with plates of food and a full tea service was destined to end in disaster. At least, he'd wisely chosen the main stairs and not the narrow servants' staircase.

"Has the new earl been down for breakfast?" she asked, glad to see Patsy tucking into the oatmeal. At least the child's appetite hadn't fled with her voice.

"Yes, my lady. I don't wish to add to your burdens, but he asked about Wellington. His batman told him the dog resides on this floor."

"Batman?" she asked.

Frame looked down his nose. "The individual he brought with him. His servant in the army, I believe. I had planned to put him in one of the rooms in the servants' wing, but Tillie…"

Emma held up a hand. "That impudent girl seems to be at the root of everything that goes awry."

"I've been on the verge of turning her off several times. If your ladyship wishes…"

Emma shook her head. "It's no longer my place to say whom you should let go. We don't want her complaining to the new earl, which is exactly what she would do if she suspected I was behind her firing."

"As your ladyship wishes. You should also be aware that Earl Gabriel thought he heard a child sobbing in the night."

Emma recalled snorting derisively when she'd learned his name was Gabriel—an angelic name for a usurper.

With a heavy heart, Emma accepted the inevitable. "We're not going to be able to stay hidden, are we, Frame?"

"It would appear not, my lady."

GABE WAS SCHEDULED to meet with the estate manager in the library at eleven o'clock, which meant he had an hour or so to explore the house and grounds. He wasn't looking forward to the meeting. He didn't wish to appear totally ignorant, but couldn't even prepare rudimentary questions. He knew nothing of the earldom's holdings, except what Rowbotham had briefly outlined.

After a breakfast served by a winking, buxom chit named Tillie, whom he definitely remembered from yesterday's introductions, he wandered out to the foyer. Feigning interest in the innumerable gilt sconces and mirrors, he felt uncomfortable in the frock coat and leggings he'd donned. Tillie's tittering told him his clothing was woefully out of fashion and the frayed cuffs didn't help matters. He wouldn't be surprised if Bradley had the cheeky girl in his bed before the week was out, though he had a suspicion the maid's sights were set higher. If she carried on making eyes at him, he'd let her know in no uncertain terms he wasn't interested. Flirts didn't appeal and he had too little time left to dally with promiscuous maids.

Speaking of Bradley, he should investigate the room assigned to his batman. The crusty soldier had served him well and deserved some comfort. Craning his neck to look up the winding staircase to the fourth floor made him lightheaded, and he didn't like the idea of Bradley being fobbed off with a cupboard in the attic. He grasped the newel post and took a deep breath, hoping he wouldn't pass out before reaching the top. It wouldn't do for the new earl to faint and tumble down the stairs. Rumors of shocking inebriation at nine o'clock in the morning would soon ensue.

He took his time, gripping the banister as he ascended, cursing the mysterious illness that robbed his legs of strength and tightened his lungs.

To his surprise, on the second floor, he encountered Frame coming down from higher up. The fellow was carrying a tray stacked with bowls, saucers and teacups, along with a silver tea service. The whole lot looked like it might topple over. He'd wager from the fastidious butler's momentary lack of composure the man wasn't happy to see him.

"Is someone upstairs ill?" he asked, eyeing the tray. That might explain the weeping he'd heard, though he doubted any of the staff were allowed to house children in their rooms.

Frame quickly regained his aplomb. "No, my lord."

Gabe wasn't sure why he felt a compulsion to explain what he was about. "I'm going up to inspect Bradley's room. Old army habits die hard and all that, don't you know, dear chap?"

Feeling like the pompous General Abercrombie many of his fellow officers often mimicked, he carried on to the fourth floor when Frame resumed his descent.

WHO ARE YOU?

OUT OF BREATH and sweating, Gabe paused after reaching the fourth-floor landing, puzzled to see only three doors. Obviously, all the servants weren't housed up here. He ought to have realized, given the size of the manor house, that there'd be a completely separate wing for servants. The question remained as to why Bradley had been billeted here, and who resided in the other rooms?

Unsure which door to try first, and not wishing to intrude on the privacy of someone who might be nursing a sick child, he was relieved when Bradley emerged from one of the rooms. The man looked positively nonplussed that Gabe had caught him in shirtsleeves and braces. He'd never seen his batman in anything but his always immaculate uniform.

"Don't worry," he said quickly, ushering his servant back into his room. "I'm here to inspect your quarters. I assume there is a servants' wing where you might find better facilities."

Bradley shut the door and reached for the jacket of his uniform. "Tillie put me in here, sir. Said I'd be closer to your chamber."

Gabe suspected Tillie had reasons of her own for putting Bradley in a room far from the other servants. "Well, she may have a point, but I intend to familiarize myself with the whole house over the next few days."

"Sir."

"We need to talk about your uniform. I see no reason for you to wear it every day. You're my valet now, not my batman. I'll speak to Frame about getting you fitted for civilian togs."

Bradley looked crestfallen, but didn't object.

"I might have to order some new outfits myself. I've worn a uniform for so long, I fear my civvies are woefully out of fashion."

"Sir."

Gabe glanced around. The room was small, as was the bed within it. But it was clean and the wardrobe looked adequate. "No W.C., though?" he asked.

"Across the landing, sir."

That explained one of the three doors. Bradley wouldn't complain. During their years in the army, they'd both been obliged to use hastily-dug latrines and shared loos with hundreds of men in less than pristine barracks. "Anyway, you're comfortable here for a few days."

"Sir. Just wish the dog…"

It was a reminder of the mysterious occupants of the third room. "I'll see what can be done."

»»»«««

AT FIRST, EMMA ignored the light tap at her door. She assumed the new earl's servant had come to complain about the dog. He'd go away if she didn't answer.

Wellington soon rendered that position untenable. He sniffed and yapped at the door, despite Patsy's efforts to pull him away. Her grunting and wailing might make the man think a child was being beaten.

She opened the door an inch, startled to see two men on the landing, one of them the new earl she'd only glimpsed yesterday through the window. He was tall, taller even than Matthew. She'd thought him a sickly-looking man but, now, she noted his chiseled features, broad shoulders, thick black hair and eyes of a color she couldn't name. They were amber, perhaps, and graced with the longest lashes she'd ever seen on a man. There was a hint of something awry, though. He was flushed and slightly out of breath. Surely climbing three flights of stairs wouldn't wind a career soldier who wasn't as elderly as she'd expected. Indeed, not elderly at all.

She swallowed hard and tried to collect her thoughts. "If it's about the dog…"

The earl shook his head. "Forgive the intrusion. I'm Gabriel Smith…er…the new earl. I was introduced to the staff yesterday, but I don't recall meeting you."

Emma kept the door open only a crack, trying to dislodge the determined Wellington with her foot. It had become clear she would have to reveal her identity, so why not get it over with? But she dithered, terrified of being thrown out of a house where she no longer had any right to stay. "I wasn't there," she replied.

"I understand you have a sick child. Is that the reason?"

It was too much. She wasn't a liar and would never be able to keep up the subterfuge. She thrust open the door, not surprised when Wellington bolted, hotly pursued by Patsy who clearly suffered no ailment anyone could see with the naked eye. "For heaven's sake," she declared, steeling herself for Gabriel Smith's censure. "I'm Lady Emma Crompton, the late earl's widow."

GABE HADN'T EXPECTED Matthew's widow to be so…what was the word…stunning. He'd never seen eyes the color of moorland heather. The anger and frustration burning in her gaze only added to her beauty. His body's instant reaction shamed him. The unrelenting black of her attire indicated she was still in deep mourning for his dead cousin.

He'd assumed she would have moved out long before now, but

then he remembered the pittance she'd been given to live on. She'd be mortified if she thought he knew of it. She was already looking down her aristocratic nose at him. The fact he was a soldier likely added to her disdain.

It would be awkward having her in the house, but he couldn't allow her to remain in an upstairs bedroom that was probably no bigger than Bradley's. Especially with a fresh-faced pigtailed child who was now climbing back up the stairs with Wellington in her arms.

"May I present my daughter, Patsy," the widow said, her intriguing eyes bleak as she laid a protective arm across the girl's shoulder. "And I believe you've already met Wellington."

"Indeed," Gabe replied, wondering what it was about the girl she wasn't telling him. "Hello, Patsy. I see you love your dog."

Patsy scrunched up her little face and asked, "Who are you?"

He didn't have a chance to answer, anxious as he was to catch Lady Emma when she fainted.

IMPROPRIETY

"M UMMY, MUMMY."

Drifting in a haze, Emma thought she heard Patsy calling her name, but…

She blinked open her eyes, overjoyed to see her daughter's anxious face at her bedside.

She sat up quickly and dragged the child into her embrace. "You can speak," she rasped, sniffling back tears.

Then, an unpleasant memory surfaced. After all her mother's coaxing entreaties, Patsy had broken her silence by asking a question of a complete stranger—an interloper. It was hurtful.

Patsy eased out of her embrace. "I wanted to know who the nice man was," she replied, as if that explained everything. "He told me he's the new earl."

Emma tensed, wondering what had been said after she'd apparently swooned.

"He says he likes Wellington, though he didn't want to hold him."

Emma was almost tempted to smile. Men weren't known to be overly fond of poodles. Matthew detested the dog. It was astonishing Patsy had offered to let Gabriel Smith hold her pet.

"If he's the new earl," her daughter said, "I suppose that means Daddy isn't coming back."

Emma swallowed the lump in her throat, retying the black ribbons of Patsy's pigtails. "No, darling, he isn't."

"You tried to tell me so, but I kept hoping you were wrong."

Emma knew all too well the temptation of denying the reality that Matthew was dead and buried. She'd wallowed in lying to herself for weeks. Not knowing what to say, she took her little girl's hand and they sat in silence for a good while.

When a light tap sounded at the door, she was suddenly shocked to realize they were no longer in the dingy room upstairs, and the knock had come from the earl's adjacent chambers.

GABE'S RELUCTANCE TO enter the dowager countess' apartments grew when Patsy opened the door to his knock.

"Come in, Mr. Smith," she said.

He'd had virtually no contact with children while he was in the army—certainly none on Saint Helena—and wasn't sure how to respond to a girl who had only recently lost her father. The child's dark hair indicated she'd inherited her father's coloring rather than her mother's. Brought up by his stepfather, he had no memory of his own father's death and his mother never spoke of the man who'd given him life. Perhaps *brought up* was misleading. Samuel Waterman was the main reason Gabe had begged his mother for the money to buy a commission at the age of sixteen. Anything to escape the meaty fists.

Frame had told Gabe of the child's refusal to speak until now, which explained her mother's fainting spell. He also understood the deep frown marring Lady Emma's countenance as she hurriedly rose from the bed. The butler had mentioned this chamber was previously hers. He'd seen no reason not to have her brought here, though perhaps he should have heeded Frame's disapproving scowl. At the time, he hadn't considered the impropriety of his bedchamber being next door. Servants like Tillie would make sure the news was all over the village by teatime.

"You mustn't call the earl Mr. Smith," the dowager countess admonished.

Patsy looked bewildered. "But I can't call him Daddy."

Lady Emma's mouth tightened.

Gabe ached for her grief. He knew the pain of a broken heart caused by a lost love.

"No," she said, clearly making an effort to stay calm. "You must call him Lord Farnworth."

Gabe cringed, but supposed the formalities had to be observed.

"But you're Lady Farnworth," Patsy retorted. "Is he your new husband?"

Clearly, formalities didn't exist in the mind of a child.

Fury reddened the dowager countess' face. "Absolutely not. Lord Farnworth is a distant cousin of your father's."

Gabe couldn't fail to notice the emphasis she placed on the word *distant*.

>>><<<

TILLIE'S APPEARANCE WOULD be all that was needed to add to Emma's mortification. The maid didn't materialize, but the chit had probably already learned of the inappropriate situation and the news would quickly spread in the nearby village of Slade.

It was too much. Born into the emerging wealthy industrial class, Emma had worked hard at convincing Matthew's family and the local people that a mill owner's daughter was worthy of the title *Countess*.

Now, her reputation would unravel. She'd be cast as the desperate widow trying to seduce the eligible bachelor who'd become the new earl.

Eligible he might be with his stunning physique, intriguing eyes and thick, black hair...

She fisted her hands in the folds of her skirts, ashamed she'd noticed anything at all about Gabriel Smith's appearance. "I must insist on returning to my upstairs chamber, my lord," she said, though the prospect held no appeal. "Just until the will is settled and I receive my widow's portion."

She tensed when something flickered in Gabriel Smith's intriguing eyes that looked uncomfortably like pity. There was no possible way he could know of her financial circumstances and had no right to feel sorry for her. She'd rather die than be the object of this man's pity.

"I can't allow that," he said. "This is your apartment. You and Patsy will be more comfortable here."

"Wellington too," Patsy agreed.

Emma wished with all her heart her daughter wasn't witnessing her humiliation. "But it's scandalous. People will talk."

Smith's chuckle grated on her nerves. "Dear lady, having spent years in the army listening to one scandalous rumor after another being bandied about by officers, I've learned not to pay too much attention. And please call me Gabriel."

With that, he bowed and took his leave.

"As if that will happen," she muttered under her breath. "*Dear lady,* indeed."

FORMAL DINNER

G ABE RETREATED TO his chamber, where Bradley was arranging clothes in the enormous armoire. "Could I have sounded any more like old Abercrombie? I actually called her *dear lady*."

"It's hard for a man to keep his wits about him when he's had a shock, sir."

Shock indeed. He hadn't expected the dowager countess and her daughter to be still in residence. In addition, he'd mistakenly thought Matthew much older than himself, and therefore believed his countess must be middle-aged. Lady Emma was a young woman who possessed a rare beauty. Her fair skin was flawless; pleasing blonde braids peeked from beneath a widow's cap. Her shapely figure would appeal to any man. He suspected she may have been thin as a young girl. Bearing a child had filled her out in all the right places.

Tempting as it was to share these observations with Bradley, he decided it would be better to keep them to himself. He had no intention of pursuing a widow with a child—not to mention the yapping poodle. Lady Emma was above his reach and it was clear she had a poor opinion of him. Who could blame her?

There was no telling how quickly his illness might progress. He perhaps had scant months to find a wife, marry and father a son. He didn't have time or energy to waste trying to win the haughty widow over to his side.

"You'll have to do something about the proximity of your apartments, sir," Bradley observed.

Gabe glanced around. "You're right. I'm tempted to simply move out of this ghastly chamber. Does this hideous green wallpaper remind you of anything?"

Bradley chuckled. "I thought the same, sir. Could be from the same batch they used to decorate Napoleon's little hideaway on Saint Helena."

They both laughed heartily at the improbability. "Still, I'm very glad to be away from that godforsaken place," Gabe said.

"As am I, sir," Bradley replied. "Boney's welcome to it."

⫸⫷

EMMA CRIED OFF eating luncheon in the dining room but realized it would be deemed rude and petty if she insisted trays be sent to her rooms on a daily basis. Her daughter had every right to eat in the dining room of what should have been her ancestral home.

She resolved to be polite to the new earl but to remain aloof. He'd soon realize how she felt about him inheriting the earldom. Of course, she'd have to do it without revealing her dire financial straits. It was imperative she come up with a plausible reason for not moving out of the manor house.

She was heartily sick of wearing mourning, but Matthew had been dead for only seven months. Black wasn't a color that complemented her complexion, but it would hopefully remind Gabriel Smith of the reasons for his windfall. She rolled her eyes at that notion. The man likely had no idea how to manage an estate the size of Farnworth. Worse still, he might be a gambler, a wastrel who would fritter away money on sinful pursuits.

She had to admit, however, Smith didn't seem the type to indulge in sinful pursuits. Too stolidly military. There was something else about him. Now that she'd seen him up close, she was even more convinced he wasn't a well man. But that wasn't her concern—unless he died without an heir. Such a catastrophe might throw the earldom into the hands of an even worse contender. At least Smith was polite, reasonably intelligent and not unattractive. He hadn't evicted them and Patsy seemed to like him.

Upon arrival in the formal dining room in time for the evening meal, she was relieved to see Frame had heeded her request. Places for her and Patsy had been set at one end of the dining table that could accommodate twenty-four. Candles flickered in three large candelabra, their reflection mirrored in the polished surface. Gabriel Smith, in dress uniform, was already standing stiffly by his chair at the other end of the table. She had to admit there was nothing quite so pleasing to the eye as a handsome soldier in uniform.

He bowed politely when she and Patsy entered. "Good evening, Countess, Miss Crompton," he said without a trace of a smile.

Guilt flickered for a moment in Emma's heart. He was nervous and no doubt realized she was deliberately being unfriendly. She nodded and sat in the chair held out for her by a footman.

"Can I sit beside Lord Farnworth?" Patsy asked.

"I'm sure Lord Farnworth would rather eat in peace," Emma replied, wishing she'd made the need to remain aloof clear to her daughter. It was such a relief to hear the child speak, she hadn't wanted to impose too many restrictions.

"You can sit wherever you like," Smith replied, but then he glanced at Emma and added, "however, you must abide by your mother's wishes."

Pouting, Patsy took her place beside Emma.

There was no conversation as servants brought in the soup course. Emma smiled inwardly when her daughter remembered her manners and didn't reach for her spoon until the earl picked up his. She only wished the soup wasn't so hot that Patsy felt it necessary to blow on it. Emma's frown didn't stop the behavior, so she decided not to scold Patsy in front of Smith, especially since he was blowing on his own soup.

What could one expect from a man who ate with hundreds of other men?

"If I may ask," the earl said while they waited for the second course. "Is there not a dower house on the estate?"

A knot tightened in Emma's stomach.

"It burned," Patsy explained.

"Recently?"

"A few years ago," Emma replied, unwilling to reveal Matthew's widowed father had gone off his head and set fire to the house where his own mother had lived until her death. His embarrassing lunacy was something she and Matthew never spoke of. Emma suspected her husband feared he too might eventually lose his wits. Before his death, he had begun to exhibit odd behavior that led her to believe it might be true.

"Can the house not be repaired?"

"Grandpapa died in it," Patsy said.

Mortified, Emma glared at her daughter. "Lord Farnworth doesn't need to know that, dear."

"Actually," he replied, "I'm anxious to learn more of the family history. Do you mean he died in the fire, or in the house?"

"Both," Patsy obliged.

"Well," he said. "I had a brief chat with the estate manager today. We agreed to meet again on the morrow. Tragic as your grandpapa's death was, I see no reason not to repair the house if it can be salvaged. I'll ask Blair's opinion."

As the widow of the late earl, Emma was entitled to move into the dower house. The problem of a roof over her head would be solved, but she wouldn't have enough money to afford the upkeep.

Still, the prospect the dower house might be restored kindled a spark of hope, and she couldn't help but be grateful to Smith for thinking of it. However, she mustn't let him know that.

INSOMNIA

G ABE HOPED THE headache he'd nursed all day would abate once
he put his head down on the pillow. After an hour of tossing, he
accepted that wasn't going to be the case. Despite sleeping naked, he
was too hot, although his feet were cold. The warm bricks conjured by
the intrepid Bradley had failed to do their job. His throat was dry and it
was hard to swallow. These weren't new symptoms of his illness, but
he'd hoped leaving Saint Helena might improve things, especially
when the aches and pains lessened slightly aboard *Dreadnought*.

Knowing Emma and Patsy slept in the adjacent apartment didn't
help matters. He couldn't hear anything from next door, but he was
aware he snored and would be embarrassed if his sawing wood kept
them awake. Hopefully, the restoration of the dower house would
turn out to be a feasible option. Matthew's widow and child couldn't
continue living in the house with him, but he could hardly turn them
out knowing they had only a pittance on which to survive.

Resigned to another sleepless night, he slid out of the four-poster
bed and lit the oil lamp with a taper from the embers of the fire. The
sickly green wallpaper made him even more out of sorts. As well as
the bed curtains, the carpets and window draperies were green. It was
all too bilious in the eerie glow of the lamp, so he decided to investigate the library downstairs.

Since it was doubtful anyone else would be up and about, he
donned his banyan to cover his nakedness rather than getting fully

dressed. The silk felt blessedly cool on his overheated skin. He tugged on a pair of woolen hose in the hopes they might warm his feet.

Holding the lamp high, he paused in the hallway, holding his breath when he heard Wellington growl softly. Silence ensued, so he carried on down the stairs.

His meeting with Mr. Blair earlier in the day had taken place in the library, but there'd been no opportunity to peruse the shelves. The Cromptons had amassed an impressive collection of books over the years. He was confident he would find something to take his mind off his worries—or send him to sleep.

The *Confessions* of Jean-Jacques Rousseau didn't appeal. He'd already read *Gulliver's Travels* and *Robinson Crusoe*. Some brilliant military mind had deemed both books appropriate reading for soldiers marooned on Saint Helena. He'd also once embarked on Goethe's *Sorrows of Young Werther*, but the pathetic story of a man hopelessly in unrequited love made Georgina's betrayal even more painful.

The unusual number of weighty tomes on madness was surprising, but not what he wanted to read in his present state, nor was he remotely interested in learning more about Napoleon Bonaparte.

Intrigued by the frontispiece of Defoe's *Moll Flanders*—"*The Fortunes & Misfortunes of the Famous Moll Flanders, &c. Who was Born in Newgate, & during a Life of continu'd Variety for Threescore Years, besides her Childhood, was Twelve Year a Whore, five times a Wife (whereof once to her own Brother), Twelve Year a Thief, Eight Year a Transported Felon in Virginia, at last grew Rich, liv'd Honest, & died a Penitent. Written from her own Memorandums.*"—he settled on it as the perfect frivolity to take his mind off his problems.

Faced with the choice of returning to his chamber to recline on the *chaise-longue*—upholstered in green fabric of course—or settling on the cushioned window seat, he chose the latter.

EMMA WAS UNCERTAIN how she felt about sleeping in her own apartment. Patsy fell asleep as soon as she got into bed, Wellington curled up against her back.

However, there was no escaping the fact that Gabriel Smith was abed right next door. She'd always hated Matthew's bedchamber and had never spent an entire night there. On the increasingly rare occasions he'd summoned her to his bed, she'd returned to her own sanctuary immediately afterwards. There was something depressingly eerie about the décor. It was like being immersed in pea soup. She'd sometimes thought it wasn't surprising Matthew's father had gone mad after sleeping in the room for years, but her opinion wouldn't have been well received.

She listened intently but could hear nothing from the earl's chamber. A soldier was probably used to sleeping in all kinds of uncomfortable places. Clearly, Smith was sound asleep.

Insomnia had plagued her since Matthew's death. The overwhelming shock and grief had destroyed her peace of mind. She couldn't come to grips with the reason her husband had indulged in such uncharacteristic behavior. He wasn't a good rider, so she would never understand what had possessed him to gallop across country urging his aged gelding over hedgerows and stone walls. One too many as it turned out.

Then came the worry over money, a still unresolved problem. Now, she was forced to sleep in a chamber adjacent to Gabriel Smith's.

A good book would help. She'd ordered *Mansfield Park* just before Matthew's death and her copy sat unopened on a library shelf.

"Bugger it," she muttered under her breath as she threw off the linens. The memory of her father's favorite expletive brought a brief smile to her face.

Wrapped in a dressing gown and wearing only slippers on her feet, she left the chamber, intending to return before Patsy realized she was gone.

The familiar staircase was easy to navigate in the dark, but she'd never noticed the hinges of the library door desperately needed oiling. Still cringing as she stepped inside, she wondered why the room was lit. Someone had left a lamp burning. "Foolhardy," she whispered, her heart leaping into her throat when she espied Smith asleep in the window seat. One long leg dangled over the side of the cushion, exposed from stockinged foot to the top of a powerful thigh. An open book rested on a broad chest left bare by a banyan that had fallen open. The dusting of dark hair looked soft. She swallowed hard, gobsmacked at the male beauty laid out before her like a Renaissance sculpture.

She ought to flee, but her feet seemed stuck to the rug. A hasty movement might wake him. Sleep had softened the harsh lines that normally marred his chiseled features. He'd be mortified she had stumbled upon him half-naked. A ripple of unwelcome desire stirred low in her belly. If she lifted the edge of the banyan that clung tenuously to the top of his thigh…

Shame soared through her. Such sinful thoughts were enough to make Matthew turn over in his grave, but she seemed incapable of quelling the curiosity that plagued her. She swayed, perplexed that what lay at the apex of Gabriel Smith's thighs might turn out to be disappointingly similar to her late husband's male bits. She clamped a hand over her mouth to stifle the unladylike giggle that threatened to emerge. Sleeplessness and worry had obviously driven her to lunacy.

The hinges squealed.

A little voice murmured, "Mummy?"

Wellington yapped.

The banyan slipped open when the earl startled from sleep. His book fell to the floor as he hurriedly covered his body and struggled to stand.

These unfortunate events unfolded quickly, yet, for Emma, they happened in dreadful slow motion. Mortification buckled her knees.

Her gaze locked with the earl's. She acknowledged as she swooned that the male parts she glimpsed ever so fleetingly were much more impressive than Matthew's.

REMORSE

G ABE'S HEADACHE RETURNED with a vengeance. The desperate hope no one would hear the yapping poodle turned out to be futile. It took his addled brain a moment or two to realize what had happened. In the blink of an eye, the library was full of people in night attire, all glaring at him as if he'd committed murder and been caught standing over the corpse, weapon in hand.

Swathed in a velour dressing gown, her hair writhing with curling rags like Medusa's serpents, the tutting housekeeper knelt beside Matthew's widow, waving a vial of smelling salts under her ladyship's nose.

Clutching the still growling Wellington, Patsy stared at Gabe as if he were an apparition, her bottom lip quivering.

Frame directed a burly footman to assist his mistress up from the floor when she showed signs of reviving.

Clad in his army-issue bathrobe, Bradley stood in the doorway, scratching his head.

Tillie leaned against a bookshelf, a cheeky smile tugging at the corners of her mouth. The chiffon peignoir did little to conceal the skimpy black negligee beneath. Gabe fleetingly wondered how a housemaid could afford such expensive garments.

He had done nothing wrong but he'd be blamed for the fiasco. His only mistake was he'd fallen into a deep sleep.

How was he to know Matthew's widow would come down to the

library? And that her daughter would follow? Truly, it was Emma's fault for leaving the child alone.

He deemed it pointless to protest his innocence. It was the middle of the night. He was a scantily clad man in a library full of people, most of whom held a poor opinion of him in any case. A disheveled woman in a dressing gown and slippers had swooned at his feet.

The widow would likely despise him even more, although he was relieved she had managed to stand and looked none the worse for wear. He wasn't sure what to make of the silly grin on her face. Shock, he supposed.

Determined not to give credence to any suggestion of impropriety, he cleared his throat and summoned his best imitation of Abercrombie. "Will you need assistance returning to your chamber, Lady Emma?" he asked.

As if awakening from a trance, she seemed suddenly to become aware of the other people. "Er…no…please go back to bed, everyone. I apologize we disturbed you, my lord. I came for a book. *Mansfield Park*. An attack of the vapors. Come along, Patsy."

Within a minute, Gabe was the only person left in the silent library. He picked up his book from the rug. "Just you and me left, Moll," he said.

Avoiding the window seat, he sat at the desk and stared at the pages, but his muddled thoughts drifted to the widow. It was unfortunate the silk banyan had slipped off his body when he'd finally nodded off, but he wondered what Emma might have done if Patsy hadn't arrived when she did.

He shook his head. He'd thought the combination of Georgina's betrayal and his illness had long since put paid to the natural male reaction he'd experienced when jolted from sleep by the sight of an alluring woman.

EMMA DOZED FITFULLY for the rest of the night, thankful Patsy hadn't expressed any upset over what had happened. She could only be grateful she'd blocked Gabriel Smith's nudity from her daughter's view. A child would be haunted by such an image. Emma couldn't get it out of her mind.

She ought to feel repulsed but found herself embarrassingly aroused by the memory of a substantial male member. She might have known the strikingly handsome officer in dress uniform who'd greeted her in the dining room would be well formed in other parts of his body.

She was wide awake when dawn broke, exhausted and ashamed of herself. Clearly, months without sexual congress had stirred forbidden feelings. It was especially troubling that Matthew's male bits had never roused wanton yearnings. One fleeting glimpse of a well-endowed man she didn't even like and she was a mess.

The soft click of Smith's door was enough to start Wellington growling. Apparently, the new earl had spent the night in the library. Remorse tightened her throat. Her midnight excursion had unwittingly put him in an embarrassing situation, and probably done nothing for her own reputation. Tillie's tongue would soon be wagging. She hoped the rest of the staff knew her well enough to defend her sterling character. But they didn't know Smith at all and no one would step forward to defend him, except his servant, another unknown quantity. Establishing himself with the local gentry would be hard enough without malicious rumor dogging Smith's heels.

TEMPTING AS IT was to curl up and spend the day in bed, Gabe deemed it preferable to escape the bilious chamber. "There'll be repercussions from last night's contretemps," he told Bradley when his servant came to help him dress for the day. "My absence would make things worse."

"You're a soldier, sir," Bradley replied. "Time to face the foe."

That was all very well, but Gabe's enemy was faceless. "Neither Lady Emma nor I did anything wrong. However, she's well known and any malicious gossip might quickly be dismissed. I'll wager Tillie will make sure the whole village knows what happened. Or her version of events."

"I'll have a word with her, sir," Bradley promised.

Gabe raised an eyebrow. Things in that regard were apparently progressing faster than he'd expected. "I don't need to tell you to be careful with that girl."

"Understood, sir."

Gabe thought he detected a trace of annoyance in his servant's voice. "I realize we are no longer in the army, but you and I are without reinforcements here. We need to present a united front."

It was tempting to laugh when Bradley stood to attention, lifted his chin and saluted. But the message had apparently sunk in. "Good man. Now, off to breakfast."

FIGHT OR FLIGHT

HEAT FLOODED EMMA'S face when Smith entered the morning room. She had to get back to thinking of him as an interloper, not an attractive and physically well-endowed male. "Good morning, Lord Farnworth," she said in a husky voice she didn't recognize.

This had to stop.

"Morning, Mr. Smith," Patsy declared.

"Good morning, ladies," he replied before Emma had a chance to remind her daughter as to the proper form of address. "Why don't you call me Cousin Gabriel?" he suggested to Patsy.

"Are you my cousin?" she asked.

Emma struggled for a means to change the direction of the conversation. "Lord Farnworth is your papa's cousin. That's how he inherited the earldom."

Smith cleared his throat. "Actually, I'm Matthew's second cousin twice removed."

Anger at the injustice tightened Emma's throat. She gripped her fork, tempted to throw it at him.

"What does that mean?" Patsy asked with a snort.

"Young ladies don't snort," Emma reminded her, too harshly. She'd intended to apologize for her part in last night's scene, but things had veered in entirely the wrong direction. She couldn't organize her thoughts. The episode in the library had addled her brain.

"Sorry, Mummy," her daughter replied, "but how can a cousin be removed?"

"It's too complicated for me to fathom, Patsy," Smith said. "All I know is your daddy and I were related."

"So, you must be my cousin," she replied with a grin.

Emma inhaled deeply to calm her nerves. She couldn't fault Smith for his willingness to befriend Patsy. He seemed to genuinely like her daughter and she didn't believe he was simply trying to ingratiate himself. Even Wellington hadn't growled when Smith entered the morning room. It appeared the poodle had accepted him as part of the family.

She would never lower herself to that level, but couldn't escape the reality she was dependent on Smith's goodwill. "I wanted to apologize for last night," she said, squeezing the life out of the napkin on her lap.

She wasn't prepared for Smith's blush. He was perhaps worried about what she might have seen. Could he tell she'd glimpsed his most private male parts?

"Think no more of it, Lady Emma," he replied after clearing his throat. "Neither of us could have known the other intended to visit the library."

"You looked so funny in that silly dressing gown," Patsy said with a chuckle.

Emma saw the same panic in Smith's eyes that soared up her spine. Had Patsy seen more than either of them thought? "Don't be rude, darling. You mustn't..."

"No, she's right. It was remiss of me to leave my chamber dressed only in a banyan."

Emma's assumption he'd been completely naked beneath the banyan was correct. The knowledge only served to further dull her wits. "The same here," she declared, unable to control her runaway tongue. "A lady doesn't leave her chamber clad in night attire."

Intending to erase last night's memory, she had succeeded instead in reliving the fiasco.

"I was afraid when you fainted, Mummy," Patsy admitted into the uncomfortable silence. "You never faint, and it's happened twice."

Wonderful! Now Smith would think her a delicate flower.

⇻⇻⇻⫷⫷⫷

EMMA HAD COME down to breakfast dressed in a fashionable day gown of black bombazine, her hair bound up in an elaborate braided affair and topped by the widow's cap she always wore. All Gabe could see in his mind's eye was the disheveled woman clad only in a dressing gown who'd come upon him in the library. He'd had no idea her hair was so long and thick.

It was inappropriate enough for a gentleman to see a female acquaintance in her night attire, but Emma likely didn't realize he'd glimpsed bare ankles and a hint of shapely calves while she lay prostrate on the carpet.

Not only that, the dressing gown had gaped open to reveal more than a hint of her nightgown, filled out nicely by generous breasts—until Mrs. Maple had hurriedly righted the garment.

Emma's blush this morning might indicate she had realized what he'd seen—or perhaps he hadn't covered himself fast enough. Was that the reason she'd swooned?

Like a good soldier faced with a surprise attack, his cock had chosen fight rather than flight when jolted awake by the unexpected arrival of Emma and her daughter. Unfortunately, it was contemplating the same maneuver now, seemingly the only part of his anatomy not debilitated by his malady.

The sooner he got the widow out of the house the better for them both. He could hardly woo a prospective wife with Emma, Patsy and Wellington underfoot. He had no idea how to go about finding suitable candidates in this part of England and his deteriorating health couldn't take many more challenges. His head was already throbbing. "I'll get Blair to show me the dower house this morning," he said. "Then we'll see what he thinks about the possibility of restoring it."

"I DON'T WANT to live in the dower house," Patsy complained after Smith had taken his leave.

Wellington barked his agreement.

Emma decided there was little point embarking on a campaign to convince her daughter of the merits of moving to the ruined structure. The possibility the house might be restored was remote. It would probably prove to be too damaged, the repairs too costly to undertake. Smith might consider such an expense unnecessary and tear the house down. She'd never understood Matthew's reluctance to deal with the problem, though his father's descent into madness must have preyed on his mind.

She didn't blame Patsy for feeling uncomfortable about the place.

Her thoughts led in an alarming direction. During the last few months of Matthew's life, he'd adopted some of his father's manner-isms and complained of similar aches and pains. Gabriel Smith had pressed his fingers to his temples in exactly the same way Matthew and his father had done—as if afflicted by the blinding headache that often brought them low.

An icy shiver ran down her spine. Was there a curse on the Earls of Farnworth?

She dismissed the foolish notion. Lots of people suffered head-aches. The new earl had only been in residence for a day, and she'd thought from the start he wasn't a healthy man. It really was too bad; he was such a handsome specimen.

APPOINTMENTS

G ABE PACED WHILE waiting for Blair in the library. It wasn't the best place to try to forget the previous night's contretemps.

His intention to discuss the dower house faltered when Blair arrived toting an armful of ledgers. Obviously, the fellow wanted to discuss financial matters.

"Good morrow to thee, Lord Farnworth," the estate manager said jovially.

He'd struck Gabe as an affable chap during their initial brief meeting, a plain-speaking northerner who could be depended on to call a spade a spade. The task of learning about the management of the estate might not be so daunting with a man like Blair to guide him.

"Good morning," Gabe replied. "I see you've brought the ledgers, but I wondered if we might investigate the dower house first."

Blair frowned. "It's a ruin, sir."

"Yes, I understand there was a fire."

Blair narrowed his eyes, but made no reply.

Gabe got the uneasy feeling there was more to learn about the matter. Blair was a forthright man but he'd worked for the Cromptons for years. His loyalty to them was understandable. "You can explain the ledgers to me later. I'm confident all is in order. Firstly, I'd like to see the dower house. Lady Emma would probably be more comfortable there, if it can be restored."

Blair hefted the ledgers onto the desk, his glance going briefly to the window seat. Evidently, news traveled fast among the staff. "I'm not rightly sure the dowager countess would want to live in the dower house, my lord."

Gabe doubted Blair knew of the meager bequest Emma had received. "Well, yes, I understand her father-in-law perished in the fire, but she seems willing to consider the notion and it isn't appropriate for her to live here."

Blair shifted his weight, clearly uncomfortable. "I can teck thee to see it, I suppose."

"Can we walk?"

"It's about a mile, on t'other side of the park."

There was a time when Gabe could march ten miles without breaking his stride, but he doubted he'd make it there and back on foot. "Looks like rain. Perhaps you can arrange for a couple of horses."

Blair eyed him, probably of the opinion his new master was a weakling who couldn't walk a mile and was afraid of getting wet, but he nodded.

"I'll meet you in the stables in ten minutes," Gabe said.

＊＊＊＊＊＊

UPON LEAVING THE morning room, Emma encountered Smith in the foyer, surprised to see he'd changed into riding attire, the tight breeches and highly polished knee-high boots emphasizing his long legs.

"Blair and I are off to take a look at the dower house," he explained. "I'll let you know his opinion."

Emma nodded, her heart in knots. William Blair was as loyal as they came, a true-blue Lancashire lad, but he'd eventually have to reveal the circumstances of the fire to the new earl. Better Smith hear of the old earl's madness from Blair than through the local gossip mill.

She wasn't sure why she cared if he found out the truth. It wasn't her father who'd gone round the bend, although she and Priscilla often wondered what had prompted their parents' harebrained tour of India.

Her brain tended to cease functioning when she contemplated a deeply buried dread that Matthew had inherited his father's manic tendencies.

If madness ran in the family, what might become of Patsy?

She felt very alone with her fears. She and Priscilla had never been close and things had worsened after her sister's marriage. Their six boys behaved like wild things in any case. Discussing madness with Priscilla was out of the question.

She could trust Frame and Mrs. Maple, but they were servants after all.

Smith perhaps had a right to know the whole recent history of the earldom. For a soldier, he seemed a reasonable man. She'd be beholden to him if he restored the dower house, though she could never divulge the dire circumstances that would earn her gratitude.

⭆⭅

GABE AND BLAIR sought shelter in the stables of the dower house when the rain began.

"Good thing the fire didn't take the stables as well," Gabe remarked.

"Aye," Blair replied. "Just the part of the house where..."

Gabe scanned the blackened walls a few yards away. "Where what?" he asked. "I'm getting the feeling there's more to this than I've been told."

Blair looked up to the sky. "Seems to be clearing."

Gabe had often dealt with evasive answers from both subordinates and superiors. "Yes, and when it does, we'll walk over to the house and you'll tell me the whole story."

The rain stopped after a few minutes.

"Just a summer shower," Blair said nervously as they dismounted.

A rare ray of sunshine emerged from behind a cloud, bathing the ruin in a golden hue. "This was a grand house," Gabe said, inhaling the rain-freshened air as he strode away from the stables. "Built of the same local stone as the main house."

"Indeed," Blair confirmed. "But it's no longer safe to venture inside."

They walked the perimeter of the property. Sections of the cream-colored walls seemed unmarred by the flames. Peering into smoke-blackened windows and gaping holes where the glass had shattered, they saw piles of charred debris littering the floor in some rooms. Others were empty and appeared virtually untouched.

Gabe was impatient to learn how the fire had started. Blair would eventually realize he had to tell him. There was no point browbeating the chap. "It looks like the fire was extinguished before it could destroy the whole structure," he began, hoping to get the man talking.

"Aye. The groundskeeper was scything the grass when he noticed the smoke. He ran over to the main house to sound the alarm."

"But I understood the old earl was in the dower house at the time of the fire."

Blair removed his tweed cap and raked a hand through his hair. "I reckon ye'll find out soon enough, so I may as well tell thee. Lord Farnworth started the fire. The groundskeeper saw him run outside brandishing a flaming torch, shouting wild ramblings about his mother and Judgment Day. He ran back into the flames before the groundskeeper could stop him."

"And perished."

"Aye. They recovered his body a few days later."

"Was there an inquest?"

"Aye. In Preston. 'Twere ruled an accident. The family didn't want a scandal."

Gabe understood. It wouldn't do for the local gentry to know their earl had gone mad. "I suppose the groundskeeper was pensioned off?"

Blair gazed off into the distance. "Aye, but my father never recovered from what he'd witnessed. He blamed himself for not saving the earl. He died not long after."

Gabe raised an eyebrow. Blair's roots at Thicketford ran deeper than he'd realized. "I thank you for telling me the truth. It's a dark chapter in your family's history as well as the Cromptons'."

Blair nodded, but still looked ill-at-case. "Ye should know the young Lord Farnworth never came to terms with what happened to his father. I think he feared madness might run in the family."

"That's the reason he left the ruin as it is."

"Aye. I'm nay one to gossip, but some say Lord Matthew must have been off his head the day he died."

Gabe was puzzled. "A riding accident, I thought."

"That's right, but a man not known for his riding ability doesn't urge his aging mount over stone walls and hedgerows."

"What are you saying?"

Blair averted his eyes. "Nothing, my lord. I wasn't there, so I shouldn't say."

Gabe decided not to push further. "What's your opinion then. Can the house be salvaged?"

Blair's shoulders relaxed. "I think it's time."

TROUBLE

OUT OF BREATH after walking briskly beneath the willows, Tillie reached the gates at the end of the long driveway, thankful the rain hadn't materialized. She'd looked forward impatiently to her day off and had dressed in her best gown, spencer and bonnet in order to impress her lover in whose bed she hoped to spend the rest of the day.

The curmudgeon of a gatekeeper scowled at her as he unlocked the gates. "Off with yer fancy man, are ye?"

She lifted her chin. The servants were a judgmental lot, but she put their slights down to jealousy. She was the one who'd snagged the attention of a baron's son and, someday soon, she'd be rich. "That's for me to know and you to find out," she retorted, flustered when he merely chuckled.

"Ye think I don't recognize yon carriage when his lordship picks ye up?"

"Bother," she hissed when a fat raindrop landed on her bonnet.

Ignoring the chuckling codger, she hurried off in the direction of the Whiteside estate, hoping Arthur wouldn't be late this time.

WONDERING IF TILLIE would ever stop talking, Arthur Coleman rolled off the chit's lush body and looked up at the ceiling of his chamber at Withins Hall. The maid's scandalous version of an embarrassing incident between the dowager countess Farnworth and the new earl wasn't what he wanted to hear as he pumped his seed into Tillie's warm sheath. He'd resorted to ramming his tongue down her throat to shut her up.

Now, instead of doing her duty and cleansing him, she was prattling on about Emma Crompton fancying the new earl.

"I thought he was a common soldier," he remarked, immediately wishing he hadn't given her ammunition to prolong the conversation.

"A lieutenant colonel, according to his batman," she replied coyly. "A batman's a servant, by the way. In the army. And the new earl's ever so handsome in his uniform."

Arthur restrained the urge to laugh. It was comical enough the silly twit thought she had a hope of becoming Mrs. Arthur Coleman. There was a hint of something in her voice that suggested she'd set her cap at the new Lord Farnworth. As if...

He gritted his teeth. He'd done his utmost to snag the interest of the haughty Lady Emma, but she was having none of it. The bitch couldn't have made it clearer she thought a baron's son beneath her. Apparently, she had no objection to a midnight tryst with the new earl, both of them clad in night attire.

He closed his eyes, trying to ignore Tillie's meaningless ramblings about one thing after another—Napoleon Bonaparte, the insipid child who refused to speak after her father's death and the infernal poodle that had nipped at Arthur's heels during the funeral reception. And, if she complained once more that he'd been late picking her up...

One day, he'd make the snooty Lady Emma pay for rejecting him. The substantial amounts of blunt her husband had probably left her could have paid off the vowels held by certain unsavory people. Time was of the essence. Eventually, his indulgent father would learn of the large sums of family money he'd lost at the gaming tables in Manchester.

Perhaps a visit to Thicketford Manor was in order. It would be an opportunity to size up the new Lord Farnworth while once again offering his most sincere condolences. Wasn't that what neighbors did?

Utterly sick of the sound of Tillie's voice, he rose from the bed, gripped his flaccid cock and resorted to the one thing he knew would silence her for a while. "Open your mouth, wench."

An Expensive Project

E MMA WAS SITTING in the drawing room listening for the gong that
would signal luncheon was being served. Instead, Frame came to
inform her the earl had requested her presence in the library.

"Mr. Blair is there too," he added, clearly understanding the reason
for the heat that flooded her face.

Would she ever be able to enter the library again without thinking
of…

"Thank you, Frame," she replied, thrown off balance by the request for her to join what was apparently a business discussion.
Matthew had never sought her involvement in such meetings.

She'd fretted about the dower house for most of the morning. It
was doubtful Smith would be willing to spend money on the restoration. After all, there was really nothing in it for him, except to rid
himself of her and Patsy. Steeling her nerves for bad news, she entered
the library.

Smith was seated behind the large desk, Blair in the visitor's chair.
Both stood immediately. The earl looked tired and out of sorts. The
excursion to the dower house had clearly exhausted him.

Blair bowed politely. "Lady Emma," he said.

"It's so nice to see you," Emma replied. "How is your family?"

She liked and trusted Blair and knew Matthew had depended on
his judgment. She was glad Smith seemed willing to keep him on.

"They are well, thank ye for asking, yer ladyship," Blair replied.

She took heart from his smile. Perhaps the news might not be all bad. Tamping down the lunatic urge to glance at the window seat, she turned her attention to Smith, determined to keep her eyes on his face.

Blair brought a second chair and the earl gestured for her to be seated. The estate manager sat beside her, but Smith remained standing, making it difficult not to let her eyes wander to the lower part of his anatomy. She began to wish she'd brought her fan.

"I've surveyed the damage," he announced. "And I understand more of the story behind the destruction."

Emma glanced at Blair whose face had reddened considerably. "Don't worry," she assured him. "Lord Farnworth has a right to know what happened."

"Yes," Smith agreed. "Blair estimates it will cost no more than a thousand pounds to restore the house to its former glory, including new furniture."

Emma's hopes blew away like chaff on the wind. "I see."

"He also informs me the estate can well afford the expense."

His facial expression gave nothing away. Emma had no idea if he was happy or furious with the prospect of spending a small fortune, or if he even intended to give permission for the job to commence. Having decided the best course of action was to remain silent, she startled when Matthew's successor asked, "What's your opinion, Lady Emma?"

She didn't know what to make of an earl who sought the opinion of a female he barely knew. Matthew, and his father before him, made no secret of their belief women were incapable of coping with anything beyond bearing children and organizing menus. She'd never had the courage to point out that her mother's "meddling" was the main reason for her father's success as a mill owner.

She weighed her options. Moving into a refurbished dower house would solve one problem. She and Patsy could continue to live on the estate they loved. But she had no funds to pay the expenses of such a large house.

"The estate would pay for the upkeep and day to day operation, of course," Smith said, finally taking a seat.

Had he read her mind? He couldn't possibly know of her financial situation. Could he? The urge to climb over the desk and kiss him was powerful, but well-bred ladies didn't indulge in such displays—and what had happened to the resolve to remain aloof? She inhaled deeply, trying to gather her wits. "A large estate like Farnworth should, of course, have a dower house, my lord," she said. "I would feel more comfortable there, and your own wife would benefit."

She realized her *faux pas* when he frowned. She'd insinuated the earl would die before his wife. "What I mean is...er...if you had a wife, and...er...if you died before her, and..."

The need for a fan intensified when he stood abruptly. She was afraid to meet his gaze, but her eyeballs ached with the effort of not looking at his crotch directly in front of her.

"How long do you estimate the restoration will take?" the earl asked Blair.

Blair stroked his stubbled chin. "Approximately six months, I reckon."

Emma held her breath, exhaling when the new earl gave Blair permission to go ahead. It would be churlish not to thank him, and she was extremely thankful. She stood, grateful for the desk between them. "Thank you, Lord Farnworth."

He leaned forward and fisted both hands on the desk. "It's only right you and your daughter remain on the estate you love."

She wasn't sure what flickered in his eyes—weariness yes, but something else—something that set her heart racing. Was it possible this soldier might turn out to be worthy of his inheritance?

Then he slumped into the chair. She couldn't embarrass him by inquiring about his malady with Blair present. "Luncheon will be served shortly, my lord," she began nervously.

"I might skip it today," he replied, "and if we are to share this house for six months, I insist you call me Gabriel."

She could grant him that. "As you wish, Gabriel," she said before taking her leave.

CONVERSATIONS

G ABE RETIRED TO his chamber, needing to nap for a while, though it was doubtful he'd manage to fall asleep in the green hell. He removed his riding jacket but getting his boots off required more energy than he had. He preferred not to call Bradley for such a trivial task. It wouldn't be the first time he'd slept with his boots on. He opened the curtains of the four-poster, climbed onto the bed and closed his eyes.

His mind wandered. The excursion to the dower house had taxed his resources, but it had been worth it just to see relief blossom on Lady Emma's face.

However, something else had flickered in the violet eyes that raked over him in a less than seemly manner. Was she attracted to him, or was she simply a lusty woman?

His thoughts drifted to his past disastrous failure to read what was in a woman's mind when it came to sexual congress. Perhaps it was as well his fiancée had run off with his best friend. Georgina was repulsed by his whispered longings of the erotic pleasures they might indulge in once they were married. He didn't consider himself a pervert when it came to sex, but Georgina had insisted she couldn't possibly allow him to suckle her breasts. After that rebuff, he'd kept to himself his thirst to taste her intimate juices. She'd been appalled when he'd explained how babies came about. He blamed the girl's mother for that oversight.

He'd wager Emma Crompton enjoyed having a man's mouth on her nipples. He'd had a difficult time keeping his eyes off her tempting breasts. It was as well the desk had prevented him from planting a lusty kiss on her full lips.

The situation was worrisome. There could never be anything between him and Emma; she was quality, he wasn't, and she clearly despised his humble roots and military career. He was dying and Emma was still mourning her first husband. Patsy hadn't recovered from her father's death.

The mission to find a wife loomed like an impossible task. Was it ethical to marry a woman knowing he didn't have long to live? The only solution, as far as he could discern, was to approach the subject of a wife with Emma. She would be living in the house for six months at least, and it would be in her best interests for him to marry and produce an heir. The earldom needed stability.

Resigned to finding no rest in the hateful chamber, he shrugged on his jacket and set off to find the dowager countess. He decided the next project after the completion of the dower house would be the redecoration of his own apartment. The green had to go.

⫸⫷

DURING LUNCH, EMMA told Patsy about their good fortune, but her daughter wasn't enthusiastic about moving to the smaller house. "I want to stay here," her daughter whined. "With Cousin Gabriel. I like him."

Emma could hardly confide anything of their financial situation. She had to hope the child would eventually come to feel at home in the old house. "Yes, he's a nice man," she agreed, knowing it was true, "but it isn't proper for us to live here with him."

"Why?"

"Because he and I aren't married and it's unseemly for an unmarried man and woman to live in the same house."

"But you could get married."

"No, that's not possible."

"Why not? Don't you like him?"

Emma worried her bottom lip. "It isn't that I don't like him…"

She paused, looking into the expectant eyes of a child who wouldn't understand any of the excuses in her arsenal. She was beginning to reconsider them herself. The man she'd expected to despise had turned out to be very kind and very attractive—in every way. Her body heated every time she thought of what lay beneath his clothing—which was all too frequently. It was becoming an obsession. Perhaps she was ailing for something.

Miss Ince's arrival cut the conversation short. "Off you go; time for your lessons."

Coward.

"Must I?"

Emma was reluctant to remind her daughter she'd missed too many lessons because of her refusal to speak. "Miss Ince thinks you will soon make up for lost ground."

With a heavy sigh, Patsy got off her chair, picked up Wellington and traipsed out with her governess.

Trying to settle her confused thoughts, Emma finished her *crème brûlée* then decided to retrieve her copy of *Mansfield Park* from the library. Her worries about where to live were over; she could relax and enjoy the book written by an anonymous *Lady*.

DISAPPOINTED NOT TO find Emma in the dining room or the drawing room, Gabe headed for the library. Blair had promised to leave some very preliminary estimates for him to peruse.

He stopped in his tracks at the sight of Emma sitting in the window seat.

The noisy door hinges alerted her and she stood hastily, the book on her lap falling to the floor. He had a feeling she'd been gazing out the window and had to chuckle at the sense of déjà vu that swept over him.

"Lord Farnworth," she spluttered, her cheeks a lovely shade of pink that easily stirred interest in his nether regions. Had he been celibate so long that the mere sight of a beautiful woman aroused him?

"I thought we'd agreed you would call me Gabriel," he replied, stooping to pick up the book.

Unfortunately, she too reached down and they both put a hand on the book at the same moment. She glanced up at him for just a brief second, but it was enough to see that his nearness affected her. He let go of the book and stepped back. *Mansfield Park,*" he remarked. "Written by *A Lady.*"

"Yes, thank you, Gabriel," she replied, out of breath for some reason. "I've just started it, but I enjoyed her previous publications. Have you read them?"

He felt out of his depth. "Can't say I have. Does no one know the author's true name?"

"No. I've heard several female writers use male pseudonyms in order to get their works published. At least she has the courage to declare she belongs to the fairer sex." She gestured to the shelves. "*Sense and Sensibility* and *Pride and Prejudice* are here in the library somewhere."

"What's the substance of the stories?" he asked.

"Er...well, I suppose you could say they deal with prejudice, you know, class distinctions and so on."

Gabe wished he hadn't asked. This was too close to the bone and Emma's deep blush betrayed her embarrassment. However, since the topic had been broached... "Actually, that's along the lines of something I wanted to discuss with you, if you have time to sit for a while."

He was glad she chose the window seat, but his own chair behind the desk seemed too far away, so he remained standing. "I hope you don't mind if I ask your advice."

Setting the book to one side, she frowned. "I'll help if I can, but Matthew didn't share matters regarding the estate. Blair would…"

He held up a hand, surprised his cousin wouldn't have sought the opinions of his intelligent wife. "Forgive my interrupting, but my questions are of a more personal nature. It concerns marriage."

DEVELOPMENTS

E MMA SUDDENLY FELT dizzy. Surely, Gabriel Smith wasn't going to propose they marry.

"You of all people understand that I must marry soon," he began, avoiding looking at her as he paced.

She wished he would stand still so she could regain her equilibrium. "I suppose…"

"The problem is, I have no knowledge of the local gentry, whereas you do. I hoped you might assist me in finding a bride."

Emma gripped the edge of the bench on which she sat, perplexed by the disappointment churning in her heart. He sought her help to find a wife. Why did the prospect leave her feeling bereft? She swallowed hard, determined to keep her voice steady. "There are a number of eligible ladies in the county, and there will no doubt be invitations to attend various balls and musicales once people realize you've arrived to take up your duties."

He finally stopped pacing and looked into her eyes, clearly hesitant to continue. "The problem is, well, to put it bluntly, I don't have long to live."

She couldn't breathe. Her suspicions were correct, but the imminent death of a man she was beginning to like and respect was too ghastly to contemplate. She rose on trembling legs and took his hands. "I suspected there was something, Gabriel," she admitted.

He averted his gaze and inhaled deeply. "Yes, well, not to dwell on the problem. It's a mysterious malady I picked up on Saint Helena. I had hoped things might improve in England, but my condition is deteriorating. Hence, the need to find a wife quickly."

A crazed notion to offer herself bubbled in her throat but she'd never been one to make rash decisions. In any case, they belonged to different worlds. "You would have to reveal your illness to a prospective bride," she murmured, unable to think of any woman in the whole county who would marry him for love in such circumstances. There was no shortage of scheming mamas who would seize the opportunity for one of their daughters to become a wealthy widowed countess. And where would that leave Emma and Patsy?

"Yes, of course," he replied, "but the earldom needs stability. If I die without an heir…"

He choked on the words and walked away to face the bookshelves on the far wall.

She stared at his broad back, overwhelmed by the cruel fate that awaited such a gentle man in the prime of his life. "I will help you, Gabriel," she said. "But have you consulted a physician about your illness? Perhaps…"

➤➤➤◄◄◄

GABE'S HEAD WAS spinning. On the one hand, telling Emma of his malady had lightened the burden. On the other, his death sentence was now all too real. He stared at the books on the shelf in front of him, but saw only a blur of leather-bound spines. "I consulted the army physician on Saint Helena when I first began to feel out of sorts. He was mystified by my symptoms. I didn't want to pursue it too vigorously with him when things worsened."

"He would have reported it to your commanding officer," she said softly.

He didn't turn around, but her sympathetic voice sounded so near.

Would she reach out to touch him? Offer comfort? "Exactly. Jackson didn't like me very much as it was. He was jealous of my rapport with the men under my command."

He exhaled, worried he sounded like a pathetic loser.

"I think you should see a good physician," Emma said. "Any prospective bride would want to be assured you've pursued every avenue to get well. I can give you the name of Matthew's doctor in Preston."

It was a lifeline and he'd be a fool to refuse. She made a good point, but he might go mad if a physician actually confirmed his worst fears. He was about to accept when Frame knocked and entered. "Your pardon, my lord, you have a visitor. I've put him in the drawing room."

He turned to look at Emma. "What's the protocol?" he asked, hoping she wouldn't object to helping him navigate the niceties of noble society.

"Who is it, Frame?" she inquired.

The butler lifted his chin. "Arthur Coleman, my lady, Baron Whiteside's son."

Emma rolled her eyes. "A neighbor," she explained, her tone indicating her dislike of the man. "I suppose you'll have to receive him, but…"

Gabe tapped a finger to his lips. "Enough said."

ARTHUR HAD HOPED Lord Farnworth would receive him alone and was more than a little peeved when Emma Crompton swanned in on his arm. Tillie had led him to believe the dowager countess regarded the new earl with disdain, yet it was evident from the brief glance they exchanged that they shared some secret.

It was laughable. The snooty dowager countess had set her cap at a soldier when she could have had a baron's son. Her betrayal of the upper class to which they both belonged strengthened his thirst for retaliation.

"My dear Lord Farnworth," he oozed, deliberately ignoring the dowager countess as he extended a hand. "Arthur Coleman. A neighbor. May I welcome you to Lancashire?"

He wasn't prepared for the firm grip of the return handshake. Clearly, the newcomer hadn't yet learned noblemen didn't crush each other's fingers.

"Good of you," the earl replied.

"Arthur is the son of Baron Whiteside," Emma explained as she took a seat on the sofa. "Their estate borders yours."

"Thank you, Lady Emma," Arthur said, hoping she detected the irritation in his voice.

To his annoyance, the earl didn't invite him to sit. Nor did Emma make any effort to ring for tea.

"Indeed," he said, pretending not to notice their appalling manners. "The purpose of my visit today is to invite you to a musicale my father is hosting Friday next. Nothing elaborate, you understand. Just a chance to get to know some of your neighbors. Seven o'clock."

He could scarcely believe it when Farnworth hesitated and looked to Emma for guidance. If the chit advised against his attendance...

"I'd be delighted to attend," the earl said.

Arthur had expected to have to coax an acceptance and resented being thrown off balance. "Good. I'll see you then."

"Seven o'clock on Friday," the earl repeated.

Nursing bruised feelings at the earl's obvious lack of interest in pursuing a conversation, Arthur had no choice but to take his leave. All the way home, he sulked in his carriage, contemplating a way to hurt both of the rude individuals residing at Thicketford Manor.

GETTING TO KNOW YOU

EMMA ROSE FROM the sofa, hoping to pursue the matter of a physician. "Thank goodness he's gone. Shall I ring for tea?"

Gabriel hesitated. "Forgive me, Lady Farnworth, I'm not up on what's considered appropriate. Will it be deemed unseemly if we take tea together?"

She supposed some tongues might wag, but it was more important she help him in his quest to provide stability for the earldom. "Please, if you insist on Gabriel, then you must call me Emma."

He smiled. "Emma it is. I suspect our recently departed visitor won't like the idea. He has his eye on you."

She grimaced. "Matthew always said Arthur Coleman is a scoundrel and a wastrel. He tried to proposition me at the reception after my husband's funeral."

He laughed, but remained standing. "Even I have more class than that."

She loved his rich baritone laughter but wished he would sit so she could concentrate on what she wanted to say rather than on the well-muscled thighs in her direct line of sight. She rose to ring for tea. "If we are to live together in this house…er…what I mean is…"

He frowned, his cheeks flushing. "I understood what you meant. Hopefully, people will come to see we are friends working in unison for the good of the earldom."

As she regained her seat, it struck Emma she'd never had a male friend—a man who trusted her with his thoughts. Matthew had treated her as a decorative necessity, a vessel for bearing his children. She realized she'd never been privy to his innermost feelings. He'd loved and respected her in his own way, but friendship? Their marriage was more of a mutually beneficial arrangement. The notion of having Gabriel Smith as a friend who trusted her was exciting. He'd already opened up to her about his illness. "So, Baron Whiteside's musicale offers an opportunity to meet members of the local gentry. The baron is nothing like his obnoxious son. You'll like him."

Gabriel finally sat in the upholstered armchair across from her. "I was anticipating you would attend the musicale with me."

Conflicting emotions assailed her. She wanted to agree, but… "I really shouldn't. I still have five months left in my mourning period. Some will be scandalized."

He leaned forward, forearms on his thighs and looked into her eyes. "But I sense you want to go, and I'd appreciate your insights about the people I'll meet."

"Well, it is just a musicale. A ball would be out of the question, but…"

"That's settled, then."

CAUTIOUS OPTIMISM CREPT into Gabe's heart for the first time in many months. He'd convinced Emma to accompany him without much effort. Her presence would help him navigate his first social event as an earl.

A maid entered the drawing room, pushing a trolley laden with pastries as well as the tea service. He hadn't eaten lunch and the aroma of fresh baked goods whetted his appetite.

He studied Emma as she poured his tea and handed it to the maid to pass to him. He'd never had a female friend and was somewhat astonished Emma Crompton was willing to fill that role. She'd clearly considered him beneath her dignity when they'd first met, yet now seemed anxious to help him.

She was remarkably beautiful, a woman any man would be fortunate to have as a wife. Even his stricken body had no trouble responding to her. If things were different…

But that was forbidden territory. She'd just lost one husband. It would be unconscionable to expect her to suffer another bereavement. She was a young woman who deserved a virile, healthy man. Still, having her as a supportive friend might ease the journey to his final demise.

Perhaps the unfortunate episode in the library hadn't been such a catastrophe after all, though he was at a loss to explain the change in her attitude toward him.

He set the teacup down on a side table and perused the selection of sweets the maid offered, loading up his plate with half a dozen different confections.

"That will be all, Sally," Emma told the maid, eyeing Gabe's plate.

"Too tempting," he said sheepishly after Sally had left.

"I'm glad you've regained your appetite."

"You've put my mind at ease on several fronts," he replied. "Helped me relax."

"I've noticed you don't eat heartily. Is that one of your symptoms?"

"Yes," he replied, surprisingly comfortable telling her of his problems. "Along with blistering headaches, weakness in my limbs, vertigo. Even my hair has started to fall out."

When she gaped at him, he stuffed a lemon tart into his mouth. He'd perhaps said too much already. He didn't want her to think he was a total wreck.

EMMA'S THROAT CONSTRICTED. Gabriel had described many of the same symptoms Matthew and his father had complained of for months before their deaths. How could that be?

The notion there might be a curse on the Earls of Farnworth reared its ugly head again, but she wasn't about to utter such superstitious nonsense to Gabriel. It was probably just a coincidence. She tried for a light tone, though she considered the potential loss of his glossy black hair a travesty. "Well, unfortunately, lots of men lose their hair, so I don't think you should worry overmuch about that."

He nodded solemnly, his mouth still full of his second lemon tart.

"Will you agree to consult Matthew's physician? Frame can send a footman to secure an appointment. I don't know Dr. Henry well, though I've seen him at church. A midwife tended me during my confinement."

Though highly regarded throughout the county, Dr. Adrian Henry hadn't solved the mystery of Matthew's ailments, and his father had adamantly refused to even consult a doctor. She kept that knowledge to herself. Seeking a physician's opinion was preferable to doing nothing.

"I will," he replied.

It was a step forward, though Gabriel's pallor indicated he didn't agree.

HALF-MOURNING

WHEN GABE ENTERED the dining room later that evening, he was happy to note several leaves had been removed from the table. The long oblong had become a square. Roses floating in silver bowls had replaced the ornate candelabra. Patsy and her mother were already seated and a footman held out Gabe's chair across from Emma.

The other thing he found pleasing was Emma's gown. The black had given way to mauve, the bombazine to a lighter material, crepe perhaps. The décolletage was much more pleasing to the male eye. A necklace of amethyst gems sparkled on bare skin. The jet beads, widow's cap and lacy black half gloves were nowhere in evidence. "The color suits you," he remarked, delighted to see her blush. "It brings out the violet in your eyes." He deemed it wise not to mention the swell of her breasts was every bit as enticing as he'd expected.

"I've put off going into half-mourning," she said, "but I think it's time."

"Me too," Patsy echoed.

Dragging his gaze from Emma's mesmerizing beauty, he noticed Patsy was also clad in a lavender dress he hadn't seen before, a pair of prettily embroidered pantalettes showing below the hem. Purple ribbons securing her pigtails had replaced the black. "Very becoming, young lady."

The child preened. "Thank you, Cousin Gabriel."

As the courses progressed, Gabe couldn't recall the last time he'd shared a meal with family. Since adolescence, the army had been his family, his brothers-in-arms. He wasn't related to Emma, and his kinship with Patsy was too complicated to figure out, yet he felt at home with them. At least, when he died, he wouldn't be alone. Dare he hope Emma and Patsy would mourn his passing?

Deciding he was getting too maudlin, he sought to inject another optimistic note into the conversation. Emma had been so delighted with his willingness to see a physician, he wanted to bring back the same enthusiastic smile. "By the by, Bradley and I need to update our wardrobes. A soldier doesn't worry much about the cut of his civvies, but an earl, I think, should be fashionably attired."

Emma could scarcely swallow her food fast enough, clearly impatient to reply. "You could meet with Matthew's tailor in Preston when you go to see Dr. Henry," she said, dabbing tempting lips with her napkin. But then the broad smile fled. "Oh, but perhaps you don't want to use Matthew's tailor."

"Why not?" Patsy asked. "And why are you going to see Daddy's doctor?"

»»»«««

MATTHEW HAD ENCOURAGED Emma to be more circumspect about opening her mouth before speaking. In her desire to help Gabriel, she'd reverted to what her late husband referred to as "a middle-class tendency" and blurted out the first thing that came to mind. She'd been too excited about finally getting to wear something flattering and liked the admiration she'd seen in Gabriel's eyes. A woman needed to feel a man found her attractive. Matthew was dead; she wasn't.

Now, her self-absorption had set Patsy to worrying and put Gabriel in the awkward position of being obliged to purchase clothing from her late husband's tailor.

"I'd be happy to visit the man's shop," Gabriel said, before turning to Patsy. "And I'm merely planning to see the doctor about a persistent headache. It's nothing, I'm sure. Just stress brought on by the prospect of my new responsibilities."

Emma exhaled slowly. Gabriel had set everything to rights. He'd calmed her agitation and eased a child's fears without lying to her.

Her throat tightened anew when Patsy set her knife and fork correctly on her cleaned plate and declared, "Daddy had headaches too."

Emma couldn't tear her eyes away from Gabriel's puzzled gaze. She knew she was blushing. Indeed, her whole body was on fire. "Yes," she conceded. "It turned out to be nothing to worry about."

Gabriel continued with his meal, apparently satisfied by her explanation. So, why did she have the queasy feeling Matthew should have been more concerned about his headaches?

※≫≫≪≪

GABE ADDED THIS latest piece of information about his late cousin to what Blair had told him about Matthew's accident and the old earl's descent into madness. It was too much of a coincidence that he should be affected by the same malady, if Matthew had, in fact, been ill at all. Sometimes, men simply behaved out of character. His cousin had paid the ultimate price for his lapse.

Gabe's own symptoms had begun thousands of miles away in the back of beyond. He dismissed the insane possibility there was a curse on the Earls of Farnworth. The gothic, brooding exterior of Thicketford Manor was playing tricks with his common sense and he'd only resided in the place for a few days.

Still, he couldn't resist asking, "Did the old earl suffer from terrible headaches too?"

"I believe so," Emma replied too quickly, avoiding his gaze.

Now, he understood why she was so insistent he visit Dr. Henry.

READING IN BED

EMMA LAY AWAKE that night—alone. Patsy had willingly allowed Miss Ince to put her to bed in the nursery. Emma could only assume Gabriel Smith's pleasant way with the child had eased her fears.

He'd quickly won her over too, although she had to admit the episode in the library had made her more disposed to favor him. She giggled, her body heating as wanton thoughts flooded her yet again.

The sense of shame these feelings caused was ebbing. Surely it was natural for a woman to be drawn to a handsome, well-formed man, although *drawn* was perhaps an understatement. She was becoming obsessed with Gabriel, to the point she toyed with the idea of knocking on the door between their apartments and letting him know Patsy was in her own bed.

She turned over and pounded the pillow. Lusting after a man was one thing; inviting him into her bed quite another. She'd do well to remember she was a grieving widow.

It struck her that the grief wasn't as sharp now. She was starting to think shock and uncertainty had thrown her into a greater panic than her husband's demise. Admittedly, she'd never felt intense sexual feelings for Matthew. In her defense, she believed her husband had considered intercourse as a means to relieve his male needs, and for the siring of heirs. The word *passionate* didn't come to mind when she recalled their joining. *Routine* was a more apt description.

It was folly to think of sexual relations with Gabriel. She wanted to do what she could for him because he was a genuinely nice man in a challenging situation, and he was ill. If she made the mistake of caring too much, she feared the grief would be truly unbearable when he died.

In an effort to settle her confused emotions, she retrieved *Mansfield Park* from the nightstand and opened the book to the next chapter.

⟫⟫⟪⟪

GABE HAD BECOME reconciled to reading *Moll Flanders* as the only means to ease him into sleep in the green torture chamber but, this night, even the intrepid Moll couldn't get his mind off Emma Crompton.

He tasted bitter irony. He'd found a woman he was attracted to just as his life was ebbing away, although the idea of a liaison between him and Emma was out of the question. He wasn't completely up-to-date on society's views about the nobility conducting themselves thusly, but doubted anything good would come of it.

What's more, his burgeoning feelings for the dowager countess tended more toward marriage. She was too fine a person to treat as a mistress, but he'd be a cad to leave her a widow for the second time in a few short years—if he even had years left.

He had to be content with the plans in progress. Blair had assured him laborers would soon begin some of the demolition required at the dower house. The visit to the physician would confirm he was terminally ill. Better to accept it and get on with finding a wife willing to bear his children. The upcoming Whiteside musicale would move things along in that regard.

He turned his attention back to Moll's next escapade, but all he could see in his mind's eye was Emma's belly round with his child. The impossibility of it was enough to drive a man mad.

PROPPED UP ON pillows, Arthur tossed aside the book whose pages he was turning without having a clue what he was reading. "Of course," he declared.

He'd racked his brain for hours and finally come up with the perfect way to hurt Emma Crompton. What did she care about more than anything else? "Matthew's brat."

It would take careful planning, but he had Tillie inside Thicketford Manor to help him. She'd balk at the idea of kidnapping, but she'd come round once he offered her something she couldn't resist.

It was a perfect scheme. He'd ransom the little girl, of course. The notion of killing her made him queasy and, besides, he needed the blunt. The earl wouldn't pay ransom for a dead child.

Thoughts of Tillie's generous breasts produced a pleasant arousal. He dealt with it quickly and fell into a deep sleep.

FAMILY EXCURSION

ONCE BRADLEY DECLARED him presentable, Gabe went down to breakfast the next morning dressed in cream-colored riding pants and his favorite navy blue dress coat. He'd come to a decision during the night. It was time he stopped bemoaning his fate and began enjoying Emma and Patsy's companionship while he had the chance.

Emma's bright smile of welcome when he entered the morning room confirmed his decision. Patsy left her chair and took his hand.

"Good morning," he said, swallowing the lump in his throat. "I wondered if you ladies might like to ride over to the dower house later this morning. Blair assures me he's sending laborers to get started on clearing out the debris."

"I would enjoy that," Emma replied.

Patsy pouted, folding her arms across her chest. "I want to stay here."

"That's disappointing," Gabe countered, winking at Emma. "I had looked forward to you riding pillion."

A smile tugged at the corners of Emma's mouth, but she remained silent.

Patsy frowned. "On your horse?"

"Of course, but if you'd rather stay here…"

"I could wear the riding habit, the one I got before Daddy…"

Tears welling, the child looked to her mother then back at him. His heart went out to her. "I think your father would be proud to see you riding a horse."

Emma nodded, clearly struggling not to break down. "'There's my big girl,' he'd say."

"I'll come then," Patsy agreed. "If the habit still fits me."

They finished breakfast and were preparing to leave the nook when Frame entered. He informed them of the footman's return from Preston late the previous evening. Afternoon appointments had been arranged with the physician and the tailor.

"Right," Gabe replied, hoping he'd be up to a full day spent with his new family. "This morning, we'll visit the dower house. After luncheon, we're off to Preston."

⤞⤝

EMMA'S RESOLVE TO remain distant blew away the moment Gabriel entered the morning room. The linen riding breeches looked good on his tall frame and navy blue suited his dark coloring.

She had to admire the way he coaxed Patsy into riding to the dower house. For a man who had no children of his own, he had a knack of bringing out the best in her daughter. He'd shown sensitivity to Patsy's sorrow over the loss of her father. Emma had spent most of the last few months losing her patience with the child's refusal to speak, which had done no good whatsoever.

She'd readily agreed to the excursion to the dower house despite a determination to busy herself elsewhere. She ought to decline the invitation to accompany him to Preston, but she'd been cooped up in Thicketford for too long. Bradley would be going with them, so there was nothing improper about the trip. She could easily procure a shopping list from Mrs. Maple.

Within the hour, she and her daughter, both dressed in riding attire, rendezvoused with Gabriel in the stables. The ostler had saddled her mare and provided a mounting block, but Gabriel surprised her by putting his warm hands on her waist and lifting her into the saddle. When their eyes met, he hesitated to remove his hands. A wave of wanting swept over her. She longed to confess she was beginning to have feelings for him, but Patsy broke the spell. "Me next."

Smiling, he lifted her daughter into the saddle of his gelding and mounted behind her, easily swinging a long leg over the steed's broad rump. "You should ride in front of me," he said. "So you can sit side-saddle like the elegant young lady you are."

"Can Wellington ride with us?" she asked.

"I think he should follow along," Gabriel replied. "The exercise will do him good."

As they set off, Emma was filled with the joyful feeling they were embarking on a family outing, something she couldn't recall ever doing with Matthew.

>>>><<<<

GABE TOOK PLEASURE in Emma's obvious enjoyment of the ride. He got the feeling it had been a long time since she'd ridden out in Thicketford's magnificent grounds.

"Look how green the grass is, despite the cold weather," she remarked more than once to her daughter. "Listen to the birds. And those copper beeches; I'd forgotten how big they are."

Gabe didn't think the somber black of the mourning gowns flattered Emma's complexion, but, in broad daylight, the black of the riding habit emphasized every tempting curve. She sat a horse well and clearly had the mare under control.

Patsy gasped in wonder when Gabe reined to a halt and pointed to a doe with her fawn near the woods in the distance. The deer melted into the trees quickly when Wellington took off in pursuit. "Naughty dog," Patsy scolded.

The poodle trotted back, still yapping.

"We need a hunting dog for deer," Gabe remarked on a whim.

"Oh, we cannot kill them," Patsy replied.

"Don't worry. I'm not a hunter," he assured her before turning to Emma, "although a tasty bit of venison would be nice once in a while."

"What's venison?" Patsy asked.

"And here we are," Gabe declared, smiling conspiratorially at Emma.

He dismounted, lifted Patsy down, then reached up to assist Emma. They stood inches part, his hands on her trim waist, hers on his shoulders. She seemed reluctant to let go. He had to hope it was longing he saw in her magical eyes. "If things were different," he whispered.

CHASING SQUIRRELS

"**Y**ES," EMMA LONGED to say. "If only things were different." But they weren't, so she moved away from Gabriel and turned her attention to the laborers working on the ruin. "It doesn't look as bad as I expected. It's the first time I've been here since the fire," she admitted, immediately wishing she hadn't. Now, she would be obliged to share painful memories.

But Gabriel didn't pry. Instead, when Patsy cowered behind his leg, he took her hand and reassured her they wouldn't go any closer. Seemingly pacified, Patsy followed Wellington to a nearby overgrown flower bed where he started digging furiously.

Confident she could trust Gabriel, Emma began the tale. "Matthew and I were only recently married," she began. "The furor resulting from the fatal catastrophe was an inauspicious beginning to our marriage. My husband hadn't expected to inherit the earldom for many years. He had to deal with the inquest and his new responsibilities. Above all, he wanted to protect the family name. He decreed the ruin off-limits after his father's body was removed. I think it was simply too difficult for him to come here."

"And I don't suppose you were prepared to assume the role of countess so quickly," Gabriel replied thoughtfully.

Emma inhaled deeply, remembering those difficult times. "I was relegated to the background, which I accepted as understandable at the time, but it didn't make things any easier. I was seventeen and with child. I wanted to console Matthew, to help him with the burden, but he withdrew into a kind of protective shell."

From which he never truly emerged—but she wasn't about to reveal that new and alarming realization. "Without Susan, I would have been completely at sea."

"Susan?"

"Matthew's sister. She's my age and what some people might refer to as a *bluestocking*. She and I became friends, despite Matthew's objections to her intellectual pursuits."

"But she doesn't live at Thicketford?"

"The family drove her out. She became a protégée of Hannah More and lives in Somerset at the moment. She came home for Matthew's funeral, and stayed for a fortnight. Campaigning against the slave trade is her passion."

"Sounds like a firebrand," Gabriel replied.

"Opinionated for sure, but a dear friend, nevertheless. Of course, Frame was an enormous help to me as well."

"He's a good man, and clearly very fond of you," Gabriel replied.

"Cousin Gabriel," Patsy shouted from beneath a chestnut tree. "Come and see. Wellington's chasing a squirrel."

Emma chuckled. "You seem to have replaced me in the pecking order."

He shrugged, grinning like a naughty boy.

"I love your smile," she confessed.

"I feel like smiling when I am with you," he said, taking her by the hand. "Come on, let's see what Wellington is up to."

GABE CONSIDERED HIMSELF fortunate to have Emma and Patsy to brighten the final months of his life. He realized it was inappropriate to take Emma's hand, but it dawned on him he wasn't the only Earl

Farnworth who'd had the job thrust upon him. Though Matthew had grown up as an earl's son, he'd had to find his own way. And Gabe would do the same. He couldn't fret about every wrong decision he might make. His days were numbered. Gossip couldn't hurt him when he was six feet under.

Emma didn't pull away as they stood watching Patsy chase her poodle in hot pursuit of a fat squirrel. Had the dowager countess perhaps also decided not to worry about propriety?

Patsy squealed when the squirrel stopped abruptly and turned to confront Wellington. The dog skidded to a halt, nigh on going head over tail before beating a hasty retreat.

"His namesake duke would be horrified," Gabe remarked as he and Emma laughed heartily.

She sobered as they walked back to their mounts, still holding hands. "Did you fight at Waterloo?" she asked.

A lead weight replaced the lightheartedness. "I did."

"You can tell me about it whenever you wish to," she whispered.

Had she sensed he'd never spoken of the pivotal battle to anyone before? "When little ears aren't listening," he agreed when Patsy caught up to them, Wellington cradled in her arms.

"So, Miss Crompton," he said as he lifted the little girl and her dog back into the saddle. "What's your opinion of the dower house now that you've seen it?"

"I think it will be fine, once they've repaired it. Miss Ince will like it too."

"What about Wellington?" he asked as he led Emma's mare to a tree stump.

"Oh, he'll enjoy chasing the squirrels," Patsy replied.

Gabe offered a hand to help Emma climb up on the stump, which brought them face to face.

She gripped his shoulders and looked into his eyes when he put his hands around her waist.

Filling his senses with her lavender perfume, he stared at her part-ed lips, wishing they were alone.

"I doubt Wellington shares that opinion," she said with a smile as he lifted her into the saddle.

EMMA COULDN'T EXPLAIN the rush of sensory emotions that swamped her each time Gabriel put his hands on her. Her nipples tingled and a warmth blossomed in a very private place. It was insanely tempting to ask him to move his hands to her breasts.

It was as though there was an alchemy between them. She'd al-ways dismissed Priscilla's gushing account of how she'd fallen in love with her husband when she'd first set eyes on him. How anyone could love Warren was beyond Emma.

Now, she understood. She wanted Gabriel Smith with an intensity that rocked the very foundations of everything she'd been brought up to believe about how ladies should behave with gentlemen.

Watching Gabriel mount his gelding, she mentally stripped him of the breeches, thirsting for a proper look at well-muscled thighs and the prodigious male member she'd only glimpsed. She longed to run her hands over his appealing buttocks and trim hips. A soldier's body, honed by years of military discipline.

She deliberately rode behind him so she could study his broad back and capable shoulders.

When he helped her dismount in front of the stables, she stared at his chest, remembering the dusting of hair she'd glimpsed in the library.

That fateful night had changed her forever, but she couldn't find it in her heart to feel even a smidgen of regret.

CHILDREN SHOULD BE SEEN

D URING THE BRIEF luncheon, Gabe was almost afraid to give free rein to the happiness bubbling inside him. As children, he and his brothers had never been allowed to talk during meals, let alone chatter like Patsy who was reliving Wellington's adventure with the squirrel.

Given the intimidating presence of their mean-tempered stepfather, the Smith brothers hadn't dared open their mouths. Gabe had the misfortune to be the last of his siblings to leave home; mealtimes became nightmare scenarios. After joining the army, he wolfed down whatever was put in front of him. Even army rations tasted good to a boy starved of love.

As he studied Emma's happy face and bright eyes across the table, he couldn't remember his mother ever smiling, except when she played her beloved piano. He often wondered why she'd married a man she obviously feared. It was probable Samuel Waterman had punished her if he found out she'd provided her son the means to buy a commission. Michael and Raphael had run off to join the navy as common seamen, but Gabe aspired to become an officer.

For years, he'd sworn off marriage. Then, he'd met Georgina and, for a few brief months, thought she might be the one. She'd proven him wrong and restored his conviction love did not exist.

Now, he knew deep in his heart that Emma Crompton was the woman for him. If only he'd found her sooner.

>>>><<<<

Matthew had been a firm believer in children being seen and not heard, especially at the table. Emma pitied him for that. He'd missed the pleasure of listening to his daughter recount the adventures of her poodle, her giggling laughter infectious. Had he appreciated the jewel he had in his intelligent little girl, or had he looked upon her as a disappointment because she wasn't a boy?

Unfortunately, Emma knew the answer. It had been written on Matthew's face the moment he found out she'd birthed a girl.

With no son to inherit, her parents had sold off their profitable spinning mill. Her father made no bones about sharing his opinion with his daughters that women were incapable of operating a business. God had designed them for domesticity. This despite the fact his wife's advice over the years had contributed greatly to the mill's success.

She wondered about Gabriel's family. "Do you have sisters?" she asked, sorry she'd mentioned it when his smile fled.

"No," he replied. "Two older brothers. Twins."

This was puzzling. Why hadn't one of them inherited the earldom?

"Both killed during the Napoleonic Wars."

"I'm sorry," she murmured. "What a terrible loss."

He kept his eyes averted. "Yes, although I lost touch with them after they left home before me."

"Did they join the army too?"

"The navy. Michael died aboard the *Royal Sovereign* and Raphael aboard *HMS Victory*."

"All three boys named for archangels."

"My mother's idea, apparently, and one my stepfather constantly ridiculed. My brothers were just two of the five hundred British sailors who died at Trafalgar."

"How did you find out?"

He smiled but there was no humor in it. "Ironically enough, I learned of their deaths through the lawyers who conducted the search for Matthew's heir. My brothers had been dead more than ten years and I didn't even know."

"That's sad," Patsy murmured, breaking the awful silence that ensued.

Emma was heartily sorry she'd brought up the subject of his family. Clearly, he hadn't enjoyed a happy childhood. The impossibility of procreating children on whom they could both lavish love broke her heart.

He was a man born to be a father, and a lifetime of barren years loomed ahead for her. Patsy was fated to be an only child.

➤➤➤❮❮❮

GABE HAD ONLY distant memories of Michael and Raphael, but the enormity of his loss struck him full force for the first time. He'd been saddened and angry to learn of their deaths, but proud they'd sacrificed their lives in the service of their country and the heroic Horatio Nelson.

His own imminent demise presaged the end of his family line, making it all the more imperative he sire a son.

He strove to banish the ghosts of the past. "I hope you are coming with us this afternoon," he told Patsy.

The child beamed, confirming yet again how relatively easy it was to bring a smile to a child's face. It was lamentable that his stepfather had never learned that simple truth.

He dabbed his mouth with his napkin, left his seat and put his hands on the back of Emma's chair. "Enough talk of the past. We should be off to Preston."

She allowed him to pull out her chair, rose and linked her arm with his. "Let the adventure begin," she said.

PRESTON

A FTER DEPARTING THICKETFORD and passing through the village of Slade, the black-lacquered carriage began the gradual six-mile downhill journey into the town of Preston.

"I can't recall ever traveling in such comfort," Gabriel exclaimed, pressing his fingertips into the plush red seat cushions.

"Well," Emma replied with a chuckle, "this conveyance is yours now, so you may as well take advantage and ride in style."

He smiled, clearly understanding her reference to his initial desire to ride outside with Bradley, James the footman and Conrad the driver, instead of inside with Patsy, Emma, and Emma's abigail. "You ladies are certainly more attractive traveling companions," he allowed, his eyes on Emma.

Patsy and Lucy giggled. The heat rose in Emma's face, then spread across her breasts.

"Not to mention these roads are in terrible condition," Gabriel added. "The gentlemen outside will be bruised from head to toe."

"Things improve once we enter the town," she assured him.

"Preston seems to be surrounded by fields," he remarked, looking out the window.

"Yes, the medieval settlement was never walled. The people who live here are proud of their town. And I am sure you've heard of the famous Preston Guild."

"Vaguely."

"Preston Guild is a tradition that began when Henry II granted the first royal charter and established a Merchant Guild. The purpose was to license local traders, craftsmen and merchants. Only members were allowed to operate in the town."

"Like in London."

"I suppose. Every several years, the Guild reviewed the membership list. If proven eligible, members would be granted renewed membership for the usual fee. It was later decided these gatherings were only needed once in a generation. From 1542, the meeting was scheduled every 20 years. So, when someone from Preston says a thing will happen *once in a Preston Guild*, they jokingly mean almost *never*."

Gabriel enjoyed the humor. "Sounds to me you know quite a bit about the place," he said with a smile.

"Mummy was born here," Patsy explained.

"As was Lucy," Emma added.

"Aye," the maid replied, lifting her chin. "We're proud folk. Her ladyship's family built their mill hereabouts, though it don't belong to them now."

Gabriel frowned, but Emma didn't want to embark on an explanation of her parents' wanderlust. When the carriage rolled to a halt, she reiterated the plans for the day, so there would be no misunderstanding. "Patsy, Lucy, James and I will alight here in Market Place. There are several textile merchants nearby and I need to order linens and wool. Mrs. Maple gave me a list. The driver will then take you and Bradley to the tailor's shop on the corner of Friargate."

"Can we later walk to Dr. Henry's from there?" Gabriel asked.

She heard the nervousness in his voice and strove to set him at ease. "Yes, Conrad will give you directions. Dr. Henry expects you at three o'clock."

James opened the door and offered his hand to help her alight, followed by Lucy and Patsy. She gave Gabriel what she hoped was a reassuring smile before the footman slammed the carriage door shut.

>>><<<

THE SUDDEN CHILLY emptiness of the carriage brought home to Gabe how much warmth and hope Emma and Patsy had brought into his life. However, he didn't have time to dwell on it overlong when the carriage rolled to a halt a few minutes later.

"Here ye be, my lord," Conrad shouted. "Messrs. Carr and Sons."

Seconds later, Bradley had the door open and was standing to attention.

"Relax," Gabe told him, glad his valet hadn't saluted as well. "We're not going into battle, just to the tailor's shop."

"Sah!"

There was little point reminding Bradley not to address him thus. This foray into civilian life perhaps did loom like a daunting campaign for the career soldier.

"Good of Mrs. Maple to provide a list for her ladyship," his valet said unexpectedly. "She gave me some tips about current fashions for gentlemen. She's a widow, but assured me her late husband's clothing always reflected the *dernier cri*."

Gabriel laughed, slapping Bradley on the back. Apart from the first day on the steps, he couldn't recall bumping into the housekeeper since his arrival. Yet, his servant had apparently struck up a friendship with the woman who'd clearly impressed him with her knowledge of *haute couture*. He never thought he'd hear his servant utter anything in French—or at least attempt to. "Good," he replied. "Let's hope the tailor agrees with her ideas."

An hour later, they emerged from Carr's establishment having had every inch of their anatomies measured and re-measured. If Carr had sired sons, they were nowhere in evidence throughout the procedure. Gabe followed Carr's advice about fabrics since the fellow wouldn't be dissuaded from his recommendations by anything a housekeeper suggested. The diminutive gentleman (smaller in stature even than

Bradley) talked incessantly, covering every topic from the lamentable accident that had taken the late earl's life, to the blight on the landscape of his hometown caused by industrial development and the influx of what he called "working class folk". He was convinced the burgeoning cotton industry would sound the death knell of Preston's standing as the most picturesque town in Lancashire. He despaired that the piecers and spinners who slaved in the cotton mills knew nothing of fine raiment, nor could they afford it.

Carr promised to deliver a long list of items within the week: breeches, shirts, cravats, dress coats, smalls—*or drawers if his lordship prefers*—socks, waistcoats, overcoats—*necessary even now in this year with no summer*—and other articles of clothing too numerous to mention.

"He made me dizzy," Gabe confessed to Bradley as they exited the premises.

His valet grunted, deepening the scowl he'd sported since Carr pooh-poohed Mrs. Maple's suggestions.

Gabe wished the visit to the physician could be postponed, but that would be cowardly. He filled his lungs. It was time to face the inevitable.

DIAGNOSIS

I F THE ARMY had taught Gabe anything, it was patience. He'd spent many an hour cooling his heels when summoned by a superior officer to discuss some inconsequential matter.

Yet, he quickly grew impatient as he sat in Dr. Henry's starkly barren waiting room. Had his title already turned him into a demanding nobleman, or was he simply exhausted and paralyzed with dread?

"I should have made an appointment for another time," he whispered to Bradley who sat beside him like a stone statue.

"It has been a busy day, sir," his valet replied, his gaze fixed on the white wall opposite.

For the first time, Gabe realized Bradley had almost as much riding on the outcome of this appointment as he did. When Gabe died, his faithful servant might find himself out of a job. Although, there was the unknown quantity of Mrs. Maple. He chuckled inwardly at the prospect of the crusty soldier married to an efficient and possibly opinionated housekeeper.

He wished the trusty soul well. Bradley deserved happiness after the selfless service he'd given during the wars with the French.

He was plucking up courage to broach the topic of Mrs. Maple when the summons came to enter Dr. Henry's inner sanctum.

The physician was younger than he'd expected, perhaps in his late thirties. The untamed red hair bespoke a rebellious nature, though his immaculately tied cravat suggested an attention to detail and pride in his appearance. He hardly seemed old enough to have garnered a reputation as a first-class doctor. On the other hand, a younger man might be more conversant with advances in medicine.

He stood quickly and offered his hand. "Adrian Henry at your service. I'm honored to meet you, my lord."

Gabe accepted the gesture, impressed with the man's firm handshake. "And I you. I understand my late cousin consulted you."

The doctor averted his eyes for just a moment, then replied. "Yes, sad business all round. Please have a seat."

"Indeed," Gabe replied, as he sat in the leather chair Henry indicated. He gripped the arms as a wave of nausea swept over him.

The physician put a hand on his shoulder. "Can I get you anything before we begin?"

Gabe shook his head, thankful the nausea had been only momentary. "No, thank you. Let's get this over with."

Henry took a seat behind his desk and dipped a quill in the inkwell. "I can see you are anxious. Tell me what's bothering you."

Gabe took a deep breath. "Headaches, mostly. Quite severe and getting worse."

The nib made a scratching sound on the paper, then the physician looked up. "Anything else?"

"My feet are always cold, sometimes my hands, even when I experience night sweats."

"I see."

More scratching.

"Nausea often takes me unawares…"

"Like just now?"

"Yes. And I don't sleep."

"Any blood in the urine?"

"No." *Thank God.*

"Hair loss?"

"Yes. Just started recently."

"Convulsions?"

"At first, not so much lately. Dizzy spells and a feeling I might faint. Weakness in my limbs."

Henry carried on dipping the pen and scratching notes to the point where Gabe was tempted to snatch the quill out of his hand and toss it away. He got the feeling Dr. Henry had a suspicion what was wrong with him. "I'm quite prepared for you to tell me I am dying," he said quietly.

Henry looked up. "When did all these symptoms start?"

"About a year ago when I was a lieutenant colonel serving on the island of Saint Helena."

The doctor put down his pen. "Guarding Bonaparte?"

The conversation switched abruptly to a discussion of the Frenchman's exile. The physician clearly knew a great deal about Napoleon, going back a number of years to his birth on Corsica. He asked about Saint Helena, Napoleon's cottage, and Gabe's duties there.

They weren't pleasant memories and Gabe couldn't see the point, but he obliged with the details. "I had to stand watch while Boney ate his meals; he insisted an officer fulfill the duty, not a common soldier. The meals sometimes went on for hours."

Henry chuckled. "Yes, the French do enjoy drawing out their dining. Why was this vigilance necessary?"

"The powers that be feared he might attempt suicide, or someone might try to assassinate him."

"On Saint Helena?"

"There was a contingent of Frenchies sent there with him, his *entourage* if you like. He might have asked for their help to end it all, or a member of his staff might weary of the duty and want to return to France."

"Were you obliged to taste the food?"

Gabe frowned at the odd question. "No."

"Did you tire of the isolation?"

"Not at first, but gradually it wears you down."

"Especially when you feel your health is deteriorating."

And you realize the loneliness isn't helping you get over Georgina's betrayal.

"Yes."

"Have things improved or worsened since your return to England?"

"They haven't improved."

Except, I've met the most incredible woman.

Henry steepled his fingers. "This is all very curious."

Gabe braced himself for bad news. "What's your opinion?"

"Well," the physician replied, retrieving a stethoscope from the drawer of his desk. "I'll share some thoughts with you after I listen to your heart. Remove your coat, shirt, and cravat, please."

Gabe stood, shrugged out of his frock coat and pulled his shirt off over his head. He breathed in and out according to Henry's directions as he methodically moved the stethoscope over Gabe's chest, then his back.

"Did you know the late earl?" the doctor suddenly asked.

"No."

"And what's the relationship?"

"Second cousin several times removed."

"I see."

"Do you think my illness is hereditary?"

"Let me see your feet."

Gabe sat, wishing Bradley had come in with him to wrestle off the boots. He eventually managed the task.

Henry put his hands on the soles of Gabe's feet, then felt his hands. "They are cold."

Gabe's energy and patience were wearing thin. "Am I dying?"

The doctor sighed as he regained his seat. "For a young man, you seem intent on thinking the worst. You can put your clothes back on."

"I'm simply tired of not knowing what's wrong with me," Gabe replied as he dressed, not even trying to emulate Bradley's cravat tying skill.

"Your heart is strong, your lungs are clear. I don't think I am breaching any confidentiality when I tell you your cousin suffered many of the same symptoms you have described."

It was a punch in the gut. "But I understood you couldn't diagnose what was wrong with him."

"I wasn't sure, but I had some suspicions. He didn't return, I suspect because I couldn't offer an immediate diagnosis. Rumor had it his symptoms worsened. After learning of the erratic behavior that apparently led to his death, I decided to do more research and consulted a respected colleague in London's Harley Street."

"And?"

"He confirmed my thoughts."

"Which were?"

"Matthew Crompton was being poisoned."

A wave of heat rolled over Gabe, then ice flowed through his veins. He had to sit before his legs buckled. "Did you share your opinion with his widow?"

"Good heavens, no. The man's dead. It would be impossible to prove my theory."

Gabe struggled to understand. "But poison kills instantly, does it not?"

"Some do. Others act on the body slowly. Like arsenic."

Gabe shook his head. "You think I'm being poisoned?"

"You have several of the symptoms of arsenic poisoning. What I don't understand is how you and Matthew could both have been poisoned when you were thousands of miles apart." He took up his pen and began to write. "However, in the short term, we must concern ourselves with an antidote. I'll give you a note to take to the apothecary down the street. He'll prepare an electuary you should take twice a day. I'll also instruct him to compound a theriac without honey you can rub on your feet and hands, like a salve. That should improve things, and you will come back to see me in a week. Bring a list of everything you eat and drink."

Back out on the street, Gabe stared at the note he held. He must have shaken hands with Dr. Henry and thanked him but had no memory of doing so.

"Was it the news you were expecting, sir?" Bradley asked quietly, scowling at his cravat.

Gabe didn't know how to respond. It seemed he wasn't dying, but somebody apparently wanted him dead. And who had poisoned Matthew?

QUESTIONS

E MMA ACCEPTED JAMES' help to board the carriage, satisfied with her purchases. It had been a productive afternoon, and the linens Mrs. Maple required would soon be on their way to Thicketford.

Lucy and Patsy piled in after her.

"Ye did well, my lady," Lucy gushed as they settled themselves. "Never did I think they'd agree to yer demands on the price."

Emma was rather proud of her bargaining skills, but didn't want to crow. "They simply realize the value of the Farnworth account."

The irony was sobering. She'd carried on business for a wealthy earldom when, in fact, she'd been left in dire financial straits.

Bradley's unexpected arrival provided a distraction from her resentful thoughts. "Lord Farnworth's at the apothecary shop," he announced before climbing up top with Conrad and James.

"He didn't look very happy," Patsy remarked as the carriage lurched forward.

"No, he didn't," Emma agreed, deeply worried the valet's demeanor presaged bad news.

They waited a good while outside the apothecary shop. Emma's heart sank when Gabriel finally emerged. She could only assume his pallor and his failure to respond to her greeting when he boarded the carriage meant he had received the worst diagnosis.

They rode back to Thicketford in complete silence. Patsy clung to her mother's arm, seemingly sensing conversation wouldn't be welcome. Gabriel stared out the window, one hand resting on the package he'd procured from the apothecary.

Emma longed to take his hand, to utter words of comfort, but lacked the courage. She hoped he would confide in her once they reached home.

However, when they arrived, he hesitated on the front steps. "Forgive me," he said hoarsely, clutching his medication to his chest. "I'm afraid the events of the day have taken their toll. Don't wait for me at dinner."

It was all too reminiscent of Matthew's appointment with the physician, except he'd returned angry and frustrated Dr. Henry hadn't been able to help him.

She supposed the doctor had prescribed something to help ease Gabriel's pain as his illness worsened.

Feeling helpless, she watched him retreat with his valet into the house, her heart aching.

⟫⟫⟫⟪⟪⟪

ALL THE WAY back to Thicketford, the notion that Bradley was the only person who could have poisoned him played on Gabe's mind. He recognized the disappointment in his valet's eyes when Gabe dismissed him before entering his chamber.

Confusion and dismay aggravated his headache and he simply wanted to take the first dose of his medicine and lie down to think. He had no energy to even remove his boots.

The electuary tasted vile and made him cough.

He climbed onto the bed, welcoming for the first time the cocoon provided by the green draperies.

As evening drew nigh, the darkness calmed his frenzied thoughts, though he still had more questions than answers. Why and how had Bradley poisoned him? As far as he could recall, he'd never eaten or imbibed anything prepared by his batman, even here in England. Yet, if anything, his symptoms had worsened since his return from Saint Helena.

The soldier was in the middle of the South Atlantic when Matthew was being poisoned, so who was responsible for that crime? It was murder whichever way you looked at it. Dr. Henry intimated the arsenic had probably affected Matthew's brain and led to his accident.

Then there was the matter of Matthew's father, who'd also suffered some sort of mental breakdown. Had the poisoner been at work even then? That ruled out Emma. He couldn't conceive of a seventeen-year-old newly-wedded and pregnant girl slowly poisoning her father-in-law.

His heart acknowledged Emma was no scheming witch administering poison willy-nilly.

His roiling stomach gradually settled when it slowly dawned on him he wasn't in imminent danger of death. He'd been granted a reprieve and knew for certain he wanted Emma by his side as he embarked on his duties as the Earl of Farnworth.

The unexpected prospect of a full and happy life ahead was enough to make a man laugh out loud, but he sobered when it occurred to him the arsenic problem hadn't been solved.

Suddenly feeling hungry, he rose and made his way to the dining room. With any luck, Emma might still be there. He had to apologize for his earlier behavior and confide in her. She was the one person he'd trust with his life.

TRUST

EMMA KISSED PATSY goodnight. "Sleep tight, little one," she whispered.

"Is Cousin Gabriel sick?" her daughter asked.

The worry in Patsy's young eyes touched her heart. She didn't want her daughter to endure the death of another important person in her life. "We'll talk about it tomorrow. Now, off you go with Miss Ince."

Patsy pouted, but the sulking ended abruptly when Gabriel entered the dining room and she literally threw herself into his arms.

Emma was mortified; a terminally ill man didn't need a child clinging to him. However, Gabriel laughed and picked her up. "Off to bed?" he asked.

She put her arms around his neck. "Yes. Will you come and tell me a story?"

Emma gasped. Her daughter had long ago stopped asking her father to read a bedtime story, something Matthew considered a tedious chore and the sole responsibility of females.

"In a while," Gabriel replied, setting her back on her feet. "When Miss Ince has tucked you in. I want to speak to your mother first."

Patsy dragged her governess from the room.

"You're good with children," Emma remarked, not sure how the conversation was about to proceed.

"Your daughter's easy to get along with," he replied. "Now, if only we could say the same about Wellington."

It was a relief to see him more relaxed—and smiling. She had expected depression and grief and didn't know how to react. "Shall I ring for a plate?"

He sat across from her and rubbed his hands together. "I am rather hungry."

She rose and pulled the cord, feeling as though she was walking on eggshells. He'd previously only pecked at his food. "Cook made a fricassee of chicken and mushrooms, with roasted potatoes and glazed carrots."

"Sounds delicious," he replied, gazing into her eyes.

Gooseflesh marched up her spine. There was something suggestive about the way he studied her. She'd heard of medicinal preparations that brought on euphoria. Perhaps that's what ailed him. "You look better," she began.

A footman interrupted briefly, saw Gabriel at the table and hurried off to fetch his dinner.

"I feel much improved," he agreed, a smile tugging at the corners of his mouth.

She got the feeling she was being teased. Matthew never teased. It was exciting, but inherently frustrating at the same time. She took the bull by the horns. "Are you going to tell me what the doctor said?"

He laughed. "He's of the opinion I am not dying."

Only the reappearance of the footman with Gabriel's dinner prevented Emma from dissolving into tears and rushing to hug him.

EMMA STRUGGLED TO hide her emotions in the presence of the footman, but Gabe had seen enough to know she cared for him. He felt badly for teasing her; however, he'd shortly have to share the dreadful details Dr. Henry had divulged.

He picked up his knife and fork and hesitated. For a long while, he'd stared at every meal put in front of him like a condemned man contemplates his last meal. What if the food was poisoned? He dismissed it as unlikely. Emma had eaten the same meal, and it was important he rebuild his strength. He sliced into the chicken, feeling ravenous. "I take it you're happy to hear my good news?" he asked between mouthfuls.

"Of course," she replied. "What does he think is wrong?"

Suddenly, the dining room didn't feel like the right place to deliver news that would surely shock her. He polished off the last of his food, dabbed his mouth with the linen napkin and suggested, "Let's repair to the library."

Frowning, she rose and followed him across the foyer.

She sat in one of the red leather chairs, watching nervously as he poured two brandies and handed her one. "I don't drink strong liquor," she said.

"You're going to need it after you hear what I have to say," he insisted.

CAUGHT UP IN a maelstrom of emotions, Emma tried to digest what Gabriel was telling her. Everything about Matthew's death now made sense, in a way. Yet, nothing made sense. How could he possibly have been poisoned? And where would a poisoner procure arsenic?

Gabriel could barely choke out his suspicions about Bradley, and she couldn't get her head around the idea of his faithful servant trying to kill him.

It was too much of a coincidence that Matthew and Gabriel, and possibly the old earl, had all been poisoned with arsenic. "Dr. Henry must be mistaken," she murmured, taking a sip of the brandy.

The fumes stole up her nose as the liquor burned a path down her throat.

Gabriel smiled when she grimaced. "Feel better?"

"Actually, yes, strangely enough, but all this is terrifying. Frame and Mrs. Maple are the only servants left from the old earl's days, and you can't possibly think…"

It came as a relief when Gabriel shook his head. "I don't have an explanation for any of it, but I doubt they are responsible."

"I feel the same way about your man. Bradley's devoted to you."

"I have to agree. Anyway, in the meantime, Dr. Henry has given me a foul-tasting elixir, and I'm to report back in a week with a list of everything I've consumed."

"If the arsenic is in the food, why have Patsy and I never fallen ill?"

"It's part of the mystery but, now I know the reason for my problem, I have to be vigilant."

THE CAMPAIGN BEGINS

"I HOPE I'M not jumping the gun here, Emma," Gabe said as he took the empty glass from her grip and stood in front of her. "I want to talk about the future—now that I know I have one."

His years in the army had matured him, given him confidence, made him the man he was, but he suddenly felt like a raw recruit trying to account for his actions to a superior officer. He was falling in love with Emma, but she was far above him in rank and breeding. He believed she had feelings for him, but he'd thought the same to be true of Georgina.

He considered Emma's fierce blush and downcast eyes as encouraging signs. Or, perhaps, they were simply the effects of the brandy.

"As you know, I had intended to find a wife and produce an heir as quickly as possible."

Talk about starting off on the wrong foot.

"Yes," she murmured, still studying the hands clasped in her lap.

He filled his lungs and tried again. "It sounds crass to my own ears to say I had no enthusiasm for the prospect of marriage. My overreaching goal was to safeguard the earldom from further disruption."

He rolled his eyes, wishing he had the courage to stop echoing General Abercrombie and simply take Emma into his arms.

She looked up at him for the first time. "But you're still obliged to sire heirs. When we go to Whiteside's musicale…"

He shook his head and held her gaze. "I misspoke when I said I had no enthusiasm for marriage. It was rather a case of being determined not to make the woman I want to marry a grieving widow—for the second time."

She rose abruptly and glared at him, her cheeks two rosy apples. "Gabriel, we cannot discuss such matters at this juncture. I am still in mourning for my husband. Much as we might disagree with society's dictates, they exist. As the earl, you must be seen to be observing them."

Her response dampened his hopes, though perhaps it left room for a glint of optimism. "I am no stranger to obedience," he replied. "But, I give you fair warning, Lady Emma, I intend to wage a campaign to win your heart."

He cursed his inability to flout the rules when she fled the library.

EMMA MANAGED TO hold back the choking tears until she collapsed on her bed. To outward appearances, she lived a charmed life. Certainly, Priscilla and her husband were envious of her rise in the ranks. No one fully understood the unexpected challenges she'd faced during the last seven years. Coping with the judgmental attitude and eccentricities of Matthew's crusty father had been hard enough, then the man had gone off his head, killed himself and mired the family in scandal.

She'd often laid the blame for Matthew's distant behavior at the feet of his father's manic suicide, but her heart knew her husband was a cold fish by nature—and just as hidebound as his father.

He'd loved her in his own stolid way and enjoyed showing her off to the local gentry, but she'd never felt treasured, loved. He'd never looked at her with the smoldering lust she'd seen in Gabriel Smith's eyes.

Ironically, it seemed she'd become as much a slave to society's rules as her late husband. She'd ached to rush into Gabriel's embrace, smother him with kisses, blurt out her relief he wasn't at death's door. She'd mentally undressed him too many times to count but had been too craven to actually touch him.

Did she not deserve passion after so many dry years? There was only one person standing in her way—the prim and proper countess she'd become.

>>><<<

HIS HEART IN knots, Gabe slowly climbed the stairs to Patsy's nursery. His legs were still weak. He had hopefully embarked on the path to recovery, but acknowledged he faced a long road ahead.

He tapped on the door and poked his head in.

"Cousin Gabriel," Patsy squealed, her dark curls bouncing. "You came."

Wellington woofed then put his head back down on Patsy's pillow.

Smiling, Miss Ince handed over the book she'd been about to read to the child and withdrew to a rocking chair in the corner.

"Mmm," he said, perching on the edge of Patsy's bed. *Tales From Shakespeare.*"

The frontispiece declared the book was designed to introduce children to the great man's plays. Perusing the list of contents, Gabe noted several tragedies listed, among them, oh dear, *Romeo and Juliet.* He definitely didn't want to read that.

"You're not sick, are you, Cousin Gabriel?" Patsy asked unexpectedly.

"I do have an illness, but Dr. Henry has given me medicine to make me better."

"Good. I don't want you to die."

His heart swelled. "I'm not going to."

"Mummy and I like you. So does Wellington."

He'd found an ally. "And I like you both, your poodle not so much."

She grinned. "Mummy already read *The Tempest* to me. I didn't enjoy it."

"Understandable," he agreed. "So, what's next?"

She dragged her unprotesting poodle off the pillow and into her arms. *"Midsummer Night's Dream."*

He could manage that.

She giggled when he showed her the illustration of a donkey's head with two fairies whispering in its ears. Clearing his throat, he began. "There was a law in the city of Athens which gave to its citizens the power of compelling their daughters to marry whomsoever they pleased."

He paused, thinking perhaps this wasn't the best story in the circumstances.

"When I grow up, I'm going to marry whomsoever I please," Patsy declared with a yawn.

Gabe relaxed and read on. He was hitting his stride when the fairies entered the tale, until he became aware of Miss Ince standing at his elbow.

"The wee lass is asleep, my lord," she whispered.

Proud of his first successful foray into fatherhood, he kissed Patsy's forehead, tickled Wellington's pink tummy and tiptoed from the nursery.

SUSAN

D R. HENRY'S SALVE didn't help with Gabe's problem of cold extremities during the night, but he was of the opinion the elixir had mitigated the night sweats. He'd slept marginally better, and had to hold fast to the belief the treatments would eventually counteract the effects of the poison.

Shrugging on his banyan, he decided to reveal everything to Bradley, having come to the conclusion his faithful valet couldn't possibly be responsible. When Bradley entered to assist with the morning's preparations, Gabe motioned for him to sit on the *chaise-longue*. The soldier's clenched jaw and ramrod stiff back showed he was put out, no doubt because Gabe had revealed nothing of the doctor's diagnosis—or perhaps he was uncomfortable sitting while Gabe remained standing.

"I'm going to brief you on what transpired yesterday. I didn't tell you right away because you'll probably be as shocked as I was."

Bradley stood. "I'll stand, if you don't mind, sir."

Feeling weak in the knees, Gabe took his place on the settee. "It's poison."

"Sir?"

"Arsenic."

A myriad of emotions played across the servant's face— incomprehension, disbelief, then, finally, anger burning brightly in the man's eyes. "Somebody's been poisoning you, sir?" he rasped, his face on fire.

"It would appear so. First in Saint Helena, now here."

Bradley narrowed his eyes. "But I'm the only person...oh, no, sir, you don't think..."

Gabe stood. "No, I don't. You have no motive to kill me. In fact, my death might land you in a pickle. Besides, I've never had any reason to doubt your loyalty."

Bradley's knees seemed to give way as he sat. "I don't understand. Is it something you eat, or drink?"

"We don't know. Even more perplexing is that my cousin Matthew was apparently also being poisoned with arsenic."

"But that means..."

Gabe shook his head. "However, Lady Farnworth wasn't in Saint Helena, so how could she have administered poison to me?"

"In any case, she ain't the murdering sort," Bradley said, coming smartly to his feet. "Don't you worry, sir, I'll catch the culprit. You see if I don't. Nobody's going to poison my commanding officer and get away with it."

Gabe wasn't sure how much more vigilant in his duties Bradley could be, but it was a relief to have him on his side. "Good man. Now, since I am not in imminent danger of dying, I intend to make the most of life."

"Breakfast first, sir? I'll arrange with Mrs. Maple for two people to supervise the preparation of your food at all times."

"Right."

A half-hour later, Gabe breezed into the morning room, hoping to continue his campaign of convincing Emma they should give a relationship between them a chance. He was disappointed when the footman informed him Lady Farnworth and Miss Crompton had eaten earlier.

Evidently, Emma was avoiding him, but the added challenge would make the final victory that much sweeter.

>>><<<

"I'VE DECIDED IT'S high time you learn to ride a horse," Emma told Patsy. Elated when her yawning daughter's eyes lit up, she bristled when Patsy asked, "Will Cousin Gabriel teach me?"

Emma could hardly explain she'd hit upon the riding lessons as a way to avoid bumping into Gabriel. "I'm sure he doesn't have time, darling. Blair has recommended one of the experienced stable hands."

"But he made time to read me a story last night."

Rejecting Gabriel's suit suddenly became a great deal more difficult. He'd made the effort to read to Patsy because he'd promised he would. Too busy wallowing in self-recrimination, she hadn't even known of it. "Well, that's nice, but teaching someone to ride a horse takes a lot longer."

Guilt weighed heavily. She sensed Gabriel would be happy to teach Patsy how to ride and her daughter could certainly benefit from some fatherly attention. "Perhaps in a day or two, when you've started to get the hang of it. Now, run along and get Miss Ince to help you change into your riding clothes. I'll meet you in the stables behind the house."

On her way to the stables, Emma recalled Matthew's scorn when she'd purchased the riding habit for her daughter. "She's much too young," he'd said. Emma had bitten back her retort—if they'd had a son, he'd have been on horseback in nappies.

Caxton was waiting, standing beside a pony. He'd worked for the estate for years, so she was confident he wouldn't let any harm come to Patsy.

"I'll jus' lead 'er round yon paddock a few times to start wi', my lady," he said. "Flossy 'ere's very docile, so don't ye worry none."

"Thank you, Caxton," she replied, her attention drawn suddenly to the house. Patsy was running toward her, Wellington nipping at her heels. "Mummy," she shouted breathlessly, "Aunty Susan's here."

Emma's heart threatened to burst. She'd intended to write to Susan about Dr. Henry's arsenic theory. There was no one she would rather have by her side than her one true friend at this difficult time. She lifted her skirts, took Patsy's hand and ran back into the house.

She found their welcome visitor in the foyer talking to Frame. Tears flowing, she threw herself into her sister-in-law's embrace. "Susan, I can't believe you're here."

⟫⟫⟫⟪⟪⟪

GABE ALMOST STEPPED back into the morning room when he came upon the tearful scene in the foyer, but this was his house now, dammit. It would appear Matthew's sister had arrived unexpectedly, probably to determine his suitability or lack thereof. He couldn't see her face, but gray seemed to be the predominant color of her attire. He cleared his throat to alert the women to his presence.

Emma took the visitor's hand. "Susan, may I introduce Gabriel Smith, our new Lord Farnworth."

He was surprised to find himself face to face with a much younger and more attractive woman than he'd expected; she had the same dark hair and olive complexion as Patsy. The smile fled as soon as Susan set eyes on him.

Emma's blotchy face bothered him for a moment, but then he realized it was caused by tears of happiness. He executed a clipped bow. "Miss Crompton, it's my honor to meet you."

"I call him Cousin Gabriel," Patsy explained, boosting his confidence when she put her small, warm hand in his.

Susan raked her gaze over him, glanced briefly at Emma, then bobbed a curtsey. "Lord Farnworth."

"Let's not stand on ceremony," he replied, certain she'd already made up her mind about him. "I'm aware this was your home for many years and I know Emma considers you a dear friend. Please call me Gabriel."

"Gabriel," she echoed, still staring at him. Perhaps he wasn't what she was expecting. He found it amusing a woman known for voicing her opinions seemed at a loss for words.

"You can direct the footmen to put Lady Susan's trunks in her old room, Frame," Emma said, linking her arm with her friend's. "How long are you staying? Why didn't you tell me you were coming? Did you stay overnight in Manchester?"

She drew Susan toward the drawing room. "Ring for tea, Frame. Come along, Gabriel. We have so much to tell Susan."

"But my riding lesson, Mummy," Patsy complained.

Emma paused. "Oh, I forgot. Caxton's waiting for you. Off you go."

Gabe was elated Emma wanted to include him in the discussions, but he watched Patsy run off thinking he'd be the best person to teach her to ride.

DOUBLE MYSTERY

A GREAT WEIGHT lifted from Emma's shoulders. Susan always saw to the heart of any problem and would help sort through the onslaught of disturbing revelations. Her world had been set on its head in the last few days. Susan would help right it. "I can hardly believe you're here," she gushed, beginning to wonder if it had been a mistake to invite Gabriel to be part of this first conversation.

Seated on the sofa, Susan smoothed down the skirts of her gray muslin gown and looked daggers at Gabriel who had remained standing beside Emma's chair. "I had to come and see this new earl for myself."

Emma might have known Susan wouldn't beat around the bush, but she was embarrassed for Gabriel. She needn't have worried.

"I understand your misgivings, Miss Crompton," he replied. "I can think of no one less suited to the task of being an earl than myself."

Susan raised a thin eyebrow. "And yet, you accepted the title."

Gabriel shrugged. "I felt it my duty."

"And the windfall enabled you to escape Saint Helena."

"Susan," Emma chided.

"It's all right, Emma. Matthew's sister is obviously well informed. I admit I was glad to leave Napoleon's island of exile, though, in the beginning, I welcomed the isolation. However, I can assure you I would have been content to remain in the army. I was a good soldier."

"Gabriel fought at Waterloo," Emma interjected, signaling the footman to wheel the tea trolley where she could reach it. She dismissed him with the assurance she could pour. She didn't want a servant to overhear matters of private concern.

"I don't suppose you have Souchong tea?" Susan asked.

It occurred to Emma her friend had acquired some rather pretentious tastes while living with her mentor. "No, just plain pekoe, my dear."

Susan sighed. "That will have to do."

As she poured, Emma worried what Gabriel must think of Susan, although his opinion shouldn't matter.

"Frankly, Sister," Susan suddenly declared, "I understand the constraints that keep you tied to this house, but you must see how it looks to an outsider."

Emma's stomach turned over. How could Susan know about the will? She was relieved when Gabriel took the Sèvres teacup and saucer from her trembling hand and passed it to her sister-in-law.

"Lady Farnworth is living here at my request until the repairs to the dower house are complete," he said.

Susan's tea apparently went down the wrong way. She coughed, swallowing hard as her eyes watered. "The dower house?" she asked hoarsely.

➤➤➤◄◄◄

GABE SENSED EMMA was getting flustered. He had to stop Susan blurting out details of the will she seemed to have become privy to. The newcomer's opinions would obviously have an influence on the woman he loved, but he wasn't prepared to behave as if he had done something wrong. "I'm having the dower house restored," he explained. "Emma and Patsy have a right to live there."

"But..."

"I know the history, Miss Crompton. Emma and I have learned

more about the deaths of your father and brother than you are probably aware of."

Some of the belligerence left Susan's gray eyes as she took another sip of tea. "We don't talk about my father's death."

"I'm afraid we have to," Emma said.

"Yes," Gabriel agreed, accepting his cup of tea. As he began to relay the details of his time in Saint Helena and Dr. Henry's diagnosis of his and Matthew's symptoms, he wished there was a bottle of brandy nearby to fortify the beverage he didn't particularly care for.

Susan put down her cup shortly after he began his tale. Neither she nor Emma interrupted once. By the time he finished, the color had drained from Susan's face.

"Arsenic?" she asked after a long silence punctuated only by the sonorous ticking of the Perigal clock on the mantelpiece.

"Yes," Emma replied. "I understand now what was happening to Matthew. The poison was slowly driving him mad."

"Like Papa," Susan whispered, staring into nothingness.

"So," Gabriel interjected. "What we have here is a double mystery. Arsenic poisoning has clearly been going on at Thicketford for many years, which doesn't explain how I was poisoned in the middle of the South Atlantic before anyone had any inkling I would become the Earl of Farnworth."

Susan pursed her lips as she stood. "A mystery, indeed, but mysteries are meant to be solved—and solve it we shall. Come along, Emma, walk with me to my room. All this news on top of traveling has worn me out. Thank you for your excellent summation, Lord Farnworth."

He bowed. "I apologize for being the bearer of troubling tidings. And, please, call me Gabriel."

"It is troubling. However, *Gabriel*, I now understand more about these tragic deaths."

He bowed again as the ladies left, noting with satisfaction the smile on Emma's blushing face. He'd won the first sortie.

>>>×<<<

EMMA AND SUSAN encountered Mrs. Maple and two housemaids as they climbed the stairs.

"Your room is ready, Miss Crompton," the housekeeper said. "If ye'd given us more notice, I'd have aired it out, but we've put fresh linens on the bed."

"Thank you, Mrs. Maple," Susan replied, either oblivious to the housekeeper's implied criticism or choosing to ignore it. "You're a treasure."

She inhaled deeply when they entered the chamber. "It isn't long since I was here last."

Emma took hold of her friend's hands. "Yet, Matthew's funeral seems like a lifetime ago."

Susan hugged her. "Life goes on, but you must have been devastated by the terms of the will. I could cheerfully have murdered Matthew myself when I found out."

Emma bristled. "Just how did you find out?"

"Hannah badgered Rowbotham. She's related to him."

Emma realized it would be pointless to make a scene over the breach of privacy. "So, you understand why the decision to repair the dower house came as a blessing. Patsy will grow up on the Farnworth estate. Gabriel has offered to pay all the expenses."

Susan smiled knowingly. "And is Gabriel aware of your measly inheritance?"

Emma's throat tightened. "I don't think so, at least I hope not."

"I'll wager he is."

Emma clenched her jaw, stricken by the thought Gabriel's actions were motivated by pity. Adherence to the code of duty had ruled his life. He perhaps felt it his duty to marry her out of guilt. She'd ended up a charity case, whereas he...

Susan's voice broke into her thoughts. "You seem to get along well with him. I notice he calls you Emma."

"Yes. I didn't expect to, but..."

"And he thinks highly of you."

Emma shrugged, not sure where the conversation was headed. Susan was too perceptive. "We're going to a musicale at the Whiteside residence on Friday. He's asked me to help him find a wife. You could come too."

Susan snorted. "Not if the snotty-nosed Arthur Coleman will be there."

"He will, but he'll avoid you."

"Why do you say that?"

"He's always been afraid of you, I think. Remember at the funeral when he tried to proposition me and you warned him off? He fled like the hounds of hell were in pursuit."

Susan laughed as she perched on the edge of the mattress and kicked off her boots. "We did have a few run-ins when we were children."

"And you always bested him."

"He fights like a girl."

They dissolved into gales of laughter.

When they calmed, Susan's next words took her completely by surprise. "Listen, Emma, why don't you and Gabriel simply admit you're drawn to each other?"

"But..."

"I know. You're still in mourning, and I respect that, but I never saw you look at Matthew the way you look at Gabriel, and I'd say the man's smitten with you."

Emma sat beside her friend on the bed. "You see too much."

Susan patted her on the knee. "That's why you're glad I'm here. What do you suppose Gabriel meant when he said he welcomed the isolation of Saint Helena?"

LEARNING TO RIDE

L UNCHEON IN THE dining room was a lively affair. Susan bombard-
ed Gabe with questions about his duties on Saint Helena, all the
while careful not to alarm Patsy with any mention of arsenic or
poisoning. She eventually went off on a tangent, voicing her opinion
on such varied topics as the Duke of Wellington's taste in clothing, the
size of Napoleon's ego, and the lamentable state of the post-war
economy. Patsy, at first, appeared puzzled by the references to
Wellington until her mother pointed out her aunty was talking about
the victor of Waterloo.

But Susan's passion was truly in evidence when she spoke about
the evils of the slave trade.

Gradually, Gabe sensed he'd met whatever criteria Matthew's
sister had set for him. Perhaps it was loyalty to her brother's memory
that kept the sour look on her face when she addressed him.

She was actually an attractive woman when she bestowed the rare
smile on Emma and Patsy. The unrelenting gray of her garb didn't suit
her olive complexion, but he suspected she didn't care a whit about
her appearance. She probably held all men in low regard and would
never marry, which, in a way, was a pity. Life with a woman who held
strong views on everything under the sun would never be dull.

"Emma and I are off to research arsenic in the library," Susan announced as the servants were removing dishes.

Gabe had planned to spend some time going over Blair's ledgers, but didn't want the ladies to think he was tagging along. "How about you and I continue your riding lessons," he suggested to Patsy.

The child beamed a smile and slid from her chair. "Oh," she said as an afterthought. "May I be excused?"

"You may," her mother replied.

Gabe stood as Patsy sped from the room. "I'll take my leave."

"Thank you," Emma said. "You're so good to my daughter."

"As I said before, she's a lovable child." He nodded to Susan. "Let me know if I can provide any more information to help in your research. I appreciate your efforts to solve the mystery."

Susan shrugged. "Searching for answers is as much for our peace of mind."

Emma cringed, but said nothing.

"Nevertheless," Gabe replied, wondering why Susan seemed determined to project a prickly exterior.

Fifteen minutes later, he was lifting Patsy into the saddle. "How did you make out with this beast earlier?" he asked.

"All right," she replied with a grin. "Caxton just led the pony around the paddock."

"Maybe we'll start off the same way this afternoon, then you let me know when you feel ready to take the reins."

A hint of uncertainty flashed in her eyes before she nodded.

Gabe led the pony into the paddock, inhaling the smell of newly scythed grass. Looking out over the verdant fields surrounding Thicketford, it occurred to him he'd been remiss in not asking Blair to show him the estate. He should learn all he could about Farnworth now that the future looked more promising.

He glanced up at Patsy, noting the growing confidence in her riding posture. He'd never realized nurturing a child could be such an intensely rewarding experience. A new desire to sire children of his own swept over him.

"Can I try?" Patsy asked after several circuits of the paddock.

Gabe wasn't completely sure she was ready, but he put the reins in her hands and showed her how to hold them correctly. "I'll be right here beside you. Go slowly."

For a novice, she did a creditable job and he only had to reassert control of the animal once or twice. She'd feel the aftereffects of too much bouncing later. "Well done," he declared as he lifted her down. "We'll work on moving with the horse in a day or two—after your bottom stops hurting."

She giggled as she put her arms around his neck. "You said *bottom*, Cousin Gabriel."

He hugged her, reveling in the little girl's affection. "What should an earl say instead?"

"Mummy calls it my *derrière*."

"Well, Miss Patsy, your *derrière* is going to be sore for a while."

They returned to the house hand in hand.

"I'm so glad you came to us, Cousin Gabriel," she told him.

"As am I," he replied, struck by the incredible realization this little bit of England was where he was meant to be.

⤜⤛⤛

"I NEVER UNDERSTOOD until now," Susan declared.

"Understood what?" Emma replied.

Susan flipped another page of the tome she was studying. "Why Papa purchased all these learned treatises on madness."

Emma closed the book she'd been perusing. She enjoyed reading novels. This stuff was too dry for her, whereas Susan pored over page after page. "You think he suspected he was going mad?"

Susan hefted the tome aside and opened the one beneath it. "Not only that, he added this illustrated volume of poisonous plants."

"Perhaps he suspected he was being poisoned?"

"Possibly, although arsenic isn't a plant. He was probably on the wrong track."

Emma shivered. "It's eerie to think this has been going on so long."

"That is what I don't understand. Who could the poisoner be? Frame? Mrs. Maple? They are the only servants left from my father's time."

"We should ask them if they noticed when the old earl first began to act strangely."

Susan snorted. "Of course, if you asked me that question, I'd say my father always behaved unreasonably."

"He just didn't know how to deal with a daughter who had a brain and wanted to use it. I can still hear him. '*Women should know their place*', and all that rot."

Susan shrugged. "I suppose. It's a good idea to question Frame and Mrs. Maple."

"I'll arrange it," Emma replied, feeling a pang of pity for her friend. She hadn't always agreed with her own parents' logic, but at least she wasn't estranged from them. Susan could never reconcile with her deceased parents.

Emma looked up when Patsy burst through the door, followed by Gabriel.

"Cousin Gabriel let me ride by myself," her daughter exclaimed breathlessly, her cheeks aglow. "And he said *bottom*."

Susan guffawed in a most unladylike manner.

Emma frowned at Gabriel who looked almost as pleased with himself as Patsy.

"Never fear, ladies," he replied. "Patsy has assured me the correct word is *derrière*."

"What on earth brought that subject up?" Susan asked.

"My *bottom* will be sore because I bounced too much," Patsy explained.

Emma's heart thudded in her ears. She hadn't seen her daughter so happy in, well, never. Her father didn't allow such outbursts. And she had Gabriel Smith to thank for bringing joy to Patsy's face.

"Well, I'm off to find Blair," Gabriel said. "I plan to arrange a tour of the estate on the morrow."

Conscious of Susan's presence, Emma bit back a suggestion she accompany him on the tour. Instead, she reminded Patsy to get changed for dinner.

⫸⫷

GABE HAD TO admit to a grudging admiration of Susan's wit and intellect. She provoked lively discussions during the evening meal. He found it impossible to agree with all her views, but appreciated that she didn't try to ram her opinions down his throat. She agreed to disagree, which he deemed reasonable and a sign of her keen intelligence.

However, on the topic of slavery, they were of one mind. He admired her determination to do all she could to bring an end to the barbaric practice.

"Did you know that people all over England, and Scotland for that matter, own thousands of slaves?" she asked. "Many of them are genteel widows who've inherited the slaves their husbands in turn inherited when their ancestors invested in plantations in faraway lands."

He hadn't been aware of that. "So, they live in England and have never set foot in Jamaica, for example."

"Exactly, and these human beings are chattels to them. An asset that makes money. Abominable."

Gabe felt uncomfortable. He sincerely hoped slaves weren't part of Farnworth's assets. Perhaps that was one of the reasons Susan and her parents had fallen out. He'd ask Blair on the morrow. They'd arranged to tour the estate then ride on into Preston to purchase materials for the renovations.

"We're off to the Chetham Library tomorrow," Susan declared in between spoonfuls of her treacle pudding.

"I'm not familiar with it," Gabe replied.

"It's one of the world's oldest libraries," Emma explained. "In Manchester."

"Who knows what we might discover about poisons there?" Susan asked.

Gabe privately thought tracking down the poisoner was more important than learning about the poison, but he kept his opinion to himself.

RESEARCH

AS THE CARRIAGE with the Farnworth crest emblazoned on its door lurched away from Thicketford the next morning, Emma and Susan hugged each other and indulged in a purely feminine burst of glee. "I'm excited," Emma confessed. "It's been years since I traveled into Manchester."

"You'll find a great deal has changed," Susan replied. "There's a lot more industry. However, it still boasts fine cultural institutions like the Chetham."

"I confess I've never been there."

Susan patted her hand. "Not surprising. I can't see Matthew encouraging you to go. He used to fly into a rage whenever I went. Even today, I'll warrant we'll be the only women there."

Emma had always assumed the conflict was between Susan and her parents, but it didn't come as a shock that Matthew had opposed his sister's thirst for knowledge. She herself had acquiesced to her husband's insistence she not become what he described as a *"bluestocking, like my confounded sister"*.

"I wonder why men fear women who think?" she mused.

"Well," Susan replied. "We could talk all day on the subject. However, not all men are so inclined. Your Gabriel, for example, strikes me as a fair-minded man in that regard. I enjoyed sparring with him last night."

Emma suddenly felt too hot. "He's not my Gabriel," she protested.

"But you want him to be."

Emma sank back into the cushions, resigned to staying silent. Susan wasn't the kind of person one could lie to.

Two hours later, the carriage deposited them and James Footman outside the Chetham Library on Long Millgate, in the heart of Manchester's town center.

Emma looked up at the red-brick building. "It resembles a fine country house. An oasis in a desert of industry."

"Wait until you see the interior," Susan replied. "It's like going back in time to the sixteen hundreds."

They stationed James outside and entered the ancient library, earning censorious glares from every male in sight. Gazing up into the vaulted beams, Emma itched to express her awe. However, the thousands of leather-bound tomes on shelves lining the walls from floor to ceiling urged her to silence. Even a whisper would echo like a cannonball.

Susan nodded to a white-haired docent. "He'll know where we can find what we're searching for."

Emma agreed. The wrinkled fellow looked like he'd been there since the library's founding. She refrained from uttering her thoughts out loud since two or three professorial types had already turned to glare at Susan's whisper.

"Arsenic," Susan almost mouthed to the old gent.

He arched the bushiest eyebrows Emma had ever seen, revealing he really did have eyes.

"Detection?" he rasped. "Toxicology? Overdose? Homicidal use? You'll have to be more specific."

Emma's stomach turned over. The word *homicide* suddenly made Gabriel's predicament and the murder of two previous earls all too real. She didn't hear Susan's reply, but dutifully followed the old man as he shuffled along a labyrinth of narrow passageways. Emma prayed the weighty volumes stacked high on either side wouldn't come crashing down. It was akin to navigating the treacherous strait 'twixt

Scylla and Charybdis.

At length, the docent danced his hand lovingly along a shelf of books and left. It occurred to Emma they should have left a trail of breadcrumbs if they were ever to find their way out.

For two hours, she dutifully scanned the pages of various hefty volumes Susan passed to her as they sat at a well-worn wooden table. The four men seated at the table when they began their search soon departed after their hostile glares didn't silence Susan.

Emma learned nothing from the tomes they examined. Most of the language was highly scientific and far beyond her comprehension. She daydreamed about Gabriel, frustrated she couldn't seem to unearth any information that might help him.

"You're a million miles away," Susan remarked, jolting her back to the library.

"I was worrying about Patsy," she lied. "We've agreed she can ride in the afternoon if she attends to her lessons in the morning."

Susan eyed her, flipping closed a spiral-bound notebook in which she'd scribbled copious notes. "Gabriel wouldn't have allowed her to continue if he thought it wasn't safe to do so in his absence."

It was true. If Emma's thoughts had ever drifted to the remote possibility of remarrying, she'd despaired of finding a partner who would want to raise another man's child. Gabriel Smith had slipped effortlessly into the role like a fish takes to water.

"A coffee before we depart for home?" Susan asked as she stood, smoothing down the skirts of her gray muslin gown.

"Where on earth…?"

"St. Ann's Square. Five minutes away."

"Surely, only men…"

Emma stopped herself. This was Susan she was talking to. "Very well."

She narrowed her eyes against the brightness outside, fervently hoping they weren't about to get thrown out of a male bastion.

TOURING THE ESTATE

T HE FIRST PERSON Blair introduced to Gabe was Jedediah Harwood. "Jedediah manages Thicketford Farm," he explained.

Eyeing the substantial and well-maintained stone farmhouse from which Harwood had emerged, Gabe surmised the man ran a successful enterprise that contributed a great deal to the earldom's wealth. "Mr. Harwood," he said, extending a hand. "It's a pleasure to meet you."

Harwood hesitated only a few seconds before removing his cap and enveloping Gabe's hand in a meaty, callused grip. "My lord," he replied in a booming voice that caused chickens pecking nearby to squawk in protest.

It was on the tip of Gabe's tongue to insist the man use his given name but he suspected Harwood wouldn't be comfortable doing so. "Tell me about the farm," he said, "bearing in mind I'm a soldier who knows nothing about farming."

During the hour that followed, Gabe learned all there could possibly be to know about pigs, goats, sheep, crop rotation and sundry other agrarian topics as Harwood led them through barn after barn — every one chock full of healthy-looking livestock and rife with gut-churning smells. None of the animals flinched at the sound of Harwood's voice, which had grown even louder now he was in competition with them. Evidently, they were used to it. He didn't always catch the drift of Harwood's northern brogue, but the fellow clearly loved his job and took his responsibilities seriously. "I'd say you're a man content with his lot," he remarked when they returned to the expansive courtyard.

Harwood smiled for the first time. "God's country, this is. How can a *mon* not thrive here?"

Gabe scanned the fields full of sheep surrounding the farm, shading his eyes to look beyond to the Pennine moors brooding over the verdant valley. He'd expected little of these northern climes, and the scenery was definitely different from the manicured vales of Kent where he'd grown up. Yet, he already felt at home. This was a place where he too could thrive. "Indeed," he replied, his heart full. "I'm confident Thicketford Farm is in good hands."

"Aye, as long as I'm in charge, Lord Farnworth, thee needn't bother thyself—unless there's another year with no summer."

Gabe had a feeling Harwood would triumph over even that unlikely event. He shook the massive hand again and walked away with Blair, impressed by the farm manager's assurances. He guessed it was a trait of northerners to acknowledge the worth of their accomplishments. More reserved southerners might consider such behavior boastful, but Harwood was no braggart.

He met the miller next. The pride in Albert Pickering's voice as he toured his new earl around the large mill solidified Gabe's assessment of his northern workforce.

They rode through acres and acres of forest, comprised mainly of maple and beech trees, and spotted several does grazing in shady glades. At the far edge of the trees, Blair pointed to a distant field dotted with white. "Sheep," Blair explained. "Yonder the Whiteside estate. Smaller than Farnworth, but productive—at least for now."

Gabe sensed his companion would elaborate without being prodded.

"Far be it from me to speak out of turn, but I dread to think what will happen when young Arthur inherits."

Gabe had to tread carefully. He had taken an instant dislike to

Arthur Coleman but doubted members of the nobility voiced criticisms of one another. "I'll meet his father this coming Friday," he said.

"Stalwart fellow, the baron," Blair replied. "Shall we head to Preston now, my lord? Our business at the sawmill will take a while. We can visit some of the tenant farmers out on't moor another day."

"Lead on," Gabe replied, already feeling the strain of the morning's excursion. "I doubt I can manage the moor today."

He welcomed the chance to sit when Blair halted at an inn upon their arrival in Preston. "Best we eat before we embark on the next task," his estate manager suggested. "Food's always good here."

The spacious dining room was busy, but not overcrowded. Many diners at other tables greeted Blair and seemed curious about his companion, probably assuming he was the recently arrived earl.

A rosy-cheeked waitress brought them the day's *special*—a heaping plate of sausages, mashed potatoes and baked beans. "Bangers 'n' mash, *meelord*," the young woman declared with a wink and a curtsey. "'Tis my honor to serve thee."

Gabe assumed his best earl voice. "Thank you. It looks delicious."

She flounced off, clearly pleased with her brush with nobility.

Blair eyed him nervously. "Plain fare, but good."

Gabe sought to reassure him. "I spent ten years in the British Army. I've eaten bangers more times than I can count."

Blair's shoulders relaxed.

As they tucked into their food, Gabe broached the topic of slaves. Blair reassured him. "That's one time Lady Susan got her way with her father. He sold off the Jamaican plantation he owned, probably just to put an end to the endless arguments."

They ate in companionable silence but Gabe got the feeling his manager must wonder about the new earl's lack of energy and obvious ill health. He saw no reason not to take the man into his confidence. The more people on the lookout for the poisoner, the better. "I should make you aware of certain things Lady Emma and I have learned in the last few days," he began.

Blair listened to the tale of Gabe's illness and Dr. Henry's revelations regarding Matthew. Shock drained his normally ruddy complexion. He squirmed in his seat, crossing and uncrossing his arms several times. He remained silent for long minutes after Gabe finished speaking.

"So, the old earl wasn't off his head after all," he finally said.

"Well, we're just at the beginning of unraveling this mystery," Gabe replied. "But I think it's safe to say madness doesn't run in the Crompton family."

"I wish my da had known," Blair muttered. "He always said summat didn't add up."

The fellow looked so downcast, Gabe felt obliged to offer a ray of hope. "Lady Emma and her sister-in-law have gone to Chetham Library today to do some research."

Blair clenched his jaw. "I feel sorry for Lady Emma. Lord Matthew could be a difficult man at the best of times. However, if Lady Susan's on the trail, ye'll soon have yer answers."

They ate the Spotted Dick served as a sweet, then left to bargain for lumber and hardware for the renovations. "Only if ye feel up to it," Blair cautioned.

"The hearty food has renewed my energy," Gabe replied truthfully. That, and crossing a possible suspect off the list.

GETTING CLOSER

T HE CONVERSATION AT the dinner table consisted mostly of Gabriel's glowing account of his day with Blair. Emma thought he looked tired, but his enthusiasm for what he'd learned about the estate was encouraging.

She and Susan talked about their trip to the Chetham Library, describing the history of the old building and the incredible collection of books it housed.

They'd begun the meal later than usual since everyone had needed time to refresh themselves after their outings. Patsy began to yawn even before the arrival of the pudding. Emma sent for Miss Ince and Patsy was packed off to bed without objection.

"Caxton reports she did well with the pony today," Gabriel said, the pride in his voice warming Emma's heart. "Tried hard not to bounce."

Susan immediately drew out her notepad. "With the little one gone, we can tell you what we learned," she declared.

Emma didn't think they'd learned much, but there'd be no stopping Susan. She began by declaring, "It seems accidental and homicidal arsenic overdoses are common."

"Accidental?" Gabriel asked.

"Predominantly food related," Susan explained, consulting her notes. "Also, arsenic is often used by physicians to treat malignancy, leprosy and cholera. There's evidence of success using it to cure ulcers of the tongue, angina, psoriasis, scabies, and malaria. I jotted down the names of the men who wrote the treatises where I found this information, but I won't bore you with those details."

Emma was beginning to think she and Susan had gone to different libraries. She didn't recall reading any of these facts. Clearly, her sister-in-law had a sharp eye for ferreting out pertinent information. "I do recall reading the cause of death in cases of arsenic poisoning is usually attributed to intestinal inflammation," she said in an effort to prevent Gabriel thinking she was contributing nothing to the discussion.

"But it also has direct effects on the blood, the heart and the brain," Susan added.

Gabriel steepled his hands, tapping his fingertips against his full lips. "Interesting. However, I could likely tell you some of the effects myself. How can we detect the stuff?"

Susan launched into a description of a process invented by a man named Marcet who used nitrate of silver to detect the poison.

"That doesn't help much," Emma said, her attention still focused on Gabriel's lips. Her remark earned a scowl from her sister-in-law.

"One thing of note," Susan pointed out. "It seems the incidences of the homicidal use of arsenic are rising dramatically. Most often, it's the victim's food that's contaminated."

Silence reigned for long minutes, until Emma could hold her tongue no longer. "That's all well and good, but we eat the same food; Matthew, his father and I ate the same food. Yet, only the men suffer the effects."

"And my affliction began in Saint Helena," Gabriel observed, "where I consumed the same food as my men. As far as I know, none of them came down with any symptoms."

"So, we can rule out food," Susan decided. "There must be another explanation."

Yawning, Gabe excused himself from the table, citing the day's excursion as a reason to retire early. He was glad when Emma also expressed a wish to seek her bed. "I'll accompany you to your apartment, if you wish," he offered with a teasing smile. "It isn't out of my way."

"I'll just look over my notes once more," Susan said. She didn't appear shocked, leading him to believe she wasn't offended by his blatantly improper suggestion.

Emma blushed as she accepted his arm.

Her warmth felt good as they ascended the stairs. They fit together nicely. He only wished he was escorting her to his chamber. Although, on second thought, he'd prefer to bed her somewhere other than in the green box.

"How are you feeling?" she asked when they reached her door.

"The elixir seems to be easing the headaches. I'll take another dose before I get into bed."

He toyed with the idea of telling her about the salve, but then he might be tempted to ask her to massage it into his hands and feet. He'd prefer her touch to Bradley's. However, that was no way to woo a lady. Mentioning his bed was likely enough to offend her sensibilities, though she seemed in no hurry to disengage her arm from his.

"You enjoyed inspecting the estate with Blair," she said.

"I did," he replied. "It's funny, I wasn't looking forward to coming here, but I feel I belong in the north."

"I'm glad you came," she whispered, looking into his eyes.

She couldn't hide the desire lurking in the violet depths. All he had to do was bend his head and kiss those tempting, slightly-parted lips— but a cough distracted him. He looked up and saw Bradley coming down the stairs from his room. "Ready to retire, sir?" his valet asked.

Emma blushed furiously. "Lucy will arrive shortly, too," she whispered. "Goodnight."

"Goodnight," he replied as she fled into her chamber and closed the door. He turned to his valet. "Wonderful timing," he growled.

"Sorry, sir," Bradley whispered as they entered Gabe's chamber. "I'm making it my business to keep watch over you at all times."

Gabe shrugged off his jacket and handed it to his valet. "That's admirable, but we need a better plan. You can't monitor my every move. I spent the day with Blair and I'm convinced he isn't the culprit. He and I ate the same meal at a local inn in Preston and he had no opportunity to slip anything toxic into my ale." He sat on the bed so Bradley could remove his boots. "In any case, Lady Susan has come to the conclusion food isn't the means the poisoner is using."

"Blimey, it's a quandary," his valet remarked. "If it isn't food or drink, what else is there?"

"Damned if I know," Gabe replied with a yawn as Bradley gathered up the clothes he'd removed. "Be a good chap and get the salve for me—and the elixir."

As he climbed into bed, it struck him how ludicrous it was a man of his age had to depend on a valet to apply ointment to his hands and feet. It was of some consolation that the faithful Bradley had always been only too happy to meet his every need.

OPERA

"I DON'T THINK it's appropriate for me to go to the baron's musicale tonight," Emma said during breakfast.

Gabriel put down his slice of buttered toast and frowned. "But I'm counting on you accompanying me."

The disappointment in his eyes was genuine and, truth be told, she wanted to go with him. "Dressed in mourning, I'll put a damper on the occasion."

"Nonsense," he replied. "The mauve you wore the other day becomes you, and the amethyst necklace is stunning."

"But going to a social event with another man so soon after my husband's death…"

"Oh, bugger it," Susan suddenly interjected with an expletive she must have overheard Emma use. "I'll come with you, if that will ease your worries."

"There, you see," Gabriel said. "Problem solved."

"Yes," Susan agreed. "The scandalmongers will have nothing to say about the new earl escorting his predecessor's sister, and will deem it perfectly suitable for you to accompany her."

"I wish I could come too," Patsy said wistfully.

"When you're older," Emma replied.

"It will be terribly boring in any case," Susan told her niece. "Anthea Coleman will sing an aria from one of Handel's more obscure operas."

Patsy lapsed into a fit of giggles when her aunt inhaled deeply and launched into an off-key falsetto version of *As With Rosy Steps the Morn*.

Emma laughed too, pleased to see Gabriel smile and stick his fingers in his ears.

"The aria was composed for a mezzo soprano," Susan explained. "But Anthea fancies herself a soprano. After that, Baroness Whiteside will play one of Beethoven's piano sonatas. She'll warn her audience in advance that she isn't classically trained, which actually means she hits more wrong keys than right ones."

"Surely it won't be that bad," Gabriel said.

"Oh, just wait," Emma replied. "In the past, I've had to hide my amusement behind my fan."

"And the baron will beam with pride throughout the performance," Susan concluded as she rose. "I suppose I'll have to hunt up a suitable frock if I'm to come with you to this stellar event."

"Can I help, Aunty Susan?" Patsy asked.

"Yes, come along. It will be more fun with the two of us."

Hand in hand, both singing at the tops of their voices, they left the morning room.

Emma fidgeted with her napkin, aware of Gabriel's eyes on her. "I'm sure it will be a good turnout," she said. "The local gentry will be anxious to meet you."

"Size me up, you mean."

"You know how people are," she replied.

"Judgmental?" he asked with a smile.

"Yes, but you've nothing to worry about. You'll charm them."

"There's only one person I'm interested in charming," he said softly, his deep voice doing funny things to her insides.

"You've already accomplished that," she admitted as she rose and hurried away.

GABE LET OUT a long, slow breath. Susan's presence seemed to be working to his advantage. Emma was certainly more relaxed around her unconventional sister-in-law.

He'd previously dreaded the evening's social obligation, but was quite looking forward to it after Susan's hilarious impersonation.

Nevertheless, it was imperative the Crompton women be by his side to guide him through what he anticipated would be a gauntlet of curious busybodies. He anticipated Arthur Coleman in particular would delight in catching him out.

Gabe didn't care what people thought of him—he was coming to realize he could make a success of the earldom and its attendant responsibilities. However, it was important the local mucky-mucks accept him if he was ever to have a chance with Emma.

While amusing, Susan's operatic performance had left him feeling uneasy. He knew Handel and Beethoven were composers, but that was as far as it went. Fighting in the Napoleonic Wars hadn't left much time for opera. Cultural events on Saint Helena were nonexistent. Gabe's stepfather was a wealthy gentleman farmer but his idea of entertainment was an evening spent drinking at the local inn with his cronies, then coming home to dish out backhanders to anyone he thought looked at him the wrong way. Gabe and his brothers soon learned to be abed long before Samuel Waterman staggered home.

Opera was just one of the challenging topics that might come up in the conversation at the musicale.

⇥⇥⇥⇤⇤⇤

"YOU NEEDN'T BE nervous about this evening," Susan said as she, Emma and Patsy ate luncheon.

"I'm just worried Gabriel is missing his meal, and dinner will be lighter fare since there'll be plenty of food at the musicale. He needs to keep up his strength."

151

"Where is he?" Patsy asked.

"He and Blair have gone to the dower house to supervise delivery of the lumber and other materials," Emma explained.

"He's a grown man," Susan said. "He can always go to the kitchens if he's hungry."

"Did you decide what to wear tonight, Mummy?"

"Yes, the lavender silk."

"And the amethysts? Cousin Gabriel really liked that necklace. Did Daddy give it to you?"

"No. The stones belonged to my grandmother," Emma replied, unreasonably pleased Gabriel wouldn't have to be concerned her late husband had given her something he liked. "When I'm too old to wear them, I'll pass them on to you."

Patsy beamed a grin. "I'd like that."

"I'm glad you decided to attend," Susan said. "You could have gone without me acting as chaperone."

"I suppose I could," she admitted. "I don't know why I am so worried about what people think."

"Because society has drummed these expectations into women's heads for years. You've honored Matthew's memory for seven months and you were a good and faithful wife to a man who would sometimes try the patience of a saint."

"Susan," Emma chided with a sideways glance at Patsy. "Little ears."

"I'm sorry, but my brother could be very demanding. I personally thought he was lucky to have you."

It was the first time Susan had shared these thoughts. Emma had always considered herself lucky to have married the son of an earl, a man far above her in rank. Perhaps her sister-in-law was right—social status wasn't what made a person noble.

STEPPING OUT

"**Y**OU LOOK VERY distinguished, sir, if I may say so."

Gabe took the compliment from Frame as high praise indeed.

Bradley glowed, straightening his master's epaulettes for what seemed like the hundredth time.

"Hopefully, I won't be the only man at the musicale in uniform," Gabe replied, though he felt comfortable in the familiar red and gold jacket and navy blue trousers. An extra dose of the elixir had banished his headache and there'd fortunately be no dancing tonight.

"It will be to your advantage if you are," Susan declared as she descended the stairs to join the men in the foyer. "Especially when they hear you fought at Waterloo."

Gabe privately hoped the conversation didn't turn to the decisive battle. He'd sooner forget the slaughter than keep regurgitating it for people who could have no inkling of the horror. He was about to compliment Susan on the mauve gown she was wearing—he hadn't suspected the generous cleavage her décolletage revealed –but the words died in his throat when he espied Emma dithering on the landing above. The amethyst gems twinkled at her throat as she bent to kiss Patsy goodbye.

Surprised he wasn't drooling, he extended a hand, hoping to calm her nerves. "Come, my lady, you look magnificent."

Lifting the hem of the lavender silk gown, she began the descent, smiling when she reached the foyer and took his hand. He fervently wished they weren't both wearing gloves.

"And you look very handsome," she replied.

"Pah!" Susan exclaimed. "Handsome? He looks positively delicious. A prize catch for any woman."

Emma's fierce blush spread across her modest décolletage.

Gabe was at a loss for words. Did Susan believe he was going to the musicale to hunt for a bride, or did she suspect the growing attraction between him and Emma? Or was she setting her own sights on him? Stimulating as it was to spar with her in conversation, he wasn't attracted to her.

"You lovebirds needn't worry," Susan teased with a wink. "Just because I have no intention of marrying doesn't mean I can't appreciate a man's good looks."

"Susan," Emma chided. "Really. Gabriel and I aren't...er...lovebirds, as you put it."

Susan rolled her eyes. "Then don't get jealous when the women fawn over him," she warned.

Gabe couldn't recall ever being fawned over, but then social occasions with a lot of females present were few and far between in the army. Most men might find the prospect appealing but there was only one woman whose admiration he increasingly craved.

Frame coughed politely. "The carriage awaits, my lord."

Chilly evenings followed the cool daytime temperatures. Maidservants swathed the ladies in fur wraps. Bradley carefully arranged Gabe's cape on his shoulders, brushing off lint invisible to all but him.

When everyone was ready, Gabe offered an arm to both Crompton women. "I'll wager I'm the only man who'll arrive with two beautiful women on his arms."

Stepping outside, he filled his lungs with the clean air. He'd successfully completed the first phase of his campaign to establish himself as the Earl of Farnworth. He and Patsy got along famously; even her poodle tolerated him. He'd formed a good working relationship with Blair. Emma and Susan were both in his camp. The servants were warming to him. All this had happened despite his ill health. Basically, he'd just been himself.

Tonight, he faced the next challenge—winning over the local gentry. That might require different tactics.

⟫⟫⟩⟨⟨⟨

EMMA HOPED THE giddiness swirling in her heart wasn't evident on her face. She'd never had the opportunity for a London season and was filled with a new appreciation for the excitement debutantes must feel on the way to their first ball. She'd attended Whiteside's musicales on previous occasions, but tonight felt different—special somehow.

She had become the envy of everyone in her social circle when she attracted the attention of a titled gentleman. Her parents were agog when Matthew asked for her hand. His courtship had been exciting, but she realized now she'd been more in love with the idea of marriage than with the reserved man she was to marry. A young woman who hadn't snagged a husband before the age of twenty had to be deficient in some way. Emma certainly didn't want to end up a spinster, maiden aunt to Priscilla's brats. Marriage to a titled gentleman was a coup, and she'd been grateful to Matthew for the comfortable life he'd provided. But she'd come to realize over the years he would never allow his true emotions to show. If he loved her, he'd never said so. Nor could she recall ever telling him she loved him. For the most part, she'd been comfortable with her husband—until his behavior became erratic.

Stepping out with Gabriel Smith was generating excitement of a different kind. She felt a girlish thrill at being escorted by a handsome man. But the emotions ran deeper than simply feeling comfortable, and she was mature enough now to recognize them for what they were. Desire…trust…respect…love.

However, it wouldn't do to let Baron Whiteside's guests see how completely besotted she was becoming with the new earl.

MUSICALE

"THE FARNWORTH ESTATE borders Whiteside lands," Emma explained, "but the gateway leading to Withins Hall is on the far side. It will take us about fifteen minutes."

Gabe wouldn't mind if it took an hour. He'd have preferred to sit next to Emma in the carriage, instead of across from her. During the journey to Preston, he'd been careful not to stretch out his legs. He deliberately made no such effort this time. The intimate contact between them was having an effect on her, despite boots and crinolines forming a barrier between them—he could see it in her violet eyes that looked everywhere but at him. She didn't move her legs away from his.

Susan kept up a constant stream of chatter about the Coleman family, particularly Arthur. She had only bad memories of him as a child—spiders and cruel tricks played on animals loomed large in most of the horror stories—and, apparently, he'd become an even more despicable character as he'd grown to manhood. By the time Conrad halted their carriage at the front entryway of Withins Hall, Gabe felt he knew what to expect of his neighbors. However, he had no notion of who else might be in attendance.

As he stepped from the carriage, Gabe noted Withins Hall was smaller than Thicketford, though built of the same gritstone. The two-story house also boasted three large attic dormers jutting out from the slate roof. Both main floors had generous mullioned windows. Two enormous chimneystacks, one on each gabled end, anchored the dwelling.

James and another Farnworth footman assisted Susan and Emma to alight and Gabe escorted the women up the steps to the open doorway. So far, he was rather enjoying this outing.

His optimism faded when they entered the crowded foyer. He narrowed his eyes against the bright light of hundreds of candles in crystal chandeliers and silver candelabra. It wouldn't take much to resurrect his headache and it was important he create a good impression this evening. Emma squeezed his arm; the tantalizing warmth of her breast pressed against him restored his confidence.

A portly, balding gentleman hurried to greet them. "Lord Farnworth, welcome," he boomed, causing a lull in the general conversation as curious heads turned to peruse the new earl in their midst.

Gabe assumed the friendly fellow pumping his hand was his host. "Baron Whiteside, thank you for inviting us. You know the dowager countess, Lady Emma, and of course, Lady Susan Crompton."

"Please, call me Bertrand. We are neighbors, after all."

"Bertrand," Gabe replied.

"My dear Countess, how well you look," the baron gushed, brushing a kiss on her gloved knuckles. "And Lady Susan, I didn't know you were home. Nice to see you back in our beautiful county."

To Gabe's surprise, Bertrand Coleman winked at him. "Lucky fellow, escorting two of the most beautiful ladies in Lancashire."

Apparently, their neighbor didn't think there was anything scandalous about Emma's attendance at the musicale, and Gabe was relieved to see some of the apprehension leave her face.

Seemingly taking their cue from their host, several people approached to be introduced and to welcome Emma and Susan. He met and chatted with country squires, landed gentry, gentleman farmers, and a few cotton mill owners. The baron obviously had no qualms about fraternizing with the *nouveau riche*. Gabe noted some of the industrialists had come from as far away as Bolton and Blackburn—a sure sign of their desire to mingle with the aristocracy and perhaps make new contacts. He resolved to speak to Blair about the estate's investments in the cotton industry.

All in all, he was pleased with the way the evening had gotten underway and relieved no one had pressed him for details of Waterloo. "It seems my uniform has won them over," he whispered to Emma when the baron ushered everyone into the salon where the performances were to take place.

"I'm sure the uniform didn't hurt, but your demeanor put them at ease."

"I just tried to be myself."

"That's what she means," Susan chimed in. "Too often, members of the upper classes tend to speak as if they have a mouthful of marbles and a ramrod up their arse."

Gabe chuckled. Susan would have fit right in to any officers' mess—if women were allowed.

"Susan," Emma chided, though a smile tugged at the corners of her mouth and laughter danced in her eyes.

"Here comes a prime example now," Susan declared as they espied Arthur Coleman making a beeline toward them.

⤜⤜⤜

EMMA STEELED HERSELF not to cringe when Coleman seized her hand and slobbered a kiss, leaving a wet stain on her white silk gloves. "Emma," he crooned, pointedly omitting her title. "Welcome."

"Arthur," she replied coldly.

Gabriel tensed beside her. He could no doubt set Arthur Coleman straight in thirty seconds, but she preferred to avoid a scene.

"You remember my sister-in-law, Susan," she said.

Arthur ogled Susan's *décolletage* before making a perfunctory bow. "Ah yes. I thought you had run off to cohabit with some other bluestocking in Somerset."

"Ever the gentleman, I see," Susan replied. "You haven't changed a bit."

Fearing Gabriel was on the point of challenging Arthur's rudeness, Emma linked arms with him and Susan and pulled them both toward the salon. Arthur clenched his jaw as he watched them go.

Apparently sensing Gabriel's annoyance, Susan told him, "Pay no attention to Arthur. He has always been a twerp, but he's harmless enough."

They weren't able to locate three chairs together until the baron chivvied several people in the front row to move into the vacant seats between them.

Emma would have preferred a more discrete location near the back of the dozen or so rows of chairs, but she and Susan took their seats either side of Gabriel.

The baron called for quiet when everyone was seated. "Thank you, dear friends and neighbors for honoring us with your presence this evening." He gestured to Gabriel. "I am particularly pleased to welcome our new Lord Farnworth."

Gabriel stood and turned to acknowledge the polite applause with a nod of the head before regaining his seat.

"You're a natural at this," Emma whispered.

"Without further ado, may I introduce my lovely daughter, Anthea, who will sing an aria from Handel's beloved opera, *Theodora*."

Emma recognized most of the guests from previous musicales. She wasn't surprised when there was a good deal of shifting in seats and coughing as Anthea Coleman, blushing fiercely, emerged to stand before the audience. Her doting father clapped louder than anyone, shouting *"Brava"* before the performance had even begun.

"It's as if time has stood still," Susan whispered, rolling her eyes.

Anthea had gained weight and become rather pear-shaped. A solution to the acne that had plagued her since early adolescence had apparently not been found. Her frizzy hair was the same nondescript brown Emma remembered. "She's a sweet girl," she whispered to a wide-eyed Gabriel.

Wringing her hands, Anthea cleared her throat. "Er, *Theodora* isn't actually an opera, Papa, it's an oratorio in three acts."

Utter silence.

"You see, in Act One, Valens—he's the Roman governor of Antioch—issues a decree that all citizens must offer a sacrifice to the goddess Venus, on pain of death."

"Good Lord," Susan muttered, too loudly.

"Clearly not a comedy," Gabriel whispered.

"It's in honor of Diocletian's birthday, you see...er...Diocletian was the emperor, by the way. But, Theodora is a Christian, and Didymus is in love with her. He's a Roman soldier, but he's become a Christian too...er...not because he loves Theodora..."

After a comprehensive ten-minute synopsis of the entire plot, Anthea explained she was about to offer a rendition of *Defend Her, Heaven*, an aria sung by Irene, who was Theodora's friend. "Er...she's a Christian too, but she doesn't die."

She then introduced her mother as her accompanist.

"I see who Anthea takes after," Gabriel whispered during the polite applause as the baroness settled her large posterior on the piano bench.

As the off-key performance progressed, Gabriel crossed one long leg over the other and pressed a knuckle to his lips. The chairs were placed close enough that their upper arms touched. Emma felt him tremble as he struggled not to laugh. Susan was biting her fist, her face beet red. If Gabriel lost control, Emma knew she would dissolve into a fit of snorting giggles.

It was the most fun she'd had in many a year, made all the more pleasant by the stimulating presence of the noble man seated next to her.

FROM HIS VANTAGE point at the rear of the salon, Arthur seethed with resentment as he watched the three people in the front row. He didn't blame them for mocking his brainless sister. Did the silly girl not realize she'd rambled on about the plot of *Theodora* at every musicale? She'd memorized the arias of Handel's English opera, but Italian presented too much of a challenge.

As for his mother! Whatever made her think she could play the piano, he'd never know. The only good thing about being born into such a family was the title he would inherit, and the fortune that came with it.

That brought his thoughts back to his dire need to replenish the estate's coffers before his father found out he'd gambled much of it away.

Since no one would lend him any blunt, he'd have to resort to extortion. Who better to prey on than the promiscuous woman who'd spurned his suit and who now flirted with the common soldier sitting beside her? He couldn't see their faces, but their heads almost touched each time Emma leaned toward the upstart who thought he could be an earl.

As for the uppity Susan Crompton, a few good fuckings would soon put her straight as to who ruled the world. He was just the man to administer such a lesson. His dick twitched at the prospect.

He decided to pursue his plan to take revenge and exploit Emma's Achilles heel. She'd pay any price to save her daughter's life, if she believed it was under threat.

He folded his arms and leaned against the door frame, chortling with satisfaction. The next step would be to elicit more information from his accomplice within Thicketford Manor.

The unsavory characters he owed money to in Manchester would gladly provide manpower if they believed it would result in repayment of his debts. He had only to work out the details.

SARTORIAL PITFALLS

T HE SUN WAS well up by the time Gabe rose the morning after the musicale. He'd enjoyed the outing and couldn't recall the last time he'd laughed so heartily. He'd derived almost as much pleasure from Emma and Susan's giggles when the three of them indulged in a sherry in the drawing room after their return home.

Perched on the edge of his bed, he admitted the late brandy on top of a full evening hadn't been a good idea. Exhausted when he finally retired, he'd forgotten about applying the salve and taking a final dose of the elixir. As a result, he'd hardly slept a wink, his head ached like the devil and his stomach didn't feel too good about some of the different foods he'd sampled.

It was of some consolation the encounter with the local *Who's Who* had gone well. He'd had jovial and productive conversations with everyone he'd met, except Arthur Coleman. Susan claimed the fellow was harmless, but there was something evil about him that sent a shiver up Gabe's spine. He'd learned to size men up quickly in the army. When your life was on the line…

He pitied the kind-hearted baron. His son wasn't to be trusted, and the daughter—well, enough said.

It would be easy to dismiss his concerns about Arthur, but the Whiteside estate bordered Farnworth. He foresaw problems when the unpleasant young man inherited his father's title. The possibility roused protective instincts. Arthur definitely had designs on Emma.

Gabe had seen it in his lecherous gaze. If the wretch so much as…

"Good morning, sir…er…my lord," Bradley chirped as he entered the chamber. "You'll be happy to hear our new togs have arrived from Preston."

James entered in his wake, his arms laden with brown paper parcels tied up with string.

Gabe hoped he'd feel more like trying on his new wardrobe once he'd taken his medicine, but he sensed Bradley had more to tell him.

"Mr. Carr is waiting downstairs. He insists it's his duty to make sure everything fits. He's brought two apprentices with him in case alterations are needed."

Gabe had to give the tailor credit. Reputation and personal service were everything to an artisan like Carr. A hearty recommendation from an earl wouldn't go amiss and it offered Gabe a way to contribute to the local economy. He sensed the tailor would face a tough road ahead as more cotton workers flooded into Preston—men who couldn't afford bespoke clothing and expensive cravats. "Bring him up," he said. "After I've taken my elixir, if you please."

As Bradley helped him don his banyan, the errant fancy occurred that Emma's presence while he tried on the new clothing would make the job much more enjoyable. His cock stirred in wholehearted agreement. This might turn out to be a good day after all.

Having taken his medicine, he was feeling a little better when Carr bustled in with his helpers and directed them to untie the string securing the parcels and lay out the items of clothing. "I'm sure everything will fit perfectly, Lord Farnworth, but one can never be absolutely sure."

Bradley coughed into his fist when the first item Carr held up was a pair of drawers. They'd both been issued drawers in the army, though Bradley had often complained he preferred to simply tuck his shirttails *over and under*. Compared to the shorter, army-issue drawers, Carr's drawers were more like a knee-length lining for a pair of trousers. They could in no way be referred to as "smalls".

"Notice the shaped waistband and open front fly," Carr said. "The waistband is fastened with two buttons, and is laced closed in the back. The seat is full, the legs tight, with sufficient fullness through the crotch for full freedom of movement."

Gabe smiled. God had been generous with his male parts and he liked the sound of that advantage.

"The fly front rise is short, with the waistband fitting around the hips and stomach. The knee-bands are designed for ties."

The two apprentices didn't blink an eye throughout this commentary. They had obviously heard it before. The red-faced Bradley, however, looked like he might burst. Gabe anticipated some good-natured ribbing after Carr left, but he felt obliged to pull on the garment and allow the tailor to fasten the waistband and lace up the rear. Bradley had helped him don his uniform in the past, but Gabe had always managed to put on his own smalls. One thing was for sure. If ever he succeeded in bedding Emma Crompton, he sure as hell wasn't going to be wearing these drawers. She'd laugh herself silly.

Next, Carr held up one of several shirts. "White linen, of course. Full in the body and sleeves."

Standing on tiptoe, the little man deftly lifted the shirt over Gabe's head, helped him shove his arms into the sleeves and buttoned it closed at the neck. "The cravat will hide the buttons," he explained. "I prefer to make the cuffs wide and, of course, they too button closed."

He had Gabe turn about so he could inspect the fit. "How does it feel?"

Every officer had, at one time or another, been subjected to the scrutiny of an army tailor, but Gabe had never been asked his opinion as to the fit. "Good," he replied truthfully.

"Now, the stockings," Carr continued. "We have thick cotton or wool stockings and, of course, silk. The cotton comes in handy to wear under the silk stockings if you wish to hide the hair on your legs."

Bradley coughed again.

"In the army, I never had to worry about that," Gabe declared. "We didn't wear breeches even when they were popular."

"Oh, but, sir," Carr retorted. "While cloth breeches are considered old-fashioned, buff leather ones are still commonly worn for morning or country attire. I've fashioned several pairs for you."

Gabe dutifully pulled on the cotton stockings, then the silk, then a pair of knee-length buckskin breeches.

He lifted his arms when Carr took over, tucking in the shirt. "Two buttons at the waistband, like so, and then the fall comes up to cover a gentleman's privates, like this, and buttons like so."

Bradley stepped forward to help Gabe lift the braces over his shoulders to keep the breeches up.

"Waistcoats next. I made some single, others double breasted. All button up the front. I prefer ties in the back rather than buckles. Easier to manage. You will like the decorative silks I chose for the fronts. Jacquards for the most part. Not too gaudy, as befits a gentleman of your status. I sensed you're not a man for peacocks and the like. Plain in the back, of course."

Gabe had to admit the tailor had chosen tasteful colors and patterns that would suit him. "Not what I'm used to wearing, but they'll be a welcome change."

Carr beamed, turning next to ease Gabe's arms into a royal blue dress coat with brass buttons. "Cutaway tails in the back, as you see. All wool. I dislike linen. I made them all double breasted. More manly."

Gabe moved toward the cheval mirror but stopped when Carr tutted. "No ensemble is complete without the cravat, my lord."

He produced a long rectangle of material and showed Gabe the horsehair pad sewn inside. "Brummell has made starch popular but I still prefer the padding."

His valet bristled when Carr proceeded to fasten the cloth around

Gabe's neck. If there was one thing Bradley boasted of, it was his ability to tie the perfect cravat.

"White only," Carr went on as he worked. "Color is for the working classes, dandies and the sporting set."

Finally allowed to inspect his appearance in the mirror, Gabe's spirits rose. Perhaps it was true that clothes made the man. He actually felt better physically. He'd seen the admiration in Emma's eyes when he'd appeared in uniform. Wait until she saw him in this outfit.

"The way things are with our abysmal weather, you'll need this before winter," Carr said, straining to hold up an ankle-length overcoat. It was hard to tell if the diminutive fellow's forced smile meant he was happy or irritated when Bradley hurried to help him lift it onto Gabe's shoulders.

"And the beaver hat, *de rigueur,* of course, sir," Carr said. "I brought buff and brown gloves. I'm not partial to the yellow. I can recommend William Timpson and Sons for boots. For the moment, I'm sure you have your own we can try with your new ensemble."

Minutes later, with Bradley's help, Gabe's Hessians were on his feet and he stood. "You cut a dashing figure, sir," his valet said.

"You might also want to purchase a pair of John Bulls," Carr suggested. "I personally prefer boots that reach the knee. Otherwise, we expose a good deal too much calf, don't you agree?"

Gabe nodded his agreement, though he'd never given the matter much thought. Clearly, the sartorial aspects of inheriting a title were laden with pitfalls he hadn't considered.

He thanked the tailor profusely for his efforts as Bradley stowed clothing in the armoire and the chest of drawers. "Everything fits perfectly, Mr. Carr," he said, thinking privately the apprentices had been brought along as part of the performance, not because Carr thought they'd be needed. "As for the bill."

The little man smiled. "Don't worry about that, my lord. I'll send it to Mr. Blair as usual."

"For my valet's wardrobe, as well."

"Of course."

"Speaking of which, Bradley, are we going to see you in your new outfits?"

"No sir," his valet replied after a moment's hesitation. "Mr. Frame and Mrs. Maple are waiting below stairs to help with my fashion parade."

Gabe raised an eyebrow, but made no comment about his often misogynistic valet seeking the opinion of the housekeeper. "Perhaps you can take Mr. Carr's apprentices to the kitchens on your way and get cook to give them some of her lemon tarts."

⟫⟫⟨⟨⟨

"OUR EARL CUTS quite the dashing figure in his new frock coat," Susan remarked after Gabriel had finished his luncheon and excused himself, intending to go to Preston to purchase a pair of boots. Patsy had gone in search of her dog who'd suddenly run off during the meal.

Emma privately thought *dashing* was an understatement, but it wouldn't do to gush about how breathtakingly handsome Gabriel looked. "Yes. The blue is very becoming."

"Why didn't you tell him?"

Emma shrugged. "I'm sure he doesn't need me to compliment him."

"He wanted your approval."

It was true. Emma had seen it in his eyes. However, she was quite certain he'd recognized the glow of admiration in her own gaze.

"Why don't you act on your attraction?" Susan asked.

Emma had kept asking herself the same question, but the answers were always the same. "I'm still mourning my husband."

Susan rolled her eyes. "We've been over this."

"Gabriel might not feel the same way."

168

"Nonsense."

"People will talk."

"Let them."

"It's easy for you to say. You don't live here."

Susan snorted her disagreement. "It was never easy for me. I know how hard it is to challenge society's norms, but I've never regretted being myself. And maybe I will return to live at Thicketford."

Relief swept over Emma as she reached to squeeze her sister-in-law's hand. "That would be wonderful. I need a friend close by."

Susan chuckled. "You won't think so once you and Gabriel…"

All conversation ceased when Patsy returned to the table, Wellington in her arms. "I tracked him down in the kitchens," she explained. "Cook wasn't happy. He frightened her cat."

Her head filled with visions of lying abed in Gabriel's arms, Emma rubbed Wellington's ears and said, "That's nice, dear."

FILTH

Having spent the morning cleaning ashes out of four grates and scrubbing the hearths clean, Tillie decided to spend her brief lunch break napping in her room. She needed sleep more than she needed to spend thirty minutes with the other servants, especially Frame and Mrs. Maple. It was obvious the two of them had assigned her to the filthiest, backbreaking menial duties, no doubt hoping she would give notice. Hah! And just where would she go? Unless Arthur could find her a position at Withins Hall. That would make trysting easier.

Lost in these thoughts, she ambled along the deserted corridor of the servants' quarters. Her heart stopped when she bumped into a solid male wall. A gasp emerged from her constricted throat—she recognized the footman's Whiteside livery. "What are you doing here?" she asked, looking around nervously.

"Ye're to come with me," he muttered, seizing her arm.

"Don't be daft," she retorted, struggling unsuccessfully to pull free.

"My master's waiting," he growled.

Confused thoughts swirled in her head. "But today isn't my day off...I..."

"He's in his carriage. Get a move on."

Tillie held up sooty hands, aware her face must be equally smudged. "Let me wash."

"No time," he replied, bustling her along to the rear entrance.

Within minutes, they were hurrying beneath the weeping willows lining the driveway. She could barely keep up with his long strides. Breathless, her heart beating too fast, she ignored the gatekeeper's snort as the brute opened the smaller gate designed for foot traffic and dragged her into the roadway.

"How much further?" she gasped as he strode away.

He made no reply, leaving her with no choice but to follow. At the end of her tether, calves on fire, she nigh on cried with relief when Arthur's carriage came into view around the next bend. The footman bundled her inside. Gasping for breath, she slumped into the seat, relieved at last to be with the lover who so desperately wanted to see her.

The smile died on her lips when Arthur sneered.

She wished she'd at least removed the soiled apron.

➤➤➤✦◀◀◀

"DON'T COME NEAR me," Arthur warned. "You're filthy."

For an instant, he feared she might cry. Perhaps he had been too harsh. Much as it pained him, he needed the chit's help.

He was relieved when she stiffened her spine and glared at him. She had moxie, he had to admit. "I thought you were a lady's maid," he said. "You look like you've been cleaning chimneys."

Her pouting scowl confirmed his suspicion she was less than happy with her masters at Thicketford. "Dearest Tillie," he crooned. "What can you tell me about young Patsy Crompton?"

She folded her arms. "What?"

Praying for patience, he tried again. "What does the little girl do during the day? Does she have a governess?"

"Why do you want to know?"

Arthur sought a clean spot and stroked her cheekbone with the backs of his fingers. "Just curious."

As he'd hoped, lust flared in her eyes. "Miss Ince gives 'er lessons but she's more like a nanny than a governess."

Arthur withdrew his hand quickly when she moved to touch him. "The child must do other things."

"She spends a lot of time playing with 'er dog."

"Indoors or out?"

"Indoors, mostly, and she 'as a trunk full of toys in the nursery."

"Does she not spend any time out of doors?" he asked impatiently.

"Well," she sniffed, dragging a handkerchief from her apron pocket and blowing her nose. "She 'as riding lessons, usually in the afternoons."

Eyeing the blackened cotton square, Arthur was glad he hadn't offered to lend her one of his monogrammed linen handkerchiefs. However, this information was promising. "In the paddock behind the stables?"

"Yes, but…"

"Who is teaching her to ride?"

"Some days it's the earl, other times Caxton."

Arthur leaned back and closed his eyes, trying to formulate a plan. It would be an added bonus if the earl got roughed up.

"I 'ave to get back," Tillie murmured, studying her dusty boots. "I'll be missed."

Arthur needed more. "You'll come to Withins."

"But…"

"Do you want to spend the afternoon with me or not?" he growled, hoping she didn't detect the disgust in his voice.

"Of course. But if I lose my position…"

"I'll find you another."

She smiled, her teeth incongruously white in her mucky face.

"I'll arrange for a bath."

She fluttered sooty eyelashes. "And will you bathe me, my lord?"

Was there no end to the woman's idiocy? "You mistake me for a servant," he replied, tapping his cane on the roof of the carriage.

❯❯❯❯❮❮❮❮

"YOU CAN COME out now," Arthur said.

Tillie understood why he'd wanted her to remain hidden behind the oriental privacy screen in his chamber while potboys filled the tub in his bathing room, but the annoyance in his voice was bothersome. It was as if he didn't really want her there, which was nonsense, of course. He loved her.

"Now, tell me what else has been occurring at Thicketford."

She wasn't sure why he was suddenly so curious about her employers, but she wanted to put him in a better mood. "Well, 'is lordship and Lady Emma attended a musicale. Lady Susan went with them."

He sighed with exasperation. "I mean something I don't know."

"The earl's new wardrobe arrived. Mr. Carr from Preston made all the outfits. The earl looks smashing in 'is new blue frock coat with gold buttons."

He still didn't look pleased, then she remembered. "Oh, and a load of lumber and stuff was delivered. For the repairs to the dower 'ouse."

His smile came as a relief, though why he'd be interested in wood was beyond her. Aristocrats were hard to fathom sometimes.

"And the lumber is stored at the dower house?"

She shrugged, anxious to remove her clothes and be done with this strange interview. "I suppose so."

"Get all that dirt off before you even think of climbing into my bed," he snarled. "I have to go into Manchester and I'll be back late."

His announcement came as a shock. She was already salivating at the promise of his cock thrusting into her. "I thought…"

"No time. You are not to leave this chamber. Do you understand?"

It was hurtful, but at least he wanted her ready for him when he returned. "Yes, Arthur."

She stared at the door for a long while after he slammed it on his way out. "It's a good thing I love you, Arthur Coleman. I won't allow you to treat me so rudely when we marry."

Thrilled by the prospect of life as a baroness, she stripped off the soiled clothing and climbed into the deliciously hot water. "Wonderful," she breathed, giggling at her breasts bobbing atop the suds. "You don't know what you're missing, Arthur," she breathed as her fingers tweaked a taut nipple before wandering to the aching nub between her legs.

OVER THE HILLS

G ABE SETTLED INTO one of the comfortable upholstered chairs in the drawing room. "I dropped in to see Dr. Henry while I was in Preston," he reported as the adults indulged in a glass of sherry after Patsy had gone to bed. "Just on the off-chance he might be free."

"And was he?" Emma asked.

"We had a brief chat. I told him about Susan's belief the poison isn't being administered in our food."

"Hopefully, you didn't tell him a woman had arrived at that conclusion," Susan said sarcastically.

"Actually, I did. He seemed impressed with your research trip to the Chetham."

"Huh! A forward-thinking male!"

Gabe chuckled, lifting his leg to rest his ankle atop the opposite knee. Assuming such a relaxed posture was a measure of how quickly he'd become comfortable with these women. "We're not all misogynists, you know."

As he'd hoped, Emma's gaze fixed on his new John Bulls. "How do the boots feel?"

"Excellent. Carr's recommendation of Timpson was a good one. The man knows his boots. Anyway, back to the doctor. He's been doing some more research of his own. Apparently, arsenic has been reported in all kinds of places."

"Such as?" Susan asked.

"In 1805, a family of nine were poisoned after eating a pudding accidentally laced with arsenic."

"A pudding," Emma exclaimed. "The whole family died?"

"Apparently not, but they were all very sick, especially the children. Then there's rat poison, of course, and Henry cited one case of a weaver who was in the habit of biting the arsenic-contaminated ends of cotton before knotting them.

"But, in my opinion, the most interesting thing is that some ordinary things like candles, fly-papers, paper, clothing and furniture have been found to contain arsenic."

"So," Susan said thoughtfully, "the poisonings could be accidental rather than deliberate."

"That might explain how I was poisoned in Saint Helena and Matthew here in Lancashire."

"In other words," Emma said, "something is doing the poisoning rather than someone."

Susan frowned. "But how on earth are we supposed to know which things contain arsenic and which don't? And what are the men exposed to that the women aren't? I'll have to think on a way to solve this puzzle."

"If anyone can come up with a solution," Gabe said, "I'm confident it will be you."

⇛⇚

EMMA SIPPED HER sherry, comfortable with the silence. She was pleased to see Gabriel relax, though the seating position he'd assumed did tend to draw the eye to forbidden places. The hysterics they'd shared after the musicale had created a bond between her, Susan and Gabriel. Amusement still bubbled beneath the surface and even the casual mention of the word *opera* set them all to laughing again.

"I just noticed you have a piano in this room," Gabriel said.

"I wondered why it's in here," Susan replied. "It was always in the music room."

"Matthew had it moved just before his death," Emma explained. "I wanted Patsy to take lessons, but he insisted the music room be redecorated beforehand. He died before the work began, and I just left things as they were."

Susan swigged down the last of her sherry and leaped to her feet. "We should play our famous, or should I say infamous, duet from *The Beggar's Opera*."

Emma tensed. "It's been years. I'm out of practice."

Not to mention the tunes she and Susan sang when Matthew wasn't at home weren't exactly *bon ton*.

"Nonsense," Susan replied, patting the empty space beside her on the piano bench. "Be a good sport."

"I'd like to hear it," Gabriel said. "Unless you're the same caliber as Lady Whiteside and her daughter."

His teasing smile left her with no choice. She took up her position beside the piano as her sister-in-law tried out the opening notes. "Susan sings alto, so she takes the part of MacHeath. I sing Polly's part."

Gabriel raised his glass. "This is an opera I'm actually familiar with."

Emma rose to the challenge. "So I won't bore you with a synopsis of the plot, unlike some I could mention." Clearly, the sherry was going to her head, but she was enjoying this interlude of frivolity and teasing. Life had been too serious for too long. "Suffice it to say, MacHeath and Polly are lovers." Heat flooded her face. Had she really spoken a word no self-respecting countess would utter?

Susan played the introduction then launched into the song, deepening her voice to sound like a man.

Were I laid on Greenland's coast,
And in my arms embraced my lass,

Warm amidst eternal frost,
Too soon the half-year's night would pass.

Gabriel's eyes widened at the saucy words, but his smile betrayed his delight.

Clutching the side of the piano, Emma filled her lungs and sang only for the man who drew her like a lodestone.

Were I sold on Indian soil,
Soon as the burning day was closed,
I could mock the sultry toil
When on my charmer's breast reposed.

Susan chimed in. *"And I would love you all the day."*

Emma plucked up her courage, emboldened by the desire burning in Gabriel's amber gaze. *"Every night would kiss and play."*

Susan joined Emma in the last stanza. *"If with me you'd fondly stray, over the hills, and far away."*

⋙⋘

GABE WAS SPEECHLESS as well as aroused. Susan hit the right notes, but Emma had the voice of an angel. "You should have performed at the musicale," he said, when what he wanted to tell her was he would *fondly stray* with her right now if she'd agree.

And they needn't go over the hills and far away. Her chamber would do nicely. Kissing and playing every night sounded like just what the doctor ordered.

But now he had a problem. Blushing prettily and avoiding his gaze, Emma declared it was time they all retired. A gentleman was expected to stand as the ladies prepared to leave but, if he did so, his rampant arousal would be impossible to conceal in the comfortable but snug-fitting new breeches.

Nevertheless, he had no choice. Fortunately, both women kept their eyes averted as they left, and the giggling gradually faded as they climbed the stairs. Obviously, they'd been well aware of his plight. "Perhaps that isn't a bad thing," he mused as he finished the last of his sherry. "My need of Lady Emma Crompton must be clear to her now."

MUSIC LESSON

"**W**OULD YOU LIKE to learn to play the piano?" Susan asked Patsy at breakfast the next day.

"What a good idea," Emma exclaimed.

Patsy nibbled her toast. "I suppose," she replied with a shrug.

"That's something I always wished I had learned to do," Gabriel remarked. "My mother loved her piano."

Sadness crept into his amber eyes—another hint of unhappy memories from his childhood.

"I could teach you both," Susan suggested.

"Let's, Cousin Gabriel," Patsy declared, suddenly enthused. "Can we start today?"

Emma appreciated Gabriel's attempt to get Patsy interested in the piano, but he could hardly be expected to take lessons with a child. "I'm sure Cousin Gabriel has more important things to do," she said.

"Not until this afternoon," he replied. "Mrs. Maple is giving me a tour of the house." He turned to Susan. "I hope you're a patient teacher."

Her sister-in-law's uncharacteristic coquettish giggle set Emma's nerves on edge. If anyone was going to sit beside Gabriel on a piano bench and teach him how to play, it should be her. The intensity of her sudden jealousy came as a complete surprise. It hadn't bothered her one iota when women fawned over Matthew at any social event they attended. For all she knew, her late husband might have carried on a dalliance with any one of them. She ought to be able to summon feelings of jealous anger at the mere thought of such a possibility, but she could not. "I know how to play too," she said lamely. "Perhaps Susan will allow me to observe and assist."

"Of course," her sister-in-law replied with an all-too-knowing smile. "I'm sure Gabriel won't mind."

"Goody," Patsy exclaimed.

Susan dispatched a footman to the library to bring paper and pencils to the drawing room, where everyone convened a few minutes later.

"First of all," she said to Patsy, indicating the writing materials as she put them on the occasional table. "I want you to put your hand flat on the paper and trace around it, then do the other hand, like so."

Emma was encouraged to see her daughter kneel by the low table, eager to try, but surely Susan didn't expect…

"Pass me a sheet of paper," Gabriel said, going down on his knees beside Patsy.

Emma gripped the side of the piano, thoroughly ashamed of the abysmal, snobbish expectations she'd had of this generous man.

When Gabriel and Patsy finished tracing, Susan instructed them to write the labels LEFT and RIGHT.

"I always get that mixed up," Patsy admitted.

Gabriel extended his right hand to her. "Remember, the *right* is the one you use to *write*, and the one you shake hands with."

She laughed as he made a big show of shaking her hand vigorously.

"Now," Susan said in a schoolmarm voice, "write the number ONE on the thumbs."

"I know my numbers," Patsy said proudly as she followed the instruction.

"So you know what to put on the finger next to the thumb," Susan said.

"Two."

Emma swallowed the lump in her throat as she watched her little girl and the man she was falling in love with. Both carefully printed 2, 3, 4 and 5 on the traced fingers as they knelt with heads almost touching. It was a heartwarming scene she would never forget as long as she lived.

"Now, hold up your hand and count off the number for each finger. Right first."

Patsy smiled at Gabriel, raised her right hand and held up each digit as she counted them off.

"Now the left."

Beaming, Patsy repeated the exercise.

"My turn," Gabriel announced, seemingly not embarrassed to be completing a children's finger exercise.

⋙⋘

AS GABE COUNTED off the numbers, his mind went back to his mother. He recalled her playing jaunty tunes by ear when he was still a very small boy. It would have been easy for her to share her talent with her sons, but, of course, Samuel would never allow such a bond to exist.

By the time Gabe left home, the piano his mother loved was long gone, sold off despite her feeble protests.

But that was in the past. He'd been given the opportunity to learn alongside a bright little girl who'd secured a place in his heart.

Nor did it concern him that Patsy immediately grasped what Susan was explaining about the musical alphabet going from A to G, and something about Middle C. He'd have to beg private lessons from Emma if he was to keep up with Patsy.

"You're not listening, Gabriel," Susan admonished, jolting him out of his reverie about where such private lessons about fingering might lead.

》》》《《《

EMMA WAS DELIGHTED when Patsy quickly got the hang of locating Middle C and had no trouble putting her fingers on the correct keys with both thumbs sharing Middle C. Within ten minutes, she was able to play what Susan called a *Spider Song,* starting off with both thumbs pressing the key, then the 2's together and so on.

"You're obviously a musical prodigy," Gabriel declared as she slid off the bench to let him have his turn.

Patsy's broad smile turned to a frown. "What's a prodigy?"

"Something you'll soon see I am not," he replied, peering at the keys, clearly not completely sure how to locate Middle C.

Without forethought, Emma sat beside him, took hold of his left hand and put his thumb on Middle C. Anything she'd intended to say died in her throat as his warmth penetrated her skin. It was most unsuitable behavior and she ought to remove her hand—but couldn't. She stared at the contrast between his masculine fingers and her slender ones; tiny wisps of dark hair dusted the back of his hand. His hands were bold and strong, capable of firing a musket or killing a man in combat. Yet, there was a gentleness in Gabriel Smith that made her believe his caresses would be…

"And the right thumb like so," Susan explained, saving her from clasping Gabriel's hand to her breast.

She withdrew abruptly. He didn't look at her as he followed Susan's instructions, but something intangible passed between them as they sat side by side on the bench. It was as if their souls were communicating.

The fanciful notion sent winged creatures fluttering in her stomach. She'd never understood her mother's ramblings about soul mates—until this very moment.

TWISTED MAZE

LUNCHEON WAS A lively affair. Patsy hummed the *Spider Song* in between chatting about how simple it was to find Middle C.

"Easy for you to say," Gabe teased. "You're a faster learner than I am."

He basked in the bright smile Patsy gave him. "You'll soon learn," she said.

Gabe acknowledged he wasn't out of the woods as far as his health was concerned, and wouldn't be until the mystery of the arsenic was solved. Strangely, he didn't feel threatened by anyone at Thicketford and he considered himself a good judge of character. The contentment he'd found in this house was already working its magic. For the first time in his life, he was experiencing the everyday joy that being part of a family brought.

He had no illusions about the difficulties that lay ahead. He'd only scratched the surface of the estate's affairs; the post-war economy was in sharp decline; cold temperatures had caused widespread crop failures and famine throughout the world. Hard decisions might have to be made in the near future—decisions that would affect people he was becoming close to as well as people he didn't yet know. He wasn't afraid of making decisions. He'd made critical ones that had kept most of his men alive in moments of crisis during the carnage of Waterloo. His quick thinking had earned him the respect of subordinates.

England, and particularly Lancashire, was becoming more industrialized. It would be his responsibility to guide the earldom through never-before-seen changes. Old ways of doing things wouldn't cut it any more. That thought perked him up. He was, in a manner of speaking, a new broom. People wouldn't be surprised if he forged new paths.

Watching Emma across the table, he knew without a doubt she was the woman he needed and wanted by his side.

A loud cough interrupted his musing.

"Yes, Mrs. Maple?" Susan asked.

"Begging yer pardon," the housekeeper replied. "His lordship requested a tour."

"I did indeed," he replied as he stood. "Excuse me, ladies. Lead on, Mrs. Maple."

The housekeeper bent the knee. Gabe regretted the unkind thought that she was too broad in the beam to attempt to curtsey any lower. He should be able to keep up with her during the tour. He couldn't help thinking the portly widow didn't seem Bradley's type—though he had to admit he'd never seen his batman with a woman on his arm. "Married to the army," he muttered as they entered the foyer.

"Beg pardon, sir?" Mrs. Maple asked.

"Nothing of importance," he replied. "I'm familiar with most of the rooms on this floor. Perhaps we can start in the kitchen."

She stopped short, her ruddy complexion turning beet red. "But Cook isn't expecting us."

All the more reason to begin there. "I'm sure she won't mind."

The housekeeper dithered, chewing her bottom lip. "We'd have to take the back stairs."

Gabe suspected he'd breached some sort of protocol, which Mrs. Maple soon confirmed. "Don't rightly know as an earl should be going up and down the servants' stairs."

"Dear lady,"—he had to stop saying that—"I've slept in trenches and navigated companionways on warships in heavy seas."

"Very well, then."

She led him to a narrow door cleverly concealed as a frieze. It was located in a corner behind a large statue of some Greek god—or maybe Roman. Emma would know.

The prospect of pleasant hours spent in the library studying books on art blew away like chaff on the wind when he stepped into a dark, dingy corridor. To the right, a narrow flight of wooden steps led down, presumably to the kitchen. A landing snaked off to the left and the stairs continued upwards from there.

"The landing leads to the dining room, with a branch off to the morning room," Mrs. Maple explained. "Them stairs over there lead to the upper floors."

Gabe suddenly understood how the footmen who served meals managed to appear and disappear so efficiently. He'd never given it a thought. What kind of earl paid no attention to the servants in his employ? He looked back to the steep stairs. There was no railing and he worried his guide might not make it to the bottom in one piece. Even he would have difficulty. "The servers are obliged to carry the trays of food up those steps?"

"And the dishes back again."

Upon closer inspection, he noticed the treads were well-worn and far too narrow. "Doesn't look safe to me," he said.

"They're used to it," she replied. "They know where not to step."

He walked along the landing and peered up the dimly-lit stairs. For some reason, he thought of the windswept cliffs of Saint Helena. His posting there suddenly seemed like a bed of roses compared to a lifetime of service climbing up and down a dark and dangerous stairway. "The plaster's peeling. How long since this part of the house was painted?"

"The old earl had the service stair put in when he modernized the house. I came just after that."

"So, at least twenty years."

Even in the dim light, the rigid set of Mrs. Maple's shoulders and her tight lips suggested she was offended, or afraid he perhaps blamed her for the wretched state of affairs.

"This must have seemed very modern all those years ago."

Her jaw relaxed a smidgen. "Yes, sir. It did."

"However, this whole area needs repair. I'll speak to Blair before a maid breaks her neck."

She exhaled, clearly relieved. He decided to refrain from asking why no one had said anything before. He probably knew the answer. It was likely neither Matthew nor his father cared a whit about the working conditions of servants. He'd also wager Emma had never ventured into this twisted maze.

He held up his hand when Mrs. Maple moved to the top of the stairs going down to the kitchen. "I doubt I'd make it down there. We'll go up to the other floors by way of the main stairs. I'll visit the kitchen when repairs have been made."

"Or there's a tradesmen's entrance, round the back," she said, a hint of a smile tugging at the corners of her mouth.

"Good to know. Another day perhaps."

He followed her out to the foyer, planning to include his own suite of rooms in the list of urgent renovations.

A BUSY WEEK

OVER THE COURSE of the following week, Thicketford Manor became a hive of activity. Susan spent a lot of time in the library, eventually retreating to the Chetham when the hammering and sawing became too much for her to concentrate.

After venturing behind the hidden doorway in the foyer, Emma was appalled by the conditions the household servants had put up with for years, and heartily agreed with Gabriel's decision to proceed with repairs. Her only excuse was that Matthew had forbidden her to *trespass* into places a countess did not belong, but that did little to assuage her feelings of guilt.

In Susan's absence, Emma continued with Patsy's piano lessons. They soldiered on, doing the best they could given the noise.

For a day or two, Mrs. Maple fretted over Tillie's mysterious disappearance, but Frame's pronouncement of "good riddance to bad rubbish" seemed to set her mind at ease. Emma was privately glad to see the back of the girl. The rest of the loyal staff could be depended on not to gossip about the growing closeness between the dowager countess and the new earl. Tillie's version would have cheapened what Emma knew in her heart was a relationship based on mutual attraction and trust.

In an effort to escape the construction racket, Emma fell into the habit of accompanying Patsy to her riding lessons in the afternoons.

Gabriel was away for much of the day supervising the clearing of debris from the rooms of the dower house. On Friday evening, he reported the actual repairs would begin the following Monday. "Blair took on a couple of extra lads this week," he told Emma. "Rough-looking chaps, but they don't seem to mind the dirty work."

⇛⇚

AFTER A WEEK, Tillie's patience with Arthur was wearing thin, but his increasingly sour mood made her reluctant to say anything. He'd provided her with a Whiteside uniform and taken away her soiled clothing, but had yet to allow her to leave his chamber. He claimed to be waiting for the right moment to present her to the housekeeper. That was all fine and dandy, but what about her wages?

Having been cooped up for seven days, she supposed she should relax and enjoy what amounted to a holiday. She indulged in soaking in the tub every day; the meals Arthur brought were better than anything she'd ever been provided at Thicketford. She just wished he would stay and eat with her, but he laughed when she suggested it.

The best thing was she got to spend nights with him, and the sex was really, really good—although he'd fallen into the annoying habit of rolling over and dozing off as soon as he'd had her. She didn't like to complain about the loud snoring that kept her awake for hours. She might have to think about asking for her own apartment once they were married—it was important she get her beauty sleep.

On Saturday morning, she was puzzled when he brought her old uniform along with her breakfast. It had been washed, but not ironed.

"I don't understand," she said.

"You'll need to put it on for today when you go to Thicketford," he replied.

"I can't go back there."

He grabbed her by the arm and twisted. "You can, and you will."

His harsh tone of voice and the stern set of his jaw made her nervous so she said nothing about how badly he was hurting her.

"My lads report the Crompton girl takes riding lessons every afternoon, just as you said. Today, when the stable hand who gives her lessons is called away, you'll be there to take the reins. The lads'll do the rest."

A knot tightened in Tillie's stomach. "Called away?" she asked, though that wasn't the question praying on her mind. What did he mean *the rest*? What lads?

"Don't you worry about that," he said, finally letting go of her arm. "Get dressed. If you start walking as soon as you've eaten you should be there in time."

"But the gatekeeper…"

"No, silly girl, overland, through the trees."

⋙⋘

"I MUST ADMIT," Gabe told his ladies as they sat down to breakfast on Saturday morning, "I am looking forward to doing absolutely nothing today."

While he'd coped better than expected with the strenuous work at the dower house, his body needed rest. Dr. Henry's elixir was helping, but wasn't working fast enough for his liking.

Susan rambled on at length every time she returned from the Chetham, but seemed disappointed she hadn't yet solved the mystery.

Bradley had shadowed Gabe all week, doing more than his fair share of clearing debris. He was clearly frustrated to have caught no one behaving in a suspicious way, though he complained about the new outside workers Blair had hired, categorizing them as *shifty*.

"There'll be no hammering today," Emma said after sipping her coffee. "Everyone's taken the weekend off."

"Mummy comes to watch me ride every day," Patsy piped up, dipping a toast soldier into her boiled egg. "I was hoping you'd accompany us this afternoon, Cousin Gabriel. I don't bounce now. Caxton says I'm a good *questrian*."

"Equestrian," her mother corrected with a smile.

Gabe had missed spending time with Emma. He wanted to resume his campaign to win her over to the idea of a lasting relationship between them. "Certainly. I look forward to it. Since it's a lovely day, how about a walk to the dower house this morning so you can see the progress we've made."

Susan begged off, but Emma readily agreed.

A Pleasant Stroll

"T HIS IS THE farthest I've been able to walk in a long while," Gabriel confided when they reached the dower house.

Emma was pleased to see the exercise had put color in his cheeks. He looked invigorated rather than tired. Her craving for him had begun when he wasn't a well man. She couldn't wait to see him fit and healthy. "The elixir must be helping," she replied.

"I believe so, but I wish it would work faster."

"And that we could figure out the mystery."

"What mystery?" Patsy asked as she returned from running a little way ahead with Wellington.

Emma smiled wryly. "The puzzle of why you're such a precocious child."

"What's prec—? What does it mean?"

"It means you're clever," Gabriel supplied.

To Emma's relief, Patsy lost interest when she espied the ruin, but she tensed when her daughter hurried toward the recently delivered stacks of lumber, ladders, scaffolding and sundry other construction materials. "Stay away from there. If it falls…"

"Let's take a peek inside," Gabriel suggested. "I think you'll be surprised."

Once again, he'd easily coaxed Patsy into obedience. She ran to take his hand. Wellington couldn't seem to tear himself away from sniffing every corner of the pile of wood.

"Take my other hand," he said to Emma. "There's still some debris. I don't want you to trip."

The gleam in his amber eyes suggested he simply wanted to hold her hand, but she couldn't refuse when Patsy urged, "Yes, careful, Mummy."

Hand in hand, they walked the perimeter of the house, peering inside. She probably made suitable remarks about how much had been accomplished. She couldn't be sure because her brain wasn't functioning properly. It was too busy basking in the thrilling sensations caused by the warmth of his hand enveloping hers, and the occasional brush of his thumb in her palm. He said nothing, didn't even look at her, but she knew he was deliberately teasing her with his intimate touch. She should have been affronted by the brazenly suggestive behavior but, if he stopped, she might whimper like a babe deprived of its warm blanket.

As it was, she wanted to throw a tantrum when he suggested it was time to return to the main house.

He called a halt beside the building materials piled up ready for the workmen to begin renovations on Monday. "Looks safe enough," he remarked. "What do you think, Wellington?"

The poodle yapped his agreement and they set off for home, all three still hand in hand.

⇥⇥⇥⇤⇤⇤

ON THE WAY back to the main house, Gabe shook his head, chuckling at his own folly. He'd thoroughly enjoyed watching Emma blush and stutter each time he twirled his thumb in her palm. However, her obvious excitement had succeeded in giving rise to a rock-hard erection, the like of which he hadn't experienced for eons. While inconvenient, it was at least proof his body was coming back to life.

The walk to the dower house had been a good idea. His energy was returning. Emma's response gave him hope, and not only that she would eventually agree to marry him. The prospect she might be just the sort of passionate woman to indulge some of his more erotic fantasies did little to ease the pressure at his groin. He itched to tell Patsy she wouldn't be moving to the renovated mansion if he had anything to say about it. However, one step at a time. He didn't want to scare Emma off as he'd done with Georgina.

One thing bothered him about the stroll to the dower house. He couldn't shake the feeling someone was watching. His instinct for danger—possibly a legacy of learning to predict his stepfather's outbursts—had served him well in the military. He'd scanned the surrounding trees but seen nothing untoward. Once the work began in earnest, he might suggest Blair post a guard at night. On the other hand, perhaps the arsenic mystery was making him overly suspicious of every little thing.

He pushed aside his misgivings during luncheon. They'd learned to be patient now that meals had to be brought via a circuitous route while the stairs were under repair. Everyone jokingly agreed the smiles bestowed on the earl by the members of the household staff made the inconvenience inconsequential. Even Mrs. Maple seemed more disposed to be friendly. She had willingly organized a system that had two people overseeing everything that was prepared in the kitchens.

Another piano lesson followed the congenial meal, with Patsy showing great progress. Gabe was becoming reconciled to being a mediocre player at best.

Then it was out to the stables for the overly excited Patsy's riding lesson. Only Susan declined to accompany them, and her niece didn't seem overly disappointed by her absence.

TERROR

C AXTON HAD SET up three very low "jumps" for Patsy to coax the
pony over. Emma expressed concern, but Gabriel assured her
they presented no danger. The pony didn't need to jump to clear
them.

"I can do it, Mummy," Patsy declared.

"Miss Crompton managed one such yesterday, my lady," Caxton
confirmed.

"Very well," Emma conceded. "Let's see this equestrian in action."

Patsy beamed as Gabriel lifted her into the side saddle then went to
sit beside Emma on a wooden bench constructed for spectators
outside the paddock fence.

"Not the most comfortable," Gabriel said, "but it's good to sit."

"I hope you didn't overdo it this morning with the walk."

"I have to get back into shape," he replied with a shrug. "I've wast-
ed too much time moping about in the belief I was dying."

They dutifully applauded each time Patsy's pony made it over the
plank laid atop hay bales. "She's going to be a good rider," Emma said
proudly.

"Like her mother," he replied.

She was about to reply when she spotted someone walking
through the tall grass in the far field. The waving grass made it difficult
to make out who it was, but the intruder must have come from the
Whiteside estate. "Is that a woman?" she asked.

Gabriel stood and shaded his eyes. "If I'm not mistaken, it's Tillie."

Emma got to her feet. "Tillie? But she's been missing for a week. We assumed..."

"Mummy, Mummy, you're not watching," Patsy yelled.

Torn between focusing on her daughter or watching what the errant maid was up to, Emma was startled by the arrival of a breathless Bradley, a rifle slung across his body.

"Fire at the dower house," Gabriel's valet shouted.

Emma slumped onto the bench as dark memories threatened to swamp her.

As soon as Gabe saw the Baker rifle he knew there was mischief afoot. He hadn't been aware his batman had kept the weapon after Waterloo, nor that he'd brought it to Thicketford, but there was no time to go into that now. "Something's burning?" he asked, worried about Emma's pallor.

"I've been keeping an eye on those new men," Bradley explained. "Saw one skulking around the dower house, so I came to the house to collect my rifle. Smelled the smoke on my way back."

Frustrated he hadn't paid heed to his instincts, Gabe beckoned Caxton. "We'll need every man. There's no water to douse the flames there." He took hold of Emma's hand. "Take Caxton's place. Look after Patsy."

He was relieved when she rallied.

"Of course," she replied, getting to her feet.

He was reluctant to leave his precious girls alone, but if the whole ruin had been torched...

He kissed Emma's forehead. "Take Patsy inside," he said as he hurried away, not certain why he felt it important.

"WHAT'S WRONG?" PATSY asked.

"Nothing, darling," her mother reassured her, though her heart was thudding in her ears as the men ran off.

She reached up to help her daughter dismount, alarmed when a frantically panting Tillie appeared at her side. The girl must have sprinted from the field to get to the paddock so quickly, but what on earth was she doing here? And why did her uniform look as if she'd been dragged through a hedge backwards? Emma bristled when the maid tried to take the reins. "Stop that."

"She's to stay on the 'orse," Tillie cried.

An icy chill surged up Emma's spine. Patsy's lip quivered. The maid had clearly lost her wits. "Step away, or I'll…"

"You'll what?" Tillie cackled as she shoved Emma hard. "Dismiss me? Well, I've already got another position, so there."

Enraged at finding herself flat on her bottom thanks to an insolent servant, Emma struggled to stand. Her heart plummeted when two unsavory-looking men suddenly ran out of the stables. Adrenalin forced her to her feet when one of the thugs reached for Patsy. "No…o…o…o!" she shrieked, lunging to protect her daughter.

"Mummy," Patsy wailed as she was roughly dragged from the pony.

Without warning, Tillie launched herself at Emma, pinning her to the ground.

Outraged and terrified for her daughter, Emma struggled in vain to avoid Tillie's fists and free herself.

"Love to see bitches fight," one of the men snickered.

"No time," the other replied as they loped away with the screeching Patsy.

※※※※

GABE AND BRADLEY had run about a hundred yards when Gabe stopped abruptly. "Wait," he shouted, leaning forward with hands on his hips to gulp air into his burning lungs.

His valet turned. "I've alerted Frame. He's mustering the footmen."

Gabe straightened. "Corporal Bradley, you and I have fallen for the oldest military trick in the book."

He saw the moment realization dawned on his batman's face. "A diversionary tactic."

"Exactly. I suspect the fire at the dower house is minor, meant to draw us away from…shit! The ladies."

Spurred on by panic, he ran back to the paddock, Bradley in pursuit.

Rage engulfed him when he saw Emma grappling on the ground with Tillie. The two recently hired men were fleeing across the field, one of them carrying Patsy over his shoulder like a sack of grain.

The decision as to which problem he should address first became moot when a deafening rifle crack sent flocks of squawking birds into the air. One of the kidnappers fell to his knees with a loud yell. His accomplice glanced over his shoulder, dropped Patsy and fled.

Drawing on a sudden surge of strength, Gabe wrestled Tillie upright and thrust her into Bradley's custody. The sight of the rifle's bayonet in the valet's hand silenced her.

Emma struggled to her feet with Gabe's help and collapsed against him.

"They've let her go, my love," he told her, enfolding her in his embrace.

She sobbed when she saw Patsy running toward them.

Helping Emma to the bench, Gabe hurried to scoop up the terrified little girl he'd come to love. "I've got you. You're safe."

She clung to him, burying her head against his shoulder. Her silence worried him. She was shaking, clearly in shock. Delivering her into her sobbing mother's arms, he swore to kill the monster who had hatched this plot to terrorize his family.

CONFESSIONS

"**W**ATCH HER," BRADLEY shouted to Caxton as he loped off into the field.

Emma's heart lurched when Tillie sneered at the elderly ostler. Turning her back to shelter Patsy from the malevolent chit, she tightened her embrace on the child in her lap. Her daughter had to believe she was safe, otherwise she might retreat again into a world of silence.

Emma herself couldn't stop trembling, though Gabriel's solid presence beside her on the bench was of immense comfort. It might not be deemed appropriate to find solace in the cocoon of his embrace, but she didn't care. She needed his warmth to ward off the chill of fear. "Who would do this?" she whispered.

"I have my suspicions," Gabriel replied, stroking Patsy's hair. "Looks like the man Bradley shot is merely wounded. We'll get the truth out of him."

Reluctant to even look out into the field, she plucked up her courage. Bradley was herding the limping kidnapper toward them at bayonet point.

"I was terrified you'd been shot," she said.

"It surprised me too," he admitted. "Although, good old Bradley always was my best sniper."

"Thank God for that."

"Got him in the arse," the veteran soldier crowed, shoving the miscreant to the ground. His face reddened when he saw Emma. "Beg pardon, my lady…in the buttocks."

Patsy raised her head. "The *derrière*, you mean."

Blinking back welling tears, Emma kissed her little girl's head.

"She's brave," Gabriel said close to her ear. "Like her mother."

Emma curled into him, calmed by his warm breath on her skin and the reassuring aroma of healthy male sweat. Moments ago, she'd feared for the two people she cared most about. The loss would have been unbearable. "I need you," she murmured.

⟫⟫⟩⟨⟨⟨

ELATED BY EMMA'S admission of her feelings, Gabe's heart raced when Patsy crawled into his lap. He stretched his arms to press the two females he loved to his body. He'd never felt more needed or wanted. He rested his chin atop Emma's head, inhaling the elusive perfume that always clung to her, even now, after she'd been wrestled to the dusty ground and pummeled by a rogue maid.

"Who sent you?" Bradley demanded, pressing his booted foot on the kidnapper's bloodied behind.

The wounded man wailed. "Stop, stop, I'll tell thee. Just get the *fyking* bullet out."

This was no place for Emma and Patsy. "Let's get you inside," he said, just as a wide-eyed and breathless Susan appeared, several worried servants in her wake. "I'll explain later," he told Matthew's sister. "Cups of tea are in order, I think, and something for cuts and bruises."

"Biscuits," Patsy murmured.

"And biscuits," Gabe confirmed with a smile.

As he expected, Susan didn't lose her composure. "Frame reports the fire is out," she replied with a nod. "Someone set the new lumber ablaze. Nothing serious."

A chill raced up Gabe's spine when Caxton suddenly groaned and crumpled to the ground, clutching his privates.

"Is that Tillie?" Susan asked.

Unwilling to let go of Patsy, Gabe could only watch as the maid fled into the field.

Bradley raised the rifle, took aim, then lowered his weapon. "Sorry, sir," he said. "Can't shoot a woman."

"Understood," Gabe replied. "Don't worry. I know where she's going, and this wretch will confirm it."

>>><<<

EVERY OVERTAXED MUSCLE in Tillie's body screamed. Her legs had turned to jelly. Fearing her lungs might burst, she sobbed when Withins Hall came in sight.

She'd been afraid Arthur might no longer be at the rendezvous point, but he was still outside the folly on the hill behind the house. She faltered upon realizing he was arguing with the fool who'd abandoned the prize. However, the fiasco wasn't her fault. She'd done her part. Arthur would see that.

He stalked toward her when he espied her. His scowl wasn't encouraging, but once she got her breath back and explained…

"Useless gits, the lot of you," he yelled, felling her with a backhander across the face.

The surly brute who'd dropped the child didn't step in.

Her mind went blank. Terror-stricken, her face on fire, she crawled away when the man she loved raised his foot. She tried to speak, but no sound emerged from a throat as dry as the desert sands of Arabia.

She'd seen Arthur in a bad mood before. Now, he was beyond angry and clearly not interested in listening to anything she had to say. Once he calmed down…

"Where's the coin ye promised?" the thug asked, mercifully drawing his attention away from her. "The Watchman won't be pleased if I return empty-handed."

When Arthur raked a hand through his hair, panic tightened Tillie's throat. He couldn't hide the fear in his eyes.

"You'll get your money," he replied. "Obviously, it will take longer now that you've bungled the job."

The man leered. "Didn't sign on to be shot at. Ye said 'twould be easy. I have to take *something* to pacify my gaffer."

"Take her," Arthur spat, toeing Tillie with his foot. "Part payment, if you will. Should be useful in one of his brothels."

The blood in Tillie's veins turned to ice as the grinning brute gripped her arm and hauled her to her feet. She'd escaped the old man at Thicketford with a swift kick where men don't like to be kicked. This lout would kill her if she tried the same thing.

Overwhelmed by the bitter realization Arthur had never loved her, she welcomed the darkness as she swooned.

PURSUIT

ATISFIED EMMA AND Patsy were resting under the watchful eye of
Matthew's sister, Gabe set off on horseback, bound for Preston.
The members of the household staff were outraged upon learning of
the terrible events that had befallen Patsy and her mother. Gabe was
confident no further harm would come to the ladies with every maid,
footman, cook and scullery lad on alert under Frame's command.

Bradley accompanied him, holding fast to the reins of Patsy's pony
atop which rode their prisoner, hands tied to the pommel.

Gabe's valet had dug the bullet out of the man's arse—none-too-
gently—and dressed the wound, but the six-mile trek into the town
would still be excruciatingly painful.

What kind of treatment he'd receive once they delivered him to
the magistrate wasn't Gabe's concern. The man had readily given up
Arthur Coleman, which might count in his favor, though Gabe could
countenance no mercy for a thug who terrorized women and children.

The local justice of the peace, one of three magistrates who served
on Preston's bench, reminded Gabe of the supercilious General
Abercrombie. He changed his tune once he discovered the identity of
his titled visitor. After hearing the details of the plot to kidnap Patsy,
he summoned an escort to take the prisoner to the gaol on Ribbleton
Lane. After an hour's delay, he rounded up two more bailiffs to
accompany Gabe to the Whiteside estate.

The new Earl of Farnworth set off for Withins Hall, not looking forward to confronting his neighbor with news of his son's crime.

He was surprised when the baron himself answered the bailiff's authoritative hammering on the door. A gaunt, harried man had replaced the jovial host of the musicale. When Coleman held up a hand to interrupt the bailiff's gruff demand for entry, Gabe sensed he already knew about Arthur's crime.

"May we come in?" Gabe asked.

"Yes, but there is no need for the bailiffs. My son isn't here."

Gabe instructed Bradley to wait outside with the scowling officials and entered the house.

The baron led him to his library and offered brandy. Gabe would have preferred not to accept, but this confrontation of two titled gentlemen was new territory. He had no wish to add to Bertrand Coleman's woes, so he accepted. "I sense you are aware of what transpired earlier," he said as the baron handed him the crystal glass.

"I'd ask you to sit, but you'd probably prefer to stand."

Gabe nodded.

The baron took a sip of his brandy. "I cannot tell you how much I grieve what happened to Lady Emma and her dear little girl."

"Arthur has confessed?"

"Yes. It seems he was desperate for money and planned to ransom Patsy. You must believe he meant her no harm."

Gabe personally knew soldiers—tough, hard men—who suffered terrible nightmares after experiencing the horrors of war. The ordeal Emma and Patsy had undergone might haunt them for years, but there was nothing to be gained from haranguing the man who looked so defeated.

"It was a convoluted tale that Arthur babbled. Clearly, he is terrified of men to whom he apparently owes a great deal of money. The silly boy thought he'd depleted the entire Whiteside treasury—as if I would grant him access to more than a small portion of it. I know I've indulged my son, but I'm not a complete fool. I could have bailed him out of his debts, and I will do so."

"But you can't bail him out of his crimes this afternoon."

"Regrettably, no. So, I thought it best he take some time to travel, see the world, so to speak."

"You've helped him escape."

The baron put down his glass. "You have no children of your own, Farnworth," he said, his voice betraying his weariness. "So, perhaps you won't understand. Arthur is my son. I won't allow him to be sent to prison, or worse still, hang for what he has done. However, I can assure you life in Jamaica won't be easy. Perhaps working in the tropics will mature him."

"I assume you own a plantation on the island?"

"My younger brother does. Nathan has warned me for years about spoiling Arthur. He'll soon straighten the boy out."

Gabe had serious doubts about the successful reformation of Arthur's character, but trying to pursue him all the way to Jamaica was likely a fool's errand. The Caribbean island might be a British colony, but there was no guarantee the long arm of British law reached there. Gabe had seen enough during his tour of duty in India to know things were often done differently in the colonies when it came to crime and punishment.

"He won't be able to return home," he told the baron, determined not to let either him or his son off the hook.

Coleman slumped into a nearby armchair, clearly at the end of his tether. "I suppose we have to hope Anthea will one day produce a son to inherit my lands and titles."

Good luck with that, Gabe thought privately. He foresaw a hunt for a distant relative when the old man died—ironic in so many ways.

However, Coleman still controlled the neighboring estate. It wasn't to Gabe's advantage to alienate him. He drank the last of his brandy. "I'll convey your deep apologies to Lady Emma. No one but you and I will know you facilitated Arthur's escape. I'll simply say he has disappeared."

In any case, mentioning Jamaica in Susan's hearing would set off another tirade about slavery. He pitied any slave who might attract Arthur Coleman's ire.

The baron struggled to his feet and offered his hand. "You have my undying gratitude, Farnworth. You're a gentleman."

Gabe accepted the gesture and took his leave, as satisfied with the outcome as he could be, given the circumstances.

I DON'T WANT TO BE ALONE

THE FOOTMEN WERE about to serve the main dinner course when Gabriel arrived in the dining room. Emma and Patsy would have preferred to stay curled up on the sofa in the drawing room, but Susan had insisted they should eat. Emma didn't have the energy to argue. The scratches on her face stung like the devil, despite the cooling salve applied by the tearful cook.

Patsy left the table and greeted him with arms outstretched. "Everything's taken care of," he said softly. "We don't need to worry about those men ever again."

His safe return raised Emma's spirits; she too wanted to hold him in her arms, but his downcast expression was puzzling. Perhaps Arthur Coleman had been killed, shot by Bradley? However, she didn't wish to discuss such matters in front of Patsy, especially after Gabriel pierced her with his amber gaze and shook his head.

It became apparent even before the last course was served that Patsy couldn't stay awake and was in danger of tumbling off her chair. Gabriel gathered her up. "I'll take her to the nursery," he said.

"I'll come with you," Emma replied, humbled by the love that shone in his eyes.

She followed him as he carried Patsy up the stairs. Gabriel waited in the rocking chair, a book in his lap, while she helped Miss Ince get her daughter ready for bed. He must be exhausted, yet he intended to read a bedtime story.

Once she was tucked in, he perched next to Emma on the bed and opened the book. Patsy was asleep before he'd read two sentences. "You go to bed," he told her. "I'll sit with her for a bit."

"You're a good man," she replied. "Don't stay up too long."

She kissed her daughter's forehead and tiptoed from the nursery. She went to her apartment, though she had no intention of falling asleep.

⟫⟫⟫⟪⟪⟪

SATISFIED PATSY SEEMED to be sleeping soundly, Gabe left the nursery. The governess usually slept on a cot in the adjacent alcove and assured him she would summon him if nightmares disturbed the little girl's sleep.

Despite the upheavals of the day, Gabe felt more at peace than he had in months. Loosening his cravat and shrugging off his frock coat, he went down one flight of stairs and entered his chamber. In less than five minutes, his headache threatened to return and his breathing became labored. Clearly, he'd overdone it.

He stripped off his shirt, toying with the idea of ringing for Bradley to help him remove his boots. Too exhausted to think, he lay back on the bed, arms outstretched.

His eyelids drooped, but he was wide awake a moment later when someone tapped at the door between his chamber and Emma's.

He nigh on tumbled off the bed, reached for his banyan and hurriedly tied the sash.

His heart leaped into his throat when he opened the door and looked into violet eyes. Emma's silk negligee clung to every curve. His cock saluted the proud nipples pouting to be free of the fabric. Renewed energy surged when she took his hand and led him into her chamber.

⇶⇷

As soon as Emma took Gabriel's hand, she knew she'd made the right decision. Something passed between them—not a spark or a crackle, but a silent, invisible communication. An alchemy. "I don't want to be alone," she whispered when he moved his hands to her hips, careful to keep their bodies apart.

"I'll stay with you, if you're sure that's what you want," he replied hoarsely.

"I'm not good at explaining these things," she admitted, wanting to chase away the doubt lingering in his eyes. She pressed her mons to his hard maleness, elated to discover the prim and proper countess could arouse this handsome man. "What I meant was, I don't want to be alone ever again."

"I'll always be here for you," he vowed, gathering her into his arms. "But I'm only human, Emma."

"I've stopped denying that I am too," she admitted. "I want you."

When he leaned against the door to close it, she hesitated. "Perhaps you prefer your chamber."

She squealed when he scooped her up. "Not likely. I've fantasized about lying with you in every room in the house, except the green purgatory."

She clung to his neck when he lay her on the bed, urging him to lie beside her. "I never liked Matthew's chamber."

He pulled her into his embrace. "I think my problem is, it reminds me too much of Napoleon's cottage."

She tucked a lock of hair behind his ear, marveling at the unlikely circumstances that had brought them together. "It must have been terribly lonely out there in the middle of nowhere."

Desire spiraled into her womb when he feathered kisses on her neck. "I welcomed the loneliness, at first."

She found the remark curious. Gabriel wasn't a loner. A sixth sense told her a woman was involved. She shouldn't ask—but she did.

DRUMBEAT

G ABE GROANED INWARDLY. He was in bed with a beautiful and willing woman in his arms—a woman he'd craved from the moment he'd set eyes on her. He didn't understand why he hadn't simply told Emma how much he wanted her, although his rock-hard erection had probably alerted her to the fact. "I was engaged to a woman named Georgina," he whispered, nibbling her ear.

To his surprise, Emma didn't pull away. "She ended things?"

"Married my best friend," he replied, glad the admission no longer had the power to hurt him.

Emma looked into his eyes. "Oh, Gabriel. She was foolish to let a man like you go."

It was tempting to feel smug in the face of this declaration, but he had to be cautious. With Emma's perfume invading his nostrils and her warm, scantily clad body pressed to his, a man might assume she had passionate sex on her mind. He wanted to spend his life making love to Emma in every way a man could make love to a woman, but she might turn out to be as prudish as Georgina. "I've come to realize Georgina wasn't the woman for me. She and I had different ideas about...well...sex."

He held his breath when her eyes widened. Could he have sounded more like a philanderer? He wouldn't be surprised if the dowager countess banished him permanently to his own chamber.

He breathed again when she touched her lips to his. "Can I be honest with you, Gabriel?"

"Of course," he replied, astonished he could still form words from his dry throat. The featherlight touch of her warm lips had turned his already rigid shaft to granite. He might go mad if they didn't...

"Matthew and I," she began, quashing his hopes as she turned onto her back. "I suppose it's shameful to speak my dead husband's name while I'm lying on a bed with you, but it's important you understand."

Thirsting to suckle the nipples poking against the silk, he propped his head up on his bent arm and willed himself to remain calm. "Tell me."

"Well, he didn't like...it was usually just..."

Gabe's hopes rose. His cousin hadn't cared about his wife's pleasure. He wiped away the tear trickling down her cheek and decided to gamble that his gut feeling was correct.

He came to his knees, cupped both breasts, bent his head and suckled, first one nipple, then the other.

Her response reminded him of powder kegs he'd seen explode at Waterloo but, if he wasn't careful, he would go up in flames too soon.

EMMA LOST CONTROL of her body when Gabriel suckled her nipples. She arched her back, shouting her euphoria when an intense ache of longing blossomed low in her belly. A throbbing began in her most intimate female place that wept with longing for Gabriel's manhood to enter.

Intercourse with Matthew had been a duty; she craved the male member she'd glimpsed in the library and felt pressed to her mons only moments ago. "Come inside me," she growled.

"Soon," he promised, his husky voice heightening her need.

She whimpered when he pulled the negligee over her head to expose her body to his greedy gaze, but the love in his amber eyes was enough to make her weep. At this moment, she was the most beautiful woman in the world.

She cradled his head when he tore off the banyan and resumed his suckling, almost driven mad when he grazed her with his teeth. "I feel that here," she confessed, letting her fingers wander to a forbidden place.

She feared she'd been too brazen when he stopped abruptly and rose from the bed. She stared at the taut abdomen, broad shoulders and chiseled chest that rose and fell as he panted for breath. Hoping she saw admiration when he raked his gaze over her, she took a chance. "You are so beautifully formed."

"Emma," he purred, dropping to his knees beside the bed.

When he curled his arms around her thighs and lifted her nether lips to his mouth, she thanked all the angels and saints for the gift of this man who seemed to know instinctively how to satisfy cravings denied for too many years.

She groaned when his clever tongue teased a certain spot. Breathless, she squirmed as an intense longing built inside, but he held firm, continuing to play when euphoria burst upon her and she soared to the heavens amid a kaleidoscope of colors. "Now, now," she cried, pressing her fingers into his scalp, desperate to take him deep inside.

Breathing heavily, he left the bed. She opened her eyes, elated to see he'd unfastened the falls of his breeches and pushed them over his hips. Matthew's wife would have averted her gaze. Gabriel's lover reached to release his manhood from the confines of his smalls, startled when he took hold of her wrist.

"Before we go any further, I need to ask you something," he growled, his eyes locked with hers.

"Yes, I'm sure," she replied, hoping she didn't sound like an impatient whore. "I want you now."

"That's not my question."

꙰꙰꙰

GABE COULD SCARCELY believe he'd prevented Emma touching him. He might embarrass himself if he didn't plunge his rampant cock inside her soon. But he had to secure a commitment. Had to know she wouldn't regret her actions later. Had to secure the victory. "Will you be my countess?" he asked, realizing belatedly that standing half-naked with his boots on and his breeches around his knees was hardly a romantic way to propose marriage to a lady. An earl was probably expected to behave in a more gentlemanly manner. He had to hope she loved him enough to overlook his lack of nobility.

Her smile was encouraging, as was the lust in her eyes, but her words took him aback. "On one condition," she said.

Had he lost her? "What's that?" he forced himself to ask.

His knees threatened to buckle when she slid off the bed, knelt before him and pulled down his smalls. Predictably, his happy cock saluted when she licked the swollen tip.

He thought he might drown in the violet depths when she looked up at him and said, "That we make love every day and that you teach me ways to please you."

Struck dumb, he lifted her back onto the bed, opened her legs and plunged his shaft into her wet heat. Clinging to him, she matched his rhythm, screaming when his seed surged into her womb. He could have sworn he heard a military tattoo—or perhaps it was the thunderous beating of his own joyous heart.

LOVE IS CONTAGIOUS

L IGHT FILTERING THROUGH the silk draperies showed it was well after dawn, but Emma was reluctant to disturb Gabriel. She lay awake, basking in the warmth of his big body against her back. His steady breathing indicated he was asleep, but then she felt the evidence of his arousal. "Good morning," she whispered, pressing her bottom against his hard maleness.

He slid a hand beneath her breasts and snuggled closer. "That's the best night's sleep I've had for a long time."

She stretched languidly when he nuzzled her nape. "You've unleashed a wanton. I want you again."

He gathered her into his arms and turned her to face him. "I like the sound of that."

His gentle kiss added fuel to the yearning, but gooseflesh marched up her spine when a tap sounded at the door and a little voice called, "Mummy."

"I'd better go," Gabriel whispered, nibbling her ear before he rose from the bed.

Confidant in her nudity for the first time in her life, she rose from the bed. She studied him as he shrugged on his banyan and collected his clothing and boots, smiling as she recalled straddling his legs to pull off his boots after their first lovemaking. She could scarcely believe the dowager countess had wiggled her bare bottom at him. Bawdy comments about *derrières* had ensued. Intercourse had never been so much fun.

She ran her fingers through his hair when he bent his head to kiss a nipple. "I don't want to hide our relationship," she whispered as desire spiraled into her womb. "I want Patsy and Susan to know."

"Mummy," Patsy called again as the handle rattled. "The door's locked."

"We won't hide," Gabriel assured her, "I want to shout it from the rooftops, but discovering me here with you now isn't the best way for your daughter to be told."

When he slipped away into his own chamber, Emma turned the key in the lock and opened the door, glad she'd had the presence of mind to secure it the night before.

Patsy rushed into her embrace. "You frightened me."

Emma sighed. Her daughter had suffered enough. "I'm sorry, sweetheart. I was just…"

"You smell funny," Patsy remarked. "Like Cousin Gabriel."

Emma plucked up her courage. "Maybe that's because he kissed me."

She hoped her daughter didn't detect his scent on the linens when she climbed into her mother's bed.

"Why did he kiss you goodnight?"

Close enough.

"Because he loves me."

"He loves me too."

Emma's heart swelled. Patsy had sensed the genuine feelings Gabriel had for her.

"Do you love him in return?" she asked.

Patsy struggled to her feet on the soft mattress and jumped up and down. "Yes. I wish he was my new daddy."

Relief made Emma dizzy. Patsy trusted Gabriel, and seemed to be suffering no lingering aftereffects from yesterday's trauma. She took hold of her little girl's hands. "Well, scamp, what would you say if I told you Cousin Gabriel has asked me to marry him?"

Frowning, Patsy stopped bouncing. "Did you say yes?"

"I did."

A broad smile replaced the frown as Patsy leaped at her mother. "Aunty Susan was right!"

CURIOUS TO HEAR the conversation between Emma and her daughter, Gabe would have listened at the door. Bradley's unexpected presence in his chamber put paid to the notion. His valet had an uncanny knack of knowing when his master had arisen—not surprising since Gabe had continued the habit ingrained in him by years of getting up at the same time every day. He'd slept very late for the first time since leaving the army. A night of extremely satisfying sexual romping had apparently done him good. Emma had turned out to be the playful and passionate partner he'd always longed for.

However, he wasn't going to be able to talk his way out of this situation. "You've caught me red-handed," he confessed. "Lady Emma and I..."

"None of my business, sir," Bradley replied, "though, may I say, I'm happy for you both."

Gabe swallowed the lump in his throat. The poker-faced man who'd served him faithfully for years actually cared about him. He held out his hand in appreciation. "Thank you. That means a lot coming from you."

Grinning, Bradley accepted the gesture. "Who'd have thought what awaited two old soldiers like us here at Thicketford?"

Gabe didn't consider himself old, and he was puzzled. Had Bradley also found love? He eyed the astonishing pink rosettes blooming on his valet's cheeks. "You mean you and Mrs. Maple..."

The grin vanished. Gabe had clearly jumped to the wrong conclusion.

"Not Mrs. Maple," Bradley snorted. "No, sir. I need your permission to wed Lucy."

⇥⇥⇥⇤⇤⇤

EMMA SENT PATSY back to the nursery with strict instructions not to tell anyone yet about her and Cousin Gabriel. "Mum's the word," she said, tapping a finger to her lips.

"Our secret," Patsy agreed. "I'll only tell Wellington."

Emma chuckled. "Come back when Miss Ince has you ready and we'll go down to breakfast together."

"Then can we tell Aunty Susan?"

Emma hesitated. Gabriel might want to be the one to announce their intention to marry. "Possibly. We'll see what Cousin Gabriel thinks."

Patsy hurried away and Emma rang for Lucy to assist with the morning's preparations. It was tempting to confide in the abigail who'd served her for years, but the woman seemed preoccupied this morning. "Not your usual chatty self," she remarked as Lucy scrubbed her dry after her bath. "Is something wrong?"

"Oh, no, my lady. Just the opposite," she gushed, blushing alarmingly.

Emma wasn't sure how she knew what was coming next, but Lucy looked like she felt—the woman was in love.

"I don't rightly know if I should say aught," Lucy said as she pulled the comb through Emma's tangles. "It depends on the earl, and ye, of course. I'd never marry without..." She clapped both hands over her mouth. "I'm sorry, my lady, it just came out."

Emma laughed as she took hold of the maid's hands. "You've met a man. Do I know him?"

"It's Mr. Bradley," Lucy confessed, her gaze seemingly glued to the carpet.

Emma felt giddy. The man whose arrival she'd dreaded had brought love to an old house and a family that sorely needed it. "I'm happy for you. I'm sure the earl will grant permission for the match, and I certainly have no objection."

"Thank ye, my lady. I never thought I'd find another good man after my Alfred died, but…"

Emma did something Matthew would have considered unthinkable, and terribly middle class. She embraced her servant. "There now, don't cry. It's a time for happiness. In fact, today I'll wear the lavender silk."

Lucy blew her red nose. "But that's for special occasions."

"Exactly. And the amethysts."

BRAINSTORM

DISAPPOINTMENT FLOODED GABE when he entered the morning room and realized Emma and Patsy hadn't yet arrived.

Susan looked up when he greeted her. "My, you look very handsome today. Going somewhere special?"

A glint in her eyes led him to believe she suspected what had transpired between him and Emma. He likely hadn't helped matters by dressing in his best new waistcoat, breeches, and frock coat, his cravat immaculate.

After almost breaking his hand in a manic handshake when Gabe give permission for his valet to wed the abigail, Bradley had tied and retied his cravat a hundred times and helped him pull on his new John Bulls. The man's skinny arse didn't compare to the tempting, endearingly white bottom of the woman he loved. "Just wanted to look my best for my ladies," he replied as he sat, rising again quickly when Emma and Patsy appeared.

His intention to greet them was preempted by Patsy's outburst. "Guess what, Aunty Susan. Mummy and Cousin Gabriel are getting married."

"Patsy," Emma chided, spooning a boiled egg from the spread on the sideboard into her daughter's eggcup. "I apologize, Gabriel, I asked her to let you make the announcement."

"Sorry," the little girl murmured, looking sheepish as her mother sliced the top off her egg.

Elated by Patsy's enthusiasm and the amethysts twinkling at Emma's throat, he opened his arms. "I hope you're happy about all this. Getting a new father is a lot to take in."

Swallowing the lump in his throat, he picked her up when she hurried into his embrace and said, "You'll be a good daddy."

Susan rose and hugged a tearful Emma. "I'm glad you've finally come to your senses." She leaned across the table and offered her hand. "Welcome to the family, Gabriel."

He accepted the gesture, quite sure it was the first time he'd ever shaken a woman's hand. He wasn't surprised her grip was firmer than some men of his acquaintance.

"Now that's settled," Susan declared as everyone sat, "I propose we look at this arsenic problem logically."

Gabe imagined General Abercrombie's contemptuous snort if anyone suggested to him a woman was capable of logic. "What are you thinking?"

"What's *arsnik*?" Patsy asked.

Gabe exchanged a worried glance with Emma. "It's a noxious substance lurking somewhere in the house and we need to track down where it is," he said.

"What's *noxshus*?"

"Harmful," Emma replied. "You've no cause to worry. Just eat your egg."

Susan continued. "We've approached this without looking at the obvious. We must ascertain what my father, Matthew and Gabriel have in common. Let's brainstorm."

"Sounds painful," Emma said, slicing her daughter's toast into *soldiers*.

"It means we simply verbalize ideas, no matter how silly they might seem," Susan explained. "So, I'll begin. They are all male."

"All earls," Emma said. "With dark hair."

"All born in England," Gabe offered, though he couldn't see any relevance in that fact. "All related, though distantly."

Susan's enthusiasm wilted visibly when a long silence ensued. "There must be some other common thread."

"I know," Patsy said, dipping the toast in her egg. "They all slept in the master's chamber."

Gabe stared at the child. He hated his bedroom and hoped to be spending most of his nights in Emma's apartment until he could get his redecorated, but…

He was distracted by Susan drumming her fingertips on the table and declaring, "Clever girl."

"It's true I sleep in the same chamber now as Matthew and his father," Gabe said. "But my symptoms began in Saint Helena."

He clenched his jaw, frustrated that he couldn't grasp an important clue gnawing at the back of his brain.

"Wait," Emma interjected. "Didn't you say your chamber reminds you of Napoleon's cottage?"

A maelstrom of loose threads struggled to knot together in Gabe's head. "Yes, almost the same wallpaper—color-wise anyway."

Susan banged her fist on the table. "That's the link. How is wallpaper made?"

"I have no idea," Gabe admitted.

"Right," Susan declared. "After breakfast, I'll get Blair to hunt for the old ledgers. We'll find out where Papa purchased the wallpaper for his chamber."

A spark of optimism flared in Gabe's breast. Perhaps they were on to something. Today was the first morning for months he hadn't woken with a pounding headache, though perhaps the release of his sexual tension had more to do with his improved disposition.

CLEARLY TOO EXCITED to wait, Susan summoned Frame and asked him to locate Mr. Blair. "Tell him to find out where my father purchased the green wallpaper used to decorate the walls of the master chamber."

Gladdened by the spark of hope in Gabriel's eyes, Emma's appetite for the fried ham, tomatoes and kidneys on her plate suddenly returned. The hunger in his gaze ignited a devilish notion. "Perhaps we shouldn't wait for the details. It might be a long while before we can ascertain if the wallpaper is the problem, and Gabriel hates the green in any case."

"What are you suggesting?" Susan asked.

"She's saying we should get the offensive stuff off my walls as soon as possible," Gabriel announced with a wink in her direction. "And I agree."

Susan nodded. "You'll have to move into another chamber."

Emma's heart careened around her ribcage when Gabriel licked his lips and replied, "That won't be a problem."

Susan frowned, looking from Gabriel then to her. "Oh, I see. Good idea. However, I think you should place an announcement of your betrothal in *The Times* as soon as possible."

Gabriel reached for her hand, a hint of doubt in his amber gaze. "Are you in agreement with that, my lady?"

"Most definitely," she replied, content to see the spark return. "Though I suppose we'll have to postpone our wedding until my mourning period is over."

"Unfortunately, yes," Susan replied. "You want to avoid scandal."

Emma privately found her sister-in-law's remark ironic in view of her lifestyle that many judged scandalous, but she was right. "I suppose the time will go by quickly."

"Can I be a bridesmaid?" Patsy asked.

"Of course," Emma replied. "And Aunty Susan can perhaps be my maid of honor."

She was surprised by Susan's blush and her gushing response. "I'd be thrilled."

Their happy chatter was interrupted by Frame's polite cough. "Mr. Blair reports he has found the information you requested, my lady, but prefers not to bring the dusty ledger out of the library."

Gabriel rose. "If you'll excuse me, I'll investigate, and also ask about placing the announcement in *The Times*."

Emma itched to accompany Gabriel and she could tell Susan was equally anxious, but Patsy hadn't finished her breakfast. "We'll be along shortly," she said.

NOBLE SACRIFICE

B LAIR STOOD WHEN Gabe entered the library. "I sense this has something to do with the arsenic?"

"Ridiculous as it seems," Gabe replied, "we think the wallpaper might be tainted. Did you find the entry?"

Blair pointed to the enormous ledger open on the desk. "The renovations to the house were quite extensive, so the entries were relatively easy to find. There are a lot of them, and we know the exact time parameters."

Gabe pored over the long list of items written in a bold hand. "The bookkeeper was careful, but the ink has faded."

Blair pointed. "Here. The wallpaper was purchased from Messrs. Morris and Potter, Manchester. I'd have to track down the invoice for the address."

"Probably no need. I suspect Lady Susan will ferret out the information before the day's out."

Blair chuckled. "Indeed, sir."

"On another matter, I need an announcement placed in *The Times*."

"Certainly," the estate manager replied. "Let me move this ledger and find pen and paper."

By the time Blair had the materials he needed, Emma, Susan and Patsy had arrived. Gabe supplied Susan with the information she wanted. "Morris and Potter, in Manchester. Do you know it?"

"I do. Papa dealt with them on a regular basis."

"As did Matthew," Emma said.

"We could go this morning," Susan suggested. "I'm off to get ready."

Sensing Emma's hesitancy to follow, Gabe put his arm around her waist and took Patsy's hand. "The announcement concerns a betrothal," he told Blair whose eyebrows had arched. "Lady Emma and I are engaged to be married."

"And I'm to be bridesmaid," Patsy crowed.

Blair's smile was genuine as he rose to shake Gabe's hand. "I'm delighted, my lord, my lady. May I be the first to wish thee both every happiness?"

"You'll know the appropriate wording," Gabe said. "We just have to decide on a date for the wedding, after Lady Emma's mourning period."

Blair dipped his quill. "We can simply say the date will be announced later, although…"

"Although what?" Gabe asked.

Blair tapped the feather against his chin. "I mean no offense, but no one will think it untoward if ye marry Lady Emma. Many local people expect it of the new earl. Had ye been Lord Matthew's brother, failure to marry his widow would be deemed a poor show."

"In other words," Gabe replied, resisting the urge to grin, "marrying Lady Emma will be viewed as a noble sacrifice on my part."

He merely coughed when Emma elbowed him in the ribs. He looked forward immeasurably to being suitably castigated for his remark when they retired for the night.

》》》《《《

THE FARNWORTH CARRIAGE arrived at the premises of Morris and Potter shortly after one o'clock in the afternoon. Emma had hesitated to bring Patsy along, but her daughter had balked at being left with her governess. Gabriel was probably right—it would be some time before Patsy overcame her feelings of insecurity.

James Footman opened the door, unhooked the steps and offered his hand to the ladies. Gabriel alit last. "Well, here we are," he said, his jaw clenched.

"We are close," she assured him, aware of how vitally important it was they solve the mystery of the arsenic.

Once inside the warehouse-like structure, they were greeted by a clerk, a rotund, balding fellow who became much more obsequious upon learning the identity of the visitors. However, Gabriel's request to meet with the owner was met with a polite shake of the head. "I'm afraid Mr. Morris doesn't meet with clients. Can I be of service?"

Emma expected Susan to demand to see Morris but, fortunately, she held back and allowed Gabriel to insist. "Thicketford Manor has given this firm a great deal of business," he said. "I'm sure Mr. Morris wouldn't want that mutually beneficial relationship to end."

The clerk shuffled off. Five minutes later, a tall young man arrived and proffered his hand to Gabriel. "Sherrington Morris at your service, my dear Lord Farnworth. How may I help you?"

Gabriel shook his hand. "You're too young to have been here when one of my predecessors purchased wallpaper for the renovations at Thicketford Manor."

"That would have been my father," Morris said. "However, I can assist with any new materials you may require."

To Emma's surprise, Gabriel produced a piece of the wallpaper from his chamber. "We're on a quest of a different sort. It concerns this green wallpaper."

"Ah, the Scheele's Green. Very popular a number of years ago."

"So, you don't sell it now?"

"We do. Are you wanting to replace it? I have a more modern version, not as much flocking."

"My question is, do you use arsenic in the manufacture?"

Morris bristled. "Arsenic! Good heavens, no. That's poisonous. We use copper arsenite—perfectly harmless. It's the pigment we've used in green paints and wallpapers since our founding in 1775."

Afraid Gabriel was about to lose his temper with the snooty young man, Emma linked her arm with his. "We have our answer," she whispered. "A campaign will have to be waged against this hidden killer, but this isn't the place to begin it."

Susan leaned close. "You'll have my full support when you take your seat in the House of Lords."

※※※

GABE ACKNOWLEDGED THEY were right. He hadn't given much thought to the political power he might wield as a peer. Morris would dismiss their theories in an effort to protect his business, but Gabe had to at least sow the seeds of doubt. He settled his beaver top hat back on his head. "We've unearthed disturbing evidence that your harmless copper arsenite is more dangerous than you think. Good day."

"I didn't like him," Patsy declared as they climbed back into the carriage.

"None of us did," Susan said. "However, there are few reputable places to purchase high quality decorating materials in Lancashire."

Gabe gritted his teeth. "So, if I want to redecorate my chamber…"

"Just don't choose green," Emma suggested. "And, hopefully, Morris won't simply ignore your warning."

On the ride back to Thicketford, Gabe contemplated the emotional upheavals he'd endured over the past year. He intended to report to Dr. Henry on the morrow. The good doctor would have ideas about launching a campaign to curtail the hidden evil they'd uncovered. In the short term, there was nothing Gabe could do about Saint Helena. Abercrombie and the Foreign Office would never believe it was possible Napoleon was being poisoned by the wallpaper in his cottage. However, local people had to be warned. Thicketford likely wasn't the only grand house with green wallpaper.

He removed his hat and leaned out the window. "Take us to Withins Hall first," he shouted to Conrad.

A Practical Solution

B RISTLING, EMMA PUT a protective arm around Patsy. "We can't go to Withins Hall."

"It's too soon," Susan agreed.

"This is a good strategic move," Gabriel replied. "Trust me. The baron isn't our enemy and could turn out to be a useful ally."

"Perhaps we should stay in the carriage," Emma suggested when they arrived. "I'm not convinced this is a good idea."

"It's all right, Mummy," Patsy said. "The baron is a nice man."

Emma supposed she had to trust Gabriel's decisions, otherwise why was she marrying him? However, she held tightly to Patsy's hand as they were ushered into the foyer by the butler who then left to inform his master of their arrival.

To her surprise, her neighbor came out to meet them, looking years older than the last time she'd seen him. She was shocked when he attempted to kneel before her with only his cane for support. "Please," she said, taking his elbow, "there is no need for this."

"But there is, Lady Emma," he replied. "I want to beg forgiveness for my son's heinous actions. Can you and your lovely little girl forgive me?"

"I forgive you," Patsy said, "but it wasn't you who made me cry."

The baron mopped his eyes with a kerchief. "I spoiled Arthur. I should have kept a closer eye on him."

Emma wasn't ready to let Whiteside off the hook, but she sympathized with his predicament. "Gabriel tells me your son has disappeared. That's an added burden for you to bear. We will recover, but you might never know what has happened to him."

The baron looked puzzled, but Gabe took her hand and spoke before she had a chance to say anything further. "Can we go into the drawing room, my lord? We have something of importance to tell you—two things, actually."

Emma suddenly had an inkling what his plan might be.

⟫⟫⟩⟩⟨⟨⟨⟨

"BERTRAND," GABE BEGAN when everyone was seated except himself. He'd intentionally put the conversation on a personal footing, but this man mustn't forget he was still in Gabe's debt. "We have uncovered information that may have a bearing on the health of people residing at Withins Hall."

Shock and dismay followed puzzlement on the baron's face as Gabe recounted the tale of his illness and the subsequent discovery of the presence of copper arsenite in the manufacture of wallpaper.

Anger contorted his features when Susan explained the poison's probable contribution to the deaths of her father and brother.

"I knew there was something amiss," he growled. "I admit I began to think the Cromptons were cursed."

"Indeed," Gabe replied. "The first priority is to ensure you have none of this Scheele's Green wallpaper in your home. Or even green paint."

The baron nodded. "I'll get the search underway today."

"Secondly, as peers of the realm, we should push for an investigation into the matter. Who knows how many hidden poisons are lurking in our houses?"

Coleman brandished his cane. "By gum, it will give me a reason to take my seat in the Lords. I admit I've neglected that responsibility too. Hard to stay awake when meaningless debates drag on, to be honest."

Feeling confident Bertrand Coleman now saw him as a fellow nobleman, Gabe took Emma's hand. "Our other news concerns a betrothal."

➤➤➤◄◄◄

"BLESS MY STARS," the baron exclaimed as Emma rose to stand beside Gabriel. "I knew it the moment I saw you two together. I'm delighted."

"Me too," Patsy declared with a grin.

"You don't think people will be scandalized?" Emma asked her neighbor.

"Not at all," came the reply. "They would start to talk if the pair of you didn't tie the knot."

"There'll be an announcement in *The Times*," Gabriel said. "We're just undecided about a date for our wedding."

"Yes, of course. But you've dutifully observed the first stage of mourning, my dear, so I don't think you need worry. Here in the north, we're not as rigidly judgmental about these things as our southern neighbors. People will see your marriage as a practical solution."

"He's right," Susan agreed. "Do what is right for the two of you. Nobody down south cares about what goes on in Lancashire anyway."

➤➤➤◄◄◄

UPON ARRIVING HOME, the ladies withdrew to refresh themselves; Gabe tracked down Blair at the dower house and passed on the information about the copper arsenite.

His estate manager was outraged and agreed to arrange for every trace of green to be stripped out of the lord's chamber, starting tomorrow. They discussed hiring more tradesmen and possible alternative decorating schemes. "I have no eye for such things," Gabe admitted. "Perhaps ask the countess."

He rode home and retired to his chamber, not surprised to find Bradley laying out his attire for dinner.

He too was astounded by the news. "Always felt there was something foreboding about this bedroom," he said. "And poor old Boney. Little does he suspect."

"I'll say," Gabe replied as his valet put the finishing touches to his cravat. "They'll be starting work in here tomorrow."

His valet winked. "You'll be needing another chamber, then."

"I should reprimand you for your cheek," Gabe said with a smile. "But we've been through too much together, you and I. I'm confident I can depend on your discretion."

Bradley tapped the side of his nose. "Soul of discretion—that's me, sah!"

SUBLIME

SHORTLY AFTER EMMA dismissed Lucy for the night, Gabriel entered her apartment through the adjoining door and stood with arms akimbo. "Bradley insisted it was only proper to wear a nightshirt under my banyan," he told her, grinning broadly. "As if a visit to an unmarried lady's bedchamber has to conform to the rules. He's probably whisked Lucy off to his room in the attic already."

Emma pressed a finger to her chin and made a show of studying him from head to toe. "The banyan stays, the nightshirt goes."

"Not what I expected, but..."

She flared her nostrils as he removed the banyan then yanked the nightshirt off over his head. Despite the ordeal he'd undergone, his body was lean and well-muscled, as she might expect of a warrior who'd spent his life in the army. She licked her lips when her gaze traveled down to the proud lance at his groin.

"Are you sure you want me to put the banyan back on?" he teased, arms held wide.

Perhaps it was a foolish notion, but... "Yes."

He complied, cinching the belt at his waist.

The silk caressed his maleness as he walked toward her.

He took her into his embrace. "You're partial to my banyan," he whispered, feathering kisses along her jaw.

"I like what's underneath," she confessed, feeling playful.

He looked into her eyes. "There's something you're not telling me."

She recognized the moment understanding dawned in his amber gaze.

"The library," he murmured.

Her face on fire, she could only nod.

"I didn't cover myself quickly enough."

"Thank goodness," she replied. "I can honestly say I saw you in a whole new light after that."

His enthralling eyes widened. "You liked what you saw."

She drew him closer, pressing her mons to his arousal. "That's an understatement."

"And what's your opinion now you've had a closer inspection?"

"I'm even more impressed."

"I have a secret of my own," he confessed close to her ear.

She shivered with anticipation, thrilled she'd found a man who loved to tease and have fun. "Mmm," she replied, inhaling the lingering aroma of his aftershave.

"A glimpse of bare ankles, and shapely calves…"

She gasped in feigned outrage.

"Beautiful breasts, all the more tantalizing for being covered by a lacy nightgown. It was disappointing when Mrs. Maple closed your bed robe."

"A gentleman would have averted his gaze," she teased, regretting the glib comment as soon as it was out of her mouth. "I'm sorry, Gabriel. I didn't mean that the way it sounded. You're more of a gentleman than any man I've ever known."

"And you are the most delicious countess I have ever bedded," he quipped.

⇉⇉⇒⇐⇇⇇

THE FEEL OF the silk against Gabe's cock was pleasantly erotic, and Emma's negligee was more transparent than she probably realized, but a man could only take so much foreplay. "Let me see you," he rasped, pulling the nightgown up over her head.

She raised her arms to assist then eased the banyan off his shoulders and pressed her lovely globes against his chest. Banyan and negligee were tossed to the four winds.

She clung to his neck when he lifted her, curling her legs around his hips. His cock slid along her wet slit as he walked to the bed. She moved to lie beneath him, but he pulled her on top of him. "We'll try something different," he said, confident after last night's antics that his countess was as eager for sexual experimentation as he was. "Straddle my hips."

"Like riding astride?" she asked, blushing delightfully when she realized what she'd said.

"Exactly," he replied with a grin, his hands on her hips. "Now, lift up, then come down on me slowly."

The pure pleasure written on her face matched his own euphoria as she eased down slowly, taking all of his not inconsiderable length. Gazing into his eyes, she naturally set the perfect rhythm, so he busied his hands tweaking her thrusting nipples. "Magnificent," he growled when she arched her back and little mewling sounds emerged from deep in her throat.

He moved his hands to part her nether lips, pressing a thumb to the diamond of her desire. He held on to the last shred of his control when she played with her own nipples. It was so much more erotic if they reached the pinnacle together.

She rode him faster, her sheath tightening on his happy cock. Her breathing became erratic; the mewling turned to a growl; the nub swelled as he increased the speed of his strokes. "Come for me," he rasped as she screamed her euphoria. His seed erupted from his body. Her pulsating sheath slowly milked every last drop before she collapsed on top of him.

"Sublime," he whispered, more than grateful he'd been granted a second chance at life with a partner he loved.

ST. JOHN'S

THE DISCUSSION AT breakfast the next day centered on picking a date for the wedding.

"Ultimately, it will depend on Canon Parr," Susan remarked.

"And he is?" Gabriel asked.

"The parson at St. John's, in Preston," Emma replied.

"We have to go all the way to Preston to be married?"

"It will be expected," Susan replied. "And it's only six miles."

"We've been remiss in not going for a while," Emma confessed. "After Matthew's death, I'm afraid I couldn't abide Parr's gloom and doom pronouncements."

"But the Farnworth earldom has traditionally been a patron of St. John's," Susan explained.

"So, Canon Parr has no doubt noted my failure to appear," Gabriel said.

"His nose will be out of joint," Emma agreed with a sigh.

Patsy snorted. "His nose is too big, anyway."

Emma didn't have the heart to scold her daughter when her remark clearly amused Gabriel. "We'll have to visit him and ask for the banns to be read out."

"And eat crow, I expect," Susan observed. "Parr is an educated man. He can be easy-going and genial."

"I sense a *but*," Gabriel replied.

"He goes everywhere in a billycock and cloak, even in summer,"

236

Patsy supplied.

"Not in church though, surely," Gabriel quipped, earning a giggle from Patsy.

"He has a certain amount of narrowness and, like many parsons, can see his own way best," Susan warned.

"Not unusual."

Susan finished buttering her toast. "I advise you not to tread on his ecclesiastical bunions. He has a strong temper and can redden up beautifully."

"Well then," Gabriel announced. "I suggest we go this very after-noon and confront the foe. We'll ask him to read the first banns this coming Sunday."

The breath hitched in Emma's throat. "But that will put our wed-ding date only a month from now."

"If Parr agrees, why wait?" he asked.

Emma scanned the expectant faces around her. She had never been impetuous, but they likely couldn't carry on their clandestine lovemaking for much longer before somebody put a flea in the wrong ear. "Why, indeed. The sooner the better."

Gabriel's smile calmed her racing heart, confirming she'd made the right decision, but there was one more thing her future husband needed to know about Canon Parr. "He officiated at my marriage to Matthew."

⤐⟫⟪⟨

EMMA WAS A Preston girl and Gabe should have realized she and Matthew would have married in the town. It was stupidly unreasona-ble to feel jealous, but he did. She had never said anything negative about her relationship with her late husband, but he got the feeling it hadn't been a love match. Nor did he have any reason to doubt the sincerity of her commitment to him.

Nevertheless, from what he'd learned of the parson at St. John's, he suspected the fellow wouldn't look favorably upon an upstart soldier who sought the hand of a widowed countess. He'd been remiss in not introducing himself to the cleric shortly after his arrival, but that couldn't be helped now.

However, Gabe had faced more formidable adversaries than a hidebound English clergyman. "I'll drop in on Dr. Henry while we are in Preston," he suggested.

They set off in the carriage after luncheon.

James Footman rode with Conrad.

Gabe held Emma's hand. "It's all right to be nervous," he told her. "I am too."

"I'm simply worried about Canon Parr. He can be awkward and I tend to shy away from confrontation, as you've probably noticed. You'll charm him, though—and what if you don't? He can't refuse to marry us. And if he did, we could just go to some other church."

She took a deep breath. "I'm babbling, aren't I? But what do you have to be nervous about?"

He put her gloved hand to his lips and kissed her knuckles, inhaling her perfume. "Inheriting responsibility for an earldom was a daunting prospect but, deep down, I was confident I could handle it. However, I've never been married. I just hope I prove to be a worthy husband to a woman I treasure. I don't want to disappoint you."

She moved their joined hands to her cheek. "Gabriel Smith, you have filled my heart with a happiness I have never known, not to mention the...rapture..."

He put his arm around her, not surprised she couldn't articulate the sexual chemistry they shared. He couldn't explain it either. However, he now felt smugly certain Matthew hadn't bothered to delve into the secret desire for passion hidden in Emma's heart.

At first glance, the stately church looked benign enough to Gabe's eyes. Its impressive steeple—completed only the previous year, according to Emma—was evidently home to the traditional clattering of squawking jackdaws. "An ordinary parish church," he remarked.

"Yes," Emma agreed. "It has a wonderful set of bells."

"Hopefully, they'll peal out on our wedding day."

As they descended from the carriage, he was glad to see the prospect bring a smile to Emma's face. They walked arm in arm along the gravel pathway; he decided not to comment on the strange hobgoblin figureheads affixed to the walls. He might have to reconsider his initial impression of gentility.

Nor did the overgrown graveyard inspire confidence, many of its blackened stones overturned or split in two.

"Needs weeding," Emma murmured.

It was an understatement, but Gabe agreed something must be done to make the cemetery appear more like consecrated ground and less like a forsaken wilderness. He tucked away the earldom's contribution as a possible bargaining chip.

As luck would have it, Canon Parr came striding toward them, slowing his pace when he sighted them. "I recognize the billycock," Gabe told Emma.

"And the ever-present cloak," she replied.

Gabe extended a hand. "Gabriel, Earl of Farnworth," he intoned in his best Abercrombie voice. "You are Canon Parr, I take it."

Uncertainty flickered in the cleric's bespectacled eyes. He seemed pleased Gabe knew his name, but there was a hint of annoyance. "My Lord Farnworth," he replied, shaking Gabe's hand. "I heard you'd arrived at Thicketford. I'd hoped to meet you before this."

Feigning regret, and somewhat astonished a man with Parr's stern reputation would have a limp handshake, Gabe bowed his head. "My apologies. My new duties have taken much of my time."

Parr nodded. "Understandable, indeed. And, forgive me if I intrude, my lord, but I heard you've been unwell."

Gabe was surprised Emma didn't openly snort. "Indeed," he echoed. "But I'm on the mend now."

Parr seemed to notice Emma for the first time, or perhaps he'd deliberately ignored her. "My dear countess," he gushed, failing to bow. "Please, I bid you enter my humble church so you may apprise me of the reason for your visit."

He led the way into a massive, dimly-lit porch. Gabe squeezed Emma's hand when they passed a large, octagonal-shaped font. Patsy had probably been christened in this very spot and he hoped to bring his own children there to receive the sacrament of baptism.

He got only a glimpse of the church's interior before Parr led them down a dark corridor to his office, but his impression was of a substantial and relatively unadorned space, very different from the ritualistically embellished places of worship he'd seen in Catholic France and Spain. The place didn't matter. He would marry Emma in a barn, if it became necessary.

A Selfless Gesture

BEING BACK IN the church evoked happy memories of the day Emma had married the handsome and wealthy Matthew Crompton, Earl of Farnworth. Her parents had been ecstatic and proud, her maid of honor sister predictably poker-faced. Even Matthew's father had been unusually jovial.

The font held its own significance, although, by the time of Patsy's baptism, Emma had already begun to accept the chilling reality that life as the Countess of Farnworth would never turn out as she'd expected.

Parr indicated two rickety chairs in his dingy office and bade them sit. Emma wrinkled her nose against the odor of sweaty feet.

Gabe fired the opening salvo before the cleric had a chance to remove his billycock and cloak. "I'll get my estate manager to send gardeners to tend the graveyard."

"Er…"

"You can no doubt recommend a stonemason for repairs to the gravestones."

Emma worried Gabriel had perhaps overdone it when Parr glowered, his face reddening. However, the cleric blinked, averting his gaze. "The parish council will be grateful," he murmured.

"Not at all. Call on me for anything St. John's needs. I don't intend to be an absentee patron."

Parr frowned, apparently not sure how to respond. Perhaps he didn't want an earl watching over everything he did. "Most generous," he said finally, eyeing Emma.

"The dowager countess and I plan to wed," Gabe announced before Parr had a chance to regroup. "We'd like you to proclaim the banns this coming Sunday."

The canon gaped, his mouth opening and closing like a floundering fish. "But…"

"I must do my duty toward my cousin's widow," Gabe insisted, his jaw clenched. "I'm sure you agree."

Parr reached for the quill on his desk. "Of course, a selfless and honorable gesture on your part, my lord."

⇒⇒⇒⇐⇐⇐

SATISFIED CANON PARR had all the information he needed for the banns and delighted to have a date for the wedding settled, Gabe rose and offered his arm to Emma. "I thank you," he told the cleric, linking his future bride's arm in his.

The cleric hastily removed the bowler hat, as if he'd just realized it was still atop his head.

"Hold on until we reach the carriage, my countess," Gabe whispered conspiratorially to Emma, though his own amusement threatened to erupt as they made their way to the porch.

Standing smartly by the open door of the carriage, James frowned, clearly puzzled when Gabe and Emma broke into fits of laughter as they boarded. They heard him muttering to Conrad after he slammed the door and climbed up top.

"Probably thinks we're mad," Emma said as the carriage lurched forward.

"We are. Mad for each other."

"You were masterful," she acknowledged. "Too bad Susan wasn't present to witness your triumph. Parr simply took your assertion you were a single man at face value. Was your father's name really John?" She giggled again. "John Smith!"

Gabe shrugged. "Parr knows which side his bread is buttered. Besides, earls don't lie."

Laughing, she collapsed against him.

He'd explain later that he didn't know his birth father's identity and certainly wasn't going to have Samuel's name on his marriage documents.

"I love your laugh," he murmured, nibbling her lips. "But I love your kisses more. Let's see if we can make one last all the way to Thicketford."

She pursed her lips, excitement flashing in her eyes. "You're on, Lord Farnworth."

⋙⋘

EMMA IGNORED JAMES Footman's sly smile when he helped her alight at Thicketford. She probably looked a little disheveled, although she'd done her best to straighten her garments. There was no way the footman could know Gabe's clever fingers had brought her to ecstasy—her lover had smothered her moans with his kisses.

Her daughter and sister-in-law met them in the foyer. "How did you get on with Parr?" Susan asked.

"Fine," Gabriel replied. "The wedding is set for a month from now."

"Yippee," Patsy exclaimed, clapping her hands.

"You should have been there," Emma gushed, elated by her daughter's enthusiasm and still enthralled by the Six Mile Kiss. "Gabriel had Parr wrapped around his little finger from the outset."

"And you were right about the hat," Gabriel told Patsy as he scooped her up. "He kept it on throughout the interview."

Susan eyed Emma. "You look a little disheveled."

Annoyingly incapable of doing anything about the heat flooding her face, Emma agreed. "The journey was tiring," she replied, determined not to meet Gabriel's teasing gaze. "I need to freshen up before dinner is served."

"Me too," Gabriel said.

DEARLY BELOVED

ONE MONTH LATER, Gabe stood before Canon Parr, awaiting his bride. It was the fourth time he'd attended services at St. John's—three Sundays to be present at the reading of the banns and today, to finally pledge himself to Emma.

He'd been delighted by how readily the members of the congregation accepted him, due in large part he suspected, to the much improved state of the graveyard. If he could only think of a way to tackle the gargoyles.

Every Sunday, he and Emma were welcomed, congratulated and wished much happiness by old maids clutching a Book of Common Prayer to their copious bosoms. Elderly bachelors were full of advice as to the best way to keep one's fortune, insisting the surest route to heaven lay in the accumulation of wealth, attending church and taking the sacrament regularly. The justice of the peace Gabe had already met was an adherent, as were his fellow magistrates. There were tradesmen with domestic-looking wives who showed off smartly dressed daughters. Gabe shook hands with manufacturers who could talk of nothing but cotton. Mr. Carr never failed to draw attention to the fact it was he who had fashioned the earl's wardrobe. Lawyers, doctors, including Dr. Henry, shopkeepers, and millworkers completed the throng, though the latter were few and far between. Susan explained the cotton workers attended church only on special occasions.

As Gabe waited in the crowded church, he was chuffed—a delightful Lancashire word Susan had taught him—that his marriage had clearly been deemed a special occasion.

A few disagreements had erupted over working-class folks sitting in pews that weren't *meant for the likes of them*, but the offenders had quickly and apologetically moved from pews where generations of certain *worthier* families had apparently sat.

Gabe wondered what those worthier folks thought of his decision to ask a servant to be his best man. He couldn't think of anyone he'd rather have at his side on this momentous day than his faithful batman. The sight of the two of them in dress uniform had elicited wide-eyed admiration and polite applause from fellow parishioners upon their arrival at the church on splendidly plumed geldings. "You'd think it was the Duke of Wellington himself getting wed," Bradley remarked.

Gabe's only disappointment was one he should have expected. He'd allowed himself to hope Rowbotham's efforts to trace his mother might come to fruition. He'd have liked her to know he was happy. A small part of him also wanted to rub Samuel's nose in his good fortune.

As they waited, he contemplated Parr. The parson smiled piously, holding the Book of Common Prayer like Moses come down from the clouds with the Ten Commandments. From what he could gather, the cleric was fairly well-liked and respected by the flock he'd led for more than twenty years; Susan was of the opinion he might have been more respected in the community as a whole if he had been less critical of Dissenters and less violent in his hatred of Catholics.

A murmur of excitement rippled through the congregation. The carriage bearing the bride had arrived. Gabe straightened his shoulders and turned. All thoughts of gargoyles, graveyards and imperfect clergymen fled when he beheld Emma standing beside the font, a shimmering beacon in the shadowed porch.

IMPATIENT TO WALK down the aisle and pledge herself to the man she loved, Emma tolerated Susan's fussing over the fall of her bridal train. "It's fine," she whispered.

"It has to be just right," Susan retorted, "so everyone sees that the blue shells and flowers embroidered along the edges echo the motif on the hem of the dress."

Emma was tempted to laugh. She'd never expected to hear the word *motif* emerge from her sister-in-law's mouth. Susan normally held all things to do with women's fashions in very low esteem. Her wardrobe consisted mainly of frugal muslins.

"I still don't understand why you didn't choose white, or even silver."

"Because white is for virgin brides, not widows about to remarry, and silver is for royalty. Anyway, the ivory suits me better."

"You are beautiful, Mummy," Patsy said.

"Thank you, darling. You and your aunt will steal a few hearts in your blue satin."

Susan snorted. "Right."

"Truly, Sister," Emma insisted, "you look wonderful. One day, some lucky man…"

"Gabriel's getting impatient," Susan snarled in reply.

"Ready, my dear?" Baron Whiteside asked with a kindly smile.

"Ready," she replied, "I'm sorry the baroness couldn't be here."

"Alas," he sighed. "My dear wife's melancholia keeps her abed. She pines for her son."

There was no good answer to remedy the pain Arthur had inflicted on his parents. Inhaling deeply, she linked her arm with her neighbor's and began the measured walk down the aisle.

GABE REACHED TO take Emma's hand when the baron gave her over into his safekeeping. The thousands of miles between Preston and Saint Helena were suddenly reduced to the inches that separated them for only the next second. When her warmth penetrated his skin, he knew he'd come home for good. The things that stood between them—distance, class, status—all melted away.

He knew it for sure when Patsy beamed an angelic smile in his direction.

"Dearly beloved," Parr intoned, obliging him to drag his gaze away from Emma's violet eyes, "we are gathered here together in the sight of God…"

Most of the preamble washed over him, only the words *ordained for the procreation of children* snagging his attention and making Emma blush.

To avoid fornication gave him pause for only a moment; it was true he and Emma had slept together outside of marriage but he didn't consider their lovemaking a sin; indeed, he felt closer to God when their bodies joined than he ever had.

He let out the breath he hadn't realized he was holding when Parr asked if anyone knew of an impediment to the marriage, and there was no outcry.

"He's not worthy of her," someone might have shouted. "A mere soldier. Not even a hero."

A nudge from Bradley's elbow jolted him to his senses. Parr was addressing him. "Gabriel Smith, wilt thou have this woman to thy wedded wife, to live together after God's ordinance in the holy estate of Matrimony? Wilt thou love her, comfort her, honor, and keep her, in sickness and in health; and, forsaking all other, keep thee only unto her, so long as ye both shall live?"

"I will," he replied, never more sure of anything in his life.

"Emma Mary Louise Crompton, wilt thou have this man to thy wedded husband, to live together after God's ordinance in the holy estate of Matrimony? Wilt thou obey him, and serve him, love, honor, and keep him, in sickness and in health; and, forsaking all other, keep thee only unto him, so long as ye both shall live?"

Emma turned to look at him. "I will," she replied.

He knew he ought to fall to his knees in humble thanksgiving for the love this woman bore him but, next thing he knew, Emma's warm right hand was in his and he was repeating his vow to her. "I, Gabriel Smith, take thee, Emma Mary Louise Crompton, to my wedded wife, to have and to hold from this day forward, for better for worse, for richer for poorer, in sickness and in health, to love and to cherish, till death us do part, according to God's holy ordinance; and thereto I plight thee my troth."

Emma took his hand in hers and pledged herself to him. "I, Emma Mary Louise Crompton, take thee, Gabriel Smith, to my wedded husband, to have and to hold from this day forward, for better for worse, for richer for poorer, in sickness and in health, to love, cherish, and to obey, till death us do part, according to God's holy ordinance; and thereto I give thee my troth."

With military precision, Bradley took a step forward and placed the wedding ring on Parr's book. Gabe took the golden circle and slid it onto the fourth finger of Emma's left hand.

Looking into her loving eyes, he followed the parson's lead, though he had no need. He had practiced the words over and over in preparation. "With this ring I thee wed, with my body I thee worship, and with all my worldly goods I thee endow: In the Name of the Father, and of the Son, and of the Holy Ghost. Amen."

Drowning in Emma's violet eyes, Gabe absorbed little else, except Parr's pronouncement *that they be man and wife together.*

WEDDING BREAKFAST

"**N**O *SIX MILE Kiss* today," Gabriel whispered when the carriage pulled away from the church.

Given the presence of Susan and Patsy in the carriage, Emma had to be content with simply being held in Gabriel's arms, her head on his chest listening to the steady beat of his strong heart.

Dr. Henry had been pleased with his progress and credited the elixir and salve; the headaches were a thing of the past, the night sweats had all but disappeared. He hadn't revealed to the physician he believed the improvement in his health had more to do with sleeping in Emma's chamber every night. The change of surroundings and intensely pleasurable sexual congress had worked wonders.

"I detected a certain amount of disappointment among the congregation when we didn't issue a general invitation to Thicketford Manor for the wedding breakfast," Gabriel remarked.

"I suppose," Susan replied. "They hoped for a chance to hobnob with nobility."

"But wedding breakfasts are meant for family," Emma asserted. "People accept that."

"Besides which," Gabriel added, "Cook and Mrs. Maple would feel put upon if we turned up with hundreds of people."

Everyone agreed, but Emma noticed Patsy didn't smile. "What's wrong, Poppet? Too much excitement?"

As if he too sensed something was wrong, Gabriel beckoned Patsy to sit on his lap. "You were the happy, smiling little girl we love," he said, cradling her in his arms. "Until we came out of the church. What upset you?"

Fidgeting with the lace cuffs of her gown, she nodded. "I saw someone talking to Baron Whiteside."

"Who was it?"

"Tillie."

Her daughter's quivering lip caused Emma's heart to lurch. She exchanged a worried glance with Gabriel. "That wretched girl."

He kissed the top of Patsy's head. "She can't hurt you," he assured her. "I'll make sure of it."

⟫⟫⟪⟪

GABE FUMED. HE and Emma had gone to a great deal of trouble to ensure everything went off without a hitch on their wedding day. He wanted it to be perfect for his bride. Since the refurbishment of the servants' staircase, it seemed he could do no wrong as far as the staff was concerned. They had gone above and beyond to decorate the house inside and out with flags and festoons. Cook bubbled with excitement about the special menu she'd chosen.

Bradley reported the general consensus below stairs was that Thicketford Manor hadn't seen such a celebration since…well, no one could recall.

Tillie had cast a shadow, although Patsy seemed to recover her good spirits as the wedding breakfast progressed. Sensing Emma was still bothered, Gabe took hold of his bride's hand under the table. "I'll speak to Whiteside," he promised.

"I'd like to hear what he has to say," she replied with a smile, "although I'm not going to let the wretched girl ruin the most wonderful day of my life."

"Seems Patsy agrees with you."

She blushed beautifully. "Susan's done her best to take her mind off it."

"My mind's on other things as well," he confessed, placing her hand on his arousal.

She moved her fingers on him, putting just enough pressure to send desire soaring up his spine. "Your male mind is always on other things."

He sighed heavily, deliberately peering down the front of her décolletage. "I know. I'm an insatiable letch when it comes to my wife."

"Canon Parr has his eye on you," she warned.

"He's just jealous."

"No, that would be my pouting sister."

Hoping proceedings were drawing to a close as the footmen began clearing away the last of the dishes, he groaned when Bradley came to his feet, champagne flute in hand.

The faithful soldier cleared his throat, hesitating to begin whatever it was he planned to say when Frame bustled in the door and bent to whisper in Gabe's ear. "Pardon the interruption, my lord, there's a woman in the foyer who claims to be your mother."

UNEXPECTED GUEST

G ABE'S THROAT TIGHTENED. He gripped Emma's hand. "My mother," he echoed, scarcely able to believe she'd come. He hesitated, filled with dread that Samuel had probably accompanied her. His stepfather was the one person he definitely didn't want to see on his wedding day.

Emma rose, pulling him to his feet. "We must greet her," she exclaimed, her smiling face reflecting her joy.

He cursed the hold Samuel Waterman still had on him. He should be hurrying to greet his mother who must have traveled a considerable distance.

The murmur of surprise among the guests rose as he allowed Emma to pull him to the foyer.

An elegant, well-dressed woman waited, uncertainty plain to see in her hesitant frown. The quality of her attire, the jaunty plumed hat, the tentative smile, all assured him Samuel Waterman was dead.

"Gabriel," she said.

The pride, joy and longing in her voice was all it took to propel him across the tiled floor. He took his tearful mother into his embrace, inhaling a scent he'd remembered for more than ten years. "You came," was all he could manage out of his dry throat, grounded by the loving way his wife stroked his back and encouraged him to weep.

EMMA DIDN'T THINK it was possible to love Gabriel any more than she already did, but the obvious affection he had for his mother touched her heart. He'd shared with her something of the abuse he'd suffered at the hands of his stepfather. Yet, he clearly didn't blame his mother and was genuinely glad to see her.

When his sobs subsided, he stepped back and took Emma's hand. "I'd like you to meet my mother, Rebecca Waterman," he said hoarsely. "Mother, allow me to introduce my wife, Lady Emma Crompton Smith, Countess Farnworth."

Still clutching Gabriel's arm, his mother curtseyed. "My honor, Lady Farnworth."

Something flickering in Rebecca Waterman's amber eyes evoked an immediate feeling of kinship. Emma took her hands. "Please, there is no need for formalities. We are family. You must call me Emma."

"I'm very happy to meet you, Emma."

Baron Whiteside appeared in the foyer. "Your guests are wondering where you've gotten to."

Gabriel made the introductions, then asked his neighbor to look after his mother until the breakfast was over.

"Certainly," the baron agreed, proffering an arm. "Anthea and I would be glad of the dear lady's company."

Chatter ceased when they returned to the dining room, all eyes on the woman on the baron's arm.

"Emma and I are delighted my mother could be here today," Gabriel announced as he and Emma regained their seats. "She's come all the way from Kent."

This news seemed to satisfy everyone's curiosity and their attention turned back to Bradley.

GABE WAS ANXIOUS to reunite with his mother and learn of her current circumstances. She'd aged, which was to be expected. The raven curls were streaked with gray, but she looked happy and well. For the moment, he had to be content with that much. His immediate concern was what Bradley planned to say as he rose once more.

"My lords, ladies and gentlemen," he began confidently, before hesitating. "And ladies...er."

Polite chuckling ensued, though Gabe doubted Bradley had intended to make a jest.

"I ask you to raise your glasses in a toast to the health of Lady Emma Smith, Countess Farnworth, a lady in the true sense of the word."

"Hear, hear, Lady Emma," the guests agreed as they sipped champagne.

Assuming his valet had finished, Gabe started to rise but, apparently, Bradley wasn't done.

"There are a few things Lady Emma should know about her new husband."

Gabe tensed. He'd always striven to be a good soldier, but he wasn't a saint.

"Having served Lieutenant Colonel Smith for many years, who better placed than me to know a thing or two about him nobody else knows?"

A shiver stole up Gabe's spine as he frantically tried to recall anything scandalous he may have done in the past. Emma's curious glance didn't help. "This should be interesting," she whispered.

"From the beginning, my superior officer treated me with respect and fairness, and, believe me, that's more than can be said for most officers in the British Army.

"He brought me with him here to Thicketford Manor, made sure I had a living, when he could just as easily have left me to rot on a godforsaken rock in the South Atlantic with a bunch of Frenchies toadying to Bonaparte.

"Everyone in England hails Wellington as our national hero, and His Grace deserves all the accolades. However, those of us who fought at Waterloo witnessed many acts of bravery that will forever go unsung. I served in Lieutenant Colonel Smith's battalion and I know for a fact his actions kept many of us alive during that hell." His face reddened. "Pardon me, ladies, didn't mean to swear," he said, his voice cracking. "Please drink to the health of the finest man I know, Earl Gabriel Smith, Lord Farnworth."

Humbled, Gabe accepted the cheers and good wishes, overjoyed to see his mother's tears and the pride in his wife's violet eyes.

LOVING FAMILY

A S THE GUESTS took their leave, Emma invited her new mother-in-law into the drawing room, somewhat relieved when Priscilla and her husband declined her invitation.

"Long journey to Cheshire," Warren grunted.

Emma refrained from reminding him she'd offered guest rooms at Thicketford.

Having kissed her sister goodbye, not surprised when no well-wishes were forthcoming, she left it to Frame to see them out and returned to the drawing room.

It was gratifying to see Patsy snuggled into Rebecca's side on the sofa. "I suppose you're my grandmama," she said.

Poignant as the meeting was, Emma wanted to listen in on the conversation with Baron Whiteside. "Susan, will you take care of our guest for a few minutes?"

"Of course, I'm anxious to hear all about Kent. Last time I was there…"

Emma slipped away, relieved to see Gabriel speaking with their neighbor in the foyer. Her husband put an arm around her waist and drew her close. "The baron tells me Tillie accosted him outside the church."

"Yes," Whiteside confirmed. "Didn't know who she was. Then the chit starts babbling on about brothels and tells me I have to save her because she knows all about Arthur."

An adder writhed in Emma's stomach. "What did you say in reply?"

"Didn't have a chance. Some brute appeared and dragged her off."

"It seems she's paying heavily for her involvement in the kidnapping scheme," Gabriel observed.

"But I hope she doesn't cause more trouble for you," Emma told the baron.

He patted her arm. "Don't worry about me. Long life and happiness to you both. I hope to see you at our next little gathering. Anthea tells me she's learning a new opera."

Emma avoided the amused glint in her husband's eyes, and headed back to the drawing room while he saw the baron to the door.

Susan had rung for tea and Emma was pleased to see everyone looked relaxed. Patsy was chattering away, Wellington at her feet, eyeing the lemon tart in her hand.

Gabriel returned and sat Patsy on his lap so he could be next to his mother.

"I'm so proud of the man you've turned out to be, Gabriel," Rebecca said. "Despite what you endured at the hands of my misbegotten husband."

"I assume he's dead."

Rebecca rolled her eyes. "Fell down the back stairs in a drunken fit after two lawyers came to visit. Broke his neck."

"Lawyers?" Emma asked.

"Asking all kinds of questions about my first husband's family history. I told him John and I had three sons, but two were killed at Trafalgar. Samuel didn't like that, especially when he tumbled there was an estate involved. Of course, neither of us knew the lawyers were trying to track down an heir to an earldom.

"Samuel ranted and raved that he deserved to inherit the money, not you. He fell down the stone steps to the cellar on his way to fetch another bottle of gin."

Gabriel shook his head. "So, I'm an earl thanks to my father?"

"Yes, John was a fine man from a good family, though his parents had both died before I met him. You favor him. He contracted black measles and was gone in a week. I was terribly lonely after his death and overwhelmed by the prospect of raising three small boys myself. I suppose that's why I was taken in by Samuel when he began his wooing. The biggest mistake of my life. Can you ever forgive me?"

"There's nothing to forgive," Gabe replied. "We were able to escape, eventually. There was no reprieve for you and, for that, Samuel Waterman should rot in hell."

Rebecca rolled her eyes. "He's too well-pickled to rot."

Everyone laughed, including Patsy, though Emma doubted her daughter understood the jest.

"I can hardly credit my father's name was actually John," Gabriel admitted.

"Like his father before him, and his grandfather. That's the reason he chose the names of archangels for his sons. *'Enough Johns in this family,'* he used to say. *'With a surname like Smith, a man should have a more impressive given name.'*"

This prompted Susan to launch into a treatise on surnames, family relationships and sundry other topics.

"I'm confused," Patsy said when her aunt finally took a breath. Holding a coconut macaroon out of Wellington's reach, she asked Rebecca, "If Gabriel is my cousin, are you my cousin too?"

"I was rather hoping you'd start calling me Papa," Gabriel replied.

"I like Daddy better," Patsy declared.

"Me too," he agreed, flashing Emma a broad smile.

"And I prefer Grandmama Rebecca to Cousin Rebecca."

As the pleasant afternoon wore on, Emma drank copious amounts of tea, ate too many sweets, and absorbed the comfortable atmosphere. At last, she belonged to a loving family.

SILVER LINING

G ABE WASN'T THE only one roused from his nap by the chiming of the Perigal clock on the mantelpiece.

"Good heavens, seven o'clock," Emma murmured. "Patsy's still asleep."

"She's had a busy day. I'll carry her up," Gabe said. "My first official act as a daddy!"

Mrs. Maple popped her head in the door. "Begging your pardon, my lady, but we assumed you wouldn't want a full meal this evening. Cook has set out a small spread in the dining room."

"Thank you, Mrs. Maple," Emma replied. "I couldn't eat another morsel. I'll come up and show my mother-in-law to her room."

"No need," Susan interjected. "I could manage a few bites, and I daresay Mrs. Waterman wouldn't say no to another cuppa."

Gabe appreciated the gesture so he and Emma might withdraw all the sooner to her chamber. "Goodnight, then," he said, pecking a kiss on his mother's cheek. "We'll talk more on the morrow."

"Goodnight, my son," she replied. "Thank you for inviting me."

He was pleased when Emma embraced his mother and wished her sweet dreams. "I hope you'll stay a few days so we can get to know each other."

His mother looked hesitant. "Actually, I've sold the cottage in Kent. Too many bad memories. Samuel was a skinflint, but I easily found where he hid his coin. I was hoping to purchase a little place of my own in Lancashire. We've spent too much time apart."

"I have a splendid idea," Susan announced. "Mrs. Waterman and I could move into the dower house when its finished."

"I thought you'd be going back to Somerset," Emma replied.

"To be honest, Hannah spends most of her time napping these days. Rebecca will be much better company, and I'll become maiden aunt to your many offspring, dear Sister."

"Sounds like a good plan to me," Gabe declared. Grand as Thicketford Manor was, he preferred not to live in the same house as his mother.

"I'll wait for you in my chamber," Emma whispered, prompting his hasty departure up the stairs to give Patsy over to Miss Ince in the nursery.

Satisfied when his daughter was safely tucked in, he hurried back down one flight to Emma's chamber, hoping he wasn't too late to help with the removal of the shimmering wedding gown.

To his delight, he found his bride standing in the center of her chamber, still fully clothed. He quickly unbuttoned and removed his uniform jacket before putting his arms around her waist and drawing her to his body.

She curled her hands under his braces and leaned into him, her swaying movements playing havoc with his male urges. "I like your mother."

"I have so many questions," he admitted. "I hope you didn't mind spending the afternoon with her. Not much of a wedding night for my beautiful bride."

"It was perfect," she replied. "Besides, we're going somewhere else for our wedding night."

"We are?"

His puzzlement grew when she took his hand and led him to the door between their chambers. He held back. "It's not finished yet."

She smiled enticingly. "Yes, it is. Close your eyes."

He obeyed, but his throat tightened. Clearly, his wife and Blair had been plotting behind his back to complete the redecoration of his bedroom, but the green hell had been the source of too much torment. "Wouldn't you rather stay in your chamber?" he asked, feeling like a coward.

"Trust me," she whispered, nibbling his ear.

Her warm breath gave him courage. "Lead on."

"Smells different," he conceded after they'd taken a few steps.

"Open your eyes," she said, a hint of nervousness in her voice. She wanted him to be pleased with the changes. When Blair had asked him about colors, he'd left the choice up to the estate manager, with perhaps a vague suggestion to "ask the countess." He didn't care, so long as it wasn't green.

Not sure what to expect, he opened his eyes.

⸙

"I HOPE YOU like it," Emma murmured when Gabriel's gaze traveled from the ivory walls to the champagne draperies at the windows and the beige chaise. "Blair wanted to do it all blue. Typical. I think men would like everything painted blue, and I did concede to a thin blue line along the crown molding, but…"

Hauling her into his arms, he silenced her with a kiss that told her all she needed to know.

"I take it you are pleased," she said, slipping his braces off his shoulders when they paused for breath.

"Pleased? It's perfect," he replied, yanking his shirt off over his head. "A chamber fit for an earl."

"And his countess," she teased, splaying her hands across his broad chest.

"Yes. Thank you. You're right. I would probably have chosen blue, but this is so much better. Looks like a different room."

"A chamber suitable for making love to one's wife for the first time?" she asked coyly, brushing his nipples with her thumbs.

His nostrils flared and he leaned his forehead against hers. "Definitely. But I'll need your help unlocking the secret of how to remove your lovely gown without tearing it apart."

"I confess, I'm not too sure myself," she admitted. "It took a while to get me into it with Lucy and Susan assisting."

He stepped back and studied her. "It's almost as if you match the room."

"You noticed," she exclaimed. "Susan was sure you wouldn't."

He glanced at the ivory bed hangings and matching quilt. "It's the same material."

"Well, I am a frugal Lancashire lass, after all," she teased. "Mr. Carr was able to order a quantity of the fabric from London at a good price, so I couldn't resist."

"Speaking of being unable to resist, I need you out of these clothes now."

Now turned out not to be possible. It took the two of them fifteen minutes to wrestle with the innumerable tapes and hooks, then three seconds for Gabriel to be shucked of his boots, trousers and smalls.

They clung together for long minutes, relishing each other's nakedness before he took a deep breath, scooped her up and carried her to the bed. He knelt beside her and reached to pull the hangings closed, cocooning them in the safe haven she had designed especially.

"They're lined with silver," he exclaimed.

She reached for the proud lance her body had craved ever since she'd first set eyes on Gabriel's maleness. "Of course, every earl should have a silver lining."

Smiling, he lay down beside her and took her into his arms. Stroking each other in intimate places they knew brought delight, they began the long, slow climb to wedded bliss.

EPILOGUE

Ten months later.

G ABE OFFERED HIS guests a second glass of brandy. Adrian Henry declined. Bertrand Coleman, Baron Whiteside, accepted.

Gabe felt sorry for his kindly neighbor, though the man never spoke about the fate that had befallen his son and heir. He expressed eternal optimism that his recently acquired son-in-law would soon get Anthea with child, hopefully a son. Dr. Henry was of the opinion a grandchild might draw the baroness out of her debilitating melancholy.

Gabe never asked if Coleman had news of Arthur in Jamaica. The crime that had blighted the baron's life was never, of course, among the topics of conversation in Gabe's library.

Despite his personal trials, Whiteside had proven to be a powerful ally in Gabe's fight to get the Lords to petition Parliament. They sought to sponsor an act curbing the use of harmful substances in the manufacture of everyday materials. They'd encountered opposition from some industrial magnates, but Emma's father, recently returned from India, had pledged to help in that regard.

Meanwhile, Dr. Henry had been busy building a powerful lobby among the medical community.

Gabe enjoyed the meetings he hosted from time to time. These worthy men had become trusted friends as well as political allies.

The Liverpool to Leeds Canal was also a frequent topic of discussion. Upon its completion in October 1816, Henry had persuaded Gabe to invest in what they both saw as a great advancement in moving coal from Lancashire's collieries to the giant shipping and manufacturing firms in Liverpool.

Gabe poured himself another finger of brandy and stared into the golden liquid, contemplating the enormous changes in his life since he'd first received word of his inheritance.

Reconnecting with his mother had brought a joy he'd never expected. She and Susan had moved into the refurbished dower house. He'd been nervous that his submissive mother and the outgoing Susan Crompton might not hit it off, but they had become fast friends. There was hardly a day went by that didn't find his mother and stepdaughter playing a piano duet together. Bertrand had invited them to play at his next musicale since his bedridden wife wasn't feeling *quite the thing.*

"How's Patsy?" the baron asked, solicitous as always about the health of the child his son had schemed to kidnap.

"She's well," he replied. "Looking forward to the arrival of what she insists will be a baby brother. I fear Wellington will find himself relegated to second place once the babe arrives."

"Not long now, eh?" Whiteside asked.

"Three weeks," he replied. "The midwife arrives to take up residence in a week, and Lucy should be back by then. Bradley's taken her to Derby to introduce his new wife to his elderly parents."

"Good man, that," the baron observed.

Gabe nodded and was about to lift the crystal glass to his lips when a breathless and red-faced Patsy burst into the study. "Daddy, come quick. My brother is on his way."

Fear prickled its way across Gabe's nape. "But…"

Henry rose. "Babies have a way of not sticking to a carefully arranged schedule. It's been a while since I delivered a baby, but it's rather like riding a bicycle."

Unable to make any sense of that pronouncement, Gabe abandoned his glass and took the steps to his chamber two at a time.

>>>><<<<

EMMA HADN'T EXPECTED a man to be present at her confinement, but Adrian Henry was a trusted friend and she was confident he knew what he was about as he rolled up his sleeves. She'd been somewhat hysterical when her water broke too soon, but the doctor had quickly calmed her with his competent manner. His quiet demeanor and careful instructions also silenced the distraught maid who'd temporarily taken Lucy's place.

"You've done this before, so you know what to expect," he reminded Emma.

"And with Patsy, I was scared to death," she admitted.

"The second one will probably be quicker because you're more relaxed."

She moaned loudly, not feeling very relaxed when a vicious contraction gripped her.

The maid mopped her brow with a cool cloth and, gradually, the pain subsided.

The doctor put an ear to her belly. "All good," he declared. "Strong heartbeat. I'll just pop out and let your husband know how things are going."

He returned a few minutes later, just in time to encourage her through another contraction.

"How fares my husband?" she asked when her breathing slowed.

"Not as well as you. He's a nervous wreck. Funny how a man can stare down French soldiers at Waterloo but is reduced to a blithering idiot when confronted by childbirth. If men bore the children, the human race would be extinct in no time."

Emma appreciated his attempt at levity. "It's unfortunate Susan and Rebecca have gone off to the Chetham today. They would have been good company for him." She finally plucked up courage to bring up a worry that had plagued her for months. "He's probably worried the arsenic may have affected our babe."

Henry shook his head. "Gabriel has been in good health for a long while now. I told him weeks ago, and I'll tell you, there is no chance the babe has been affected."

She and her husband had never discussed the possibility. She now knew Gabriel had broached the topic with the doctor but hadn't wanted to distress her.

※》》※《《※

FEELING LIKE THE king of the world though it was five o'clock in the morning and he'd been up all night, Gabe strutted around the foyer, showing off his gurgling son to the assembled staff. Even Frame glowed with pride, as if the babe was his and he alone was responsible for the boy's existence.

Patsy shadowed Gabe, reminding everyone the infant was her brother, and hadn't she told everyone it would be a boy.

Whiteside emerged from the study and choked back bleary-eyed tears. Gabe was grateful the man had kept him company all night. "Treasure every moment," Bertrand advised. "The lad will grow to manhood before you know it."

"How's Lady Farnworth?" Mrs. Maple asked.

"She's doing well," Gabe replied, thankful it was true. "Dr. Henry said she came through it with flying colors."

He didn't mention his wife looked even more beautiful after her ordeal.

Unwilling to spend another minute apart from the woman he loved to distraction, he hurried back to his chamber, Patsy hard on his heels. He hoped Henry had completed what he referred to as "necessary procedures you probably don't want to see."

Patsy nodded when Gabe reminded her Wellington would not be allowed entry. She wagged a stern finger and the whimpering poodle turned away in disgust.

Cradling his son, Gabe peeked into the chamber, relieved to see Emma propped up by a mound of pillows. "You look serene," he told her as he and Patsy perched on the edge of the mattress. He feared his heart might burst for love of the incredible woman he had married.

"It's exhaustion, not serenity," she countered, reaching for her babe.

"Can I hold him?" Patsy asked.

At a nod from Emma, Gabe placed his son in Patsy's arms. He had a momentary vision of her as a woman holding a child of her own, but he kept it to himself. Whiteside was right. Patsy had already grown inches since he'd come to Thicketford. She'd be a woman soon enough.

When his babe began to fret, Emma reached for him. "I think he's hungry. I'm not sure if my milk has come in yet, but we'll try."

Suddenly sweating, Gabe took his son from Patsy and laid him at his mother's bared breast. He resisted the urge to demonstrate suckling when the babe seemed not to get the hang of it.

"What shall we name him?" Emma asked.

They thought they had weeks yet to settle on a name. Sexually aroused as he was by the vision before him, he mentally sifted through a multitude of possibilities, dismissing *Napoleon* as the ravings of a lunatic. He knew he was losing it altogether when *Dreadnought* popped into his brain.

Struggling to regain control of his wits that fatherhood seemed to have stolen, he suddenly knew. "We'll name him Raphael Michael John Smith."

"Perfect," Emma exclaimed.

As if pleased by the moniker chosen for him, the babe stopped fussing, latched on and suckled.

Historical Footnotes

CHETHAM LIBRARY
https://en.wikipedia.org/wiki/Chetham%27s_Library

COPPER ARSENITE
I'm usually a stickler for historical accuracy, but I have to confess to tweaking timelines. The problems caused by the use of copper arsenite in the manufacture of wallpaper, paste and paint weren't actually brought to light until the latter half of the 19th century. I couldn't resist tying Gabriel's predicament into the discovery of arsenic in Napoleon's body after his death, and the subsequent theory that fumes and dust from the green wallpaper in his cottage might have contributed to it. It has since been suggested that Napoleon was probably exposed to arsenic as early as his childhood in Corsica.

https://www.nature.com/articles/299626a0
https://mmta.co.uk/2016/10/14/was-napoleon-killed-by-wallpaper/
https://www.amnh.org/explore/news-blogs/on-cxhibit-posts/was-napoleon-poisoned

As for the sketches done of Napoleon aboard *HMS Northumbcrland*
http://www.armoury.co.uk/print/1808

HMS DREADNOUGHT
https://en.wikipedia.org/wiki/HMS_Dreadnought_(1801)

PRESTON GUILD
The last Preston guild was held in 2012. Perhaps I'll meet you at the next one in 2032! Google Images has lots of fun pictures of the 2012

parades.

LIVERPOOL TO LEEDS CANAL
https://en.wikipedia.org/wiki/Leeds_and_Liverpool_Canal

OVER THE HILLS
You might enjoy hearing Sir Laurence Olivier sing this song in a 1953 version of the *Beggar's Opera*.
https://youtu.be/nU6p3Ubq42U

BEGGAR'S OPERA
https://en.wikipedia.org/wiki/The_Beggar%27s_Opera

HANNAH MORE
https://en.wikipedia.org/wiki/Hannah_More

ST. JOHN'S & CANON PARR
Canon Parr is the name of a parson who served St. John's Parish, but not until later in the century. Fascinating details about this man and his church can be found here.
http://www.lan-opc.org.uk/Preston/Preston/stjohn/index.html

NAPOLEON
https://en.wikipedia.org/wiki/Napoleon#Exile_on_Saint_Helena

BAKER RIFLE
https://en.wikipedia.org/wiki/Baker_rifle

DR. HENRY
I chose the doctor's surname in honor of Dr. Bonnie Henry, British Columbia's Chief Medical Officer, who has been a strong and respected voice for calm and kindness during the pandemic. It's also the surname of an orthopedic surgeon whose skill helped me regain the use of my left hand after I shattered the bones in my wrist in 2009.

THE YEAR WITHOUT A SUMMER

https://en.wikipedia.org/wiki/Year_Without_a_Summer

GRITSTONE

Many stone buildings in Lancashire were built with gritstone, a type of sandstone which is often beige or light gray in color. Decades of industrial pollution turned the stone black by the 20th century. This, of course, was a consequence of the industrial revolution in many parts of England. In recent times, sandblasting has revealed the hidden beauty of many old stone buildings.

About the Author

Thank you for reading *Every Earl Has a Silver Lining*. It's Book One in a series. If you're curious about Lady Susan Crompton, watch for Book Two, *Wild Earl Chase*.

If you'd like to leave a review where you purchased this book, and on Goodreads and BookBub, I would appreciate it. Reviews contribute greatly to an author's success.

I'd love you to visit my website and my Facebook page, Anna Markland Novels.

Tweet me @annamarkland, join me on Pinterest, or sign up for my newsletter.

Follow me on BookBub and be the first to know when my next book is released.

I'm on Instagram too!

My interest in genealogy blossomed into the creation of steamy historical romances about family honor, roots and ancestry. I am a firm believer in love at first sight. My heroes and heroines may initially deny the attraction between them, but eventually the alchemy wins out. My novels are intimate stories filled with passion, intrigue, adventure and suspense. And the occasional chuckle.

I hope you'll escape with me to where romance began and get intimate with history. Perhaps, you'll come to know and love my cast of characters as much as I do.

I'd like to acknowledge the assistance of my critique group partners, Reggi Allder, Jacquie Biggar, LizAnn Carson, and Sylvie Grayson, and the invaluable contributions of beta reader extraordinaire, Maria McIntyre.

Made in the USA
Middletown, DE
15 October 2021